GOD IN DEEP SILENCE

Other works of Pramod Kumar Athirakam

- Pranayapoomazha(Lyrics)

- Mappu nalkoo mahamathae(collection of Malayalam poems)

GOD IN DEEP SILENCE

PRAMODKUMAR ATHIRAKAM

PARTRIDGE
A Penguin Random House Company

ISBN: Hardcover   978-1-4828-5024-6
             Softcover   978-1-4828-5025-3
             eBook   978-1-4828-5023-9

Print information available on the last page.

To order additional copies of this book, contact
Partridge India
000 800 10062 62
orders.india@partridgepublishing.com

www.partridgepublishing.com/india

Pramod Kumar Athirakam is an award winning writer and a free lance trainer. He is an author of two works so far. God in Deep Silence is his first novel in English.

Dedication

This fiction work is dedicated to the memory of my heavenly
Father Sri Narayanan Nair and to Mother Earth

Epigraph

Sun, rises in the east but sets in the west
New to come very next day and give light to the world
Wiser religions are very few and so silent, thou born on earth
Ever rise in the hearts of the best and endure till death of the earth.

Foreword

This Novel is impossible to ignore and will infuriate readers every now and then.

Preface

We have been destroying our mother earth for long years and dangerously forget that our planet is not only predestined as a dwelling place for human beings but for all living creatures. Here each generation is trying to make their own impact and foot print on the earth but un-knowingly disturbing the very basic tranquility and rhythm of nature. Over the centuries especially in the present we have begun to upset the sanctity and balance of nature. We are greedily eating out our own life saving means. Indiscriminately burning rain forests for industrial and commercial reasons, re-directing rivers, killing birds and animals erratically, injecting hormones into meat and fruits, polluting air and water, over fishing, excessive use of chemicals and pesticides and destroying nutrients forever, blazing oil fields are few examples to make this planet as the most un-fit place to live.

Mother earth also started retaliating through many ways and means. Excess rainfall, snow fall, floods, draught, earth quakes, volcano flare-up, wide spread un-known diseases, crack in the ozone layer etc. are warning signals. Now it is high time to wake up and save our planet or perish forever!

Acknowledgment

K. Mohandas has made immeasurable contribution and support to this project. Without his insight this work would never begin. I should mention my fondly Mother who grew me up, Ramachandran Master for his support and also few beautiful minds behind this novel.

Contents

1. In the Shimmering Soil 1
2. Danger Comes 10
3. Girl in the Kingdom of Day Dream 19
4. Mystifying Fade Away 30
5. In the Chariot of Venus 40
6. An Opening to Sacret Shroud..51
7. Problems Problems Every Where 58
8. Fire of Greediness.. 64
9. Halcon Days of Spring 69
10. Forever Unlock the Immense Doorway 76
11. Devotees of Satan 85
12. In the Lunatic School 91
13. Pleasure Without Pain 101
14. Fight Between Good and Bad.. 111
15. Wolf in Darkness.. 116
16. Created by Imagination 122
17. Sacred Conflict..128
18. Aunt Sally's Snobbery...133
19. In the Dale of Sin 138
20. A Memo to a Forlorn Creature 145
21. Tragedy Blooms...150
22. The Vortex of Exhoration 159
23. An Illusive Symbol 163
24. Cribe of Nameless 168
25. Doorway of an Untaint 179
26. Re-visit with Repentant 183
27. The Final Interment 189
28. Indefinite Passing Way 197
29. God in deep silence 204
30. Eternal Tranquility..215

Chapter 1

In the Shimmering Soil

Rising rhythmically, the shining moon on the eastern horizon with all immaculate elegance of clear summer night, spreading cool radiance, like dreamy reflection of splendid light from Elysian Fields.

"Oh! Today is Full moon….," Poorvapunya told herself.

Towards her, the stars were twinkling from the sky. Her poor thatched house and asphodels in the nearby lake stood, bordered by meadows dipped in the dropping deep milky distant splendor of the moon. Its lovely reflection in little dewdrops drew her attention. Though her eyes were pale as a sign of poignant poverty, the dazzling beauty of the grassy moors and lake garnished with gloriously blooming lilies, like heaven, opened her mind.

She thought:

Where is Heaven? What is Hell?

She looked at the sky and the moving lazy clouds.

"Today the sky seems like a blue blanket and white silvery clouds are moving here and there. A big cloud gives the impression of being a chariot of silver".

Poorvapunya thought:

Might it be the chariot of Minerva[1] or Athena[2] to give light and wisdom to people on the earth?

Looking at the twinkling stars she murmured:

---

[1]   https://en.wikipedia.org/?title=Minerva
[2]   https://en.wikipedia.org/wiki/Athena

"From the Heaven God may be stretching the endless divine light to the Earth, the land of sorrows, through stars for the uplift of all creatures from their miseries."
Naughty heart let down her thought and mind moved into heavenly reminiscences.

She remembered:
Perhaps, as depicted in the famous book of **Eternal tranquility**[3], souls of dead persons might be showing lantern from paradise. One stanza from memory rambled on her rosy lips:

> 'Gaze at the gleaming sky, light blue
> Lake of Heavenly spring; that glue
> With Those Lanterns lightened there
> At that portal for souls come, fair…'

Disrupting her thought, long leaf of the book, containing stories, described as questions and answers in magical words, which she had read earlier, entered into her mind with a gleaming smile. With the esteem of a swan, when it sees a snowy watered lotus-lagoon reflecting the clear blue sky, she suddenly dipped into the letters even though a shady sleep began to creep into brain, the pitiful consequence of hungry stomach, which is common among the natives drastically drowned in famine and poverty.
Leaves of the book glittered in her reminiscence and seemed to be unfolding melodiously, but loudly, before her.

Letters themselves speaks their essence.

"Tomorrow is the rare and remarkable day for mankind…! Day of the dignified victory…! Day in which it realises the supreme and radical dream, it had ever wished for. Day, to be devoted to the world of Science…! Date which would be written in golden letters by historians in future…"!
Reliable reasons…?
It is the day of rejoicing reality; the day, which opens the entrance of eminent prosperity; the day in which human beings will go to domicile in another planet away from the earth.

---

[3] Eternal tranquility, an imaginary book read by Poorvapunya

There are dales and dancing daffodils in gentle breeze; dewy dawn and dusk with delightful twilight; ravishing rains and seven colored rain-bows; spring and singing birds; tamable deer and dense emerald green woodlands; blue sky and beautiful silver-clouds; high mountain peaks as K'iche-cliff; the huge sparkling rocks seem to be blue steps towards the Elysium; mere and meek fishes floating with mirth...!

Aren't these all in our world too...?

But there are divulged differences...! Erroneous deeds of man may create disasters on the Earth such as universal flood and flames of global warming. In the final flood, sinking may begin from the bank of *Mayan Riviera*[4] of the *Land of Mesoamerica*[5]. Which planet are they going to?. Where there are no discriminations and demerit among the living beings! No hostility and harassment! No wars and wailings! No selfishness and self-conceit! No crimes and corrections! No competition and conquering! No diseases and die-outs! No sins and saviors! If so, how life and death...?

Everyone lives with the cardinal virtues and knowledge of natural truth. All statutes and tenets are followed not because of fear about the punishments but according to self conscience. None breaks any rights of the others. So there are no grievances, complaints and courts. Pearls and pebbles have equal value as no valuations exist. All deaths are normal and not before maturity. No killing. Everyone dies as per the rule after completion of moral obligations and satisfactory life.

About food and shelter...?

Food is not a necessity since the 'God of Light'[6] gives energy to all beings directly. But anybody could rely on food if wanted. There are enough flavorful fruits and edible roots. Animals and birds seldom eat, and that too edible parts of plants only. Prominent and perspicuous point is that water in ponds is pellucid. Not only fishes but animals, birds and if man is there, he also can drink water directly from rivers and rivulets. Rivers are blemish-proof as nobody is there to poison.

Food chain...?

---

[4] https://en.wikipedia.org/wiki/Maya_civilization

[5] https://en.wikipedia.org/wiki/Mesoamerica

[6] Sunlight is the main source of Prana and vital energy on this earth. Through meditation and Soorya(Sun) yoga one can take energy of the sun directly to hypothalamus and to body.

There is no such chain to constrict throat of anyone in the name of victuals. There flora and fauna are living in harmony. Lions will not run after deer for their flesh. In the dens of tigers, rabbits are rambling with relaxation.

Haughty hawks and humble doves are sleeping in one nest. Not running after prey but waiting before 'God of light' the only way to get food.

How the animals got such wisdom…?

It is from a long and marvelous history of the past golden civilization that existed in the planet earth known as Satyayuga[7]. Once there was a pedigree of wise animals. That species was blessed with revelation of natural truth. From them all good qualities descended other animal kingdoms emphasising the maxim, 'petro, which is covered by perfumed petals of jasmine, should have fragrance'. Finally nature itself bowed head before their virtual visions and made the planet, a dream-world of divine love.

Due to their total faith in God …?

They didn't believe in God blindly but realised what His will was. Respected natural justice; comprehended the meaning of life, right and wrong; perceived the permeation of pure affection.

What might religious doctrines have taught them…!?

Religious beliefs were not necessary since no one had done any sins. No bitter consequences. They need not seek the way of truth. Sun has not to seek light. If no disease why treatment…?

Subsistence without suffering…?

Every basic need could be satiated from the nature's repository. They didn't want anything which harmed nature because of awareness about the necessity to keep nature's equilibrium for existence.

Then, how their time came to an end…?

Alas! At last, man put his right foot and entered with all of his characteristic ascendancy, to know about the possibility in order to build there his permanent domain.

Why couldn't man be driven away by anyone…?

War was not their way. They retreated to another distant planet, far away from man's hand-reaching distance. It was not a defeat, because their new place

---

[7] www.newworldencyclopedia.org/entry/yuga

was more divine than the earlier, as if, for every consequence there might have been a cause in physical world. They were glad to show how to live, and to direct mankind towards the way of truth and virtues.

But, what would man have thought…?

He thought that they were not interested in participating in the man-made grandeurs. Also presumed that man is the only animal entitled to enjoy material things.

Glories and Richness are only for mankind…?

Definitions given to 'glories', by man are not real. Man's arrogance is cause of sorrows. According to Greek mythology, crops and precious metals are believed to have come from the underworld, kingdom of Pluto (God of the dead). Pluto is considered as the lord of riches. So miseries hiding behind those things are to be carefully avoided with discernment while using. All glories of man have dual aspects. In the journey to the planet for domicile, it is festive in one sense and plaintive in another. Persons, who are going, may be in a dream-world of joy expecting a new life to be realized, but become sad thinking about their separation from relatives and pets. Otherwise has to change his attitude and follow the sacrosanct system. Does men follow their sacred way of life at least in that planet…? May be reluctant but later he must, like the Latin adage, 'experience is the teacher of fools'. Anyway he will be enforced to adjust with the rule of nature, otherwise be compelled to return to his old den.

If it happens…? In the present stage, by all means he will be thrown out by his fellow beings as routed residue of eagle eaten dove.

By and then, about the journey tomorrow

It is going to happen next morning. Passengers are getting ready for their longest journey. One of them is Mr. K'iche.J.Santler, commonly called as K'iche, from bank of *Mayan Riviera, Tabasco*[8] *of El Tortuguera* in the *Land of Mesoamerica*. 'J' stands for his mother's name, *Janne*. The word, 'K'iche' denotes his aristocratic family name, *'K'ichemoor'*. This will be his first travel out of his region! He had gone to the main market s once or twice. He knows his colloquial language not completely but got admission for the degree course in the college of cosmonautics which was in every respect owned by his father. Unfortunately, he was not able to follow the complexity of the course and hence dropped studies as wise men did. His interest is not in studies but in wandering! He had his relatives in Guatemala as well in Honduras.

Then how did he get this chance…?

---

[8] https://en.wikipedia.org/wiki/Tortuguero_(Maya_site)

In our world he was the only person bearing that name at the time of selection. Thus the fortune found him. More over, the planet is known as **Venus** as it is roaming like a zany during orbicular movement and wandering all the way! Really it has no fixed orbit. This wandering nature is not bad but good for the inhabitants, for it gives subtropical climate throughout the year. It is the reason for diversity in vegetation and versatile existence of animal kingdom.

Is Mr. K'iche competent…?

Competency or capability is not at all a matter when compared to other things happening on this planet. Anyhow praise him for his calm nature while praying. Above all, though each passenger is allowed to carry only one of the most essential articles, now he selects his Bible, well preserved with hard leather-bind, to carry with.

Oh! The clock is reminding that it is half past one.

Hoping they will drop off, tomorrow's astronauts went to bed…?

Not only tiredness but triggering notions will also stimulate slumber, which creates new dreams for tomorrows. After such a snooze the sun will come, after few hours. Till that time we shall dwell here hearing hushed songs of the moon, dripping into the merry milky light.

> How is she passing into the middle of the sky…?
> 'Holding a starry umbrella, the moon jaunts
> Like queen of heaven, in the bluish expanse
> Gladly with pet rabbit, like a lily on hands,
> Singing the lullaby with voice of reticence.
>
> Tales of thousands of eons she has, to tell;
> Of golden Mars, his marvelous mansions
> Paved all with those magical meteors, jell
> And pantheons faded in pendulous seasons.'

But, yonder she is yearning to go beyond the sight above the western horizon…?

Perhaps, her pet might have slept. Let her approach adobe to set the celestial cradle for it. Now dews of the dawn are starting to fall on chill cheeks of flower-buds from tips of leaves while the naughty breeze is trying to wake them up. In the East, glare of the Sun's golden chariot is slowly beginning to reflect on clouds as opened tapestries of the sky.

Ha! People should have gathered in the space-centre…?

Space-shuttle is ready to receive passengers into its inner cabin. All travelers are hurriedly spending last moments with their relatives before departure.

Moments of pleasure and pain…?

Combination of all feelings is flashing rapidly in all faces. Waving hands, astronauts are going to the green room to get ready.

At the entrance of the craft there lies gleaming silver metal blocks

It simply read A-T-H-E-N-A

Mr. K'iche is also receiving his space-suits and handing over his carriage to the *Cargo Controller-in-Charge*. Some began to appear near the glass-covered small window in their yellow space suit.

As per schedule, time has come to close the door of the Shuttle…?

About to close but suddenly the *Ground Officer* comes with a small carriage and calls Mr. K'iche!

"Mr. K'iche…. Mr. K'iche…..…. Mr. K'iche…………."

"What…?" –K'iche comes down quickly. His eye-brows were curved.

"This is not allowed; that's all…" –the Ground Officer puts the carriage in K'iche's hands as if throwing it away.

"It is my Bible, having weight, less than five hundred grams…" –K'iche shows the carriage as if weighing with hand.

"But not allowed…"

"Books are not allowed…?"

"Allowed except this…"

"You say, the Holy Bible is not permitted…?" –K'iche's sound becomes high. Tongue dried. Voice shivered.

"No. It is covered with leather…"

"What is the matter about leather-binding…?"

"You know, the new planet is perfectly squalor-proof. Nothing is allowed which produces grime and fetidity. Even air is sweet-smelling everywhere. Since all are getting energy from light, from 'Sun God'. No need to wait for that even we do here! No excrements, food-residues and so on. If you have such things, don't throw on outside as we do here, but use approved remnant-pits and plants. Everybody has to follow the rule of nature strictly. Moreover killing is prohibited. Leather is a symbol of animal-killing and a subject for dissection…" –the *Ground Officer* explains the matter.

"You don't waste our valuable time and before *Wayeb* [9] we must leave this hell"

"I didn't understood" he was perplexed
Means before the end of 13 th b'ak'tun
His brows curved
Means well before 13.0.0.0.0 falls on December 21st 2012.
Ohhhhhhhhh!

"What does that date mean?"
"You read our calendar based on venues?"
"I didn't"
"Our leaflet will tell more on as you reach there."
"Not now?'
"Will you please shut up and come............."
How many days to reach there..?
"If we go today then we may reach as it comes close to us'
How many days...............??
About 38 million K.m from here and day is not important.
Ill omen happens…?

The scene is ending as a comedy since Mr. K'iche gives the book to his relative and the door of the Shuttle closes.
People are waiting for the 'countdown'…?

Now seconds seem to be increasing. Not only the next few minutes but also the coming few days is of anxiety and imagination to us as well as the passengers. Most of them have started reading the lessons which were studied during the training period.
Probably they might have plunged into a thrill which can not be explained…?
Their heartbeat is steady but mind unsteady. All of them have a picture of the new planet as it appears on the front page of their booklet. At the same time a vague picture is in their brain, complicated with prospective, imagination and what they have studied in the training class.
What would be their main thought…?

---

9   https://en.wikipedia.org/wiki/Maya_calendar

Mainly about their new settlements as they would be strangers to themselves in that atmosphere just as a bride going to her bride-groom's house for the first time. Though basic arrangements were made there, and they had developed communication systems, they would be in an isolated stage since they see vacant moors and meadows, deserted pavements and streets etc. contradictory to the common sight facing us in our planet.

Thought about their friends and relatives left behind…?

In the case of man's vacillating mind, it is only as a self-denial while standing in grave-yard seeing the follies of greedy life, and when he returns from there, forgets all such revulsions and relapses into his former selfish life. Above all, existing communication facility reduces the depth of separation and links the distance between them.

Man is not free from the most tarnishing selfishness even if he gets all blessings…?

When they start dwelling in the new planet, we will be able to say about the accurate nature of mankind. Till that time we have to wait to know whether 'tomorrow's raiment is weaved today by the yarn of yesterday's antiquity'.

Here on earth, what do people think about…?

While taking small concave ladles to pour gruel mixed with coconut-scrapes into plates placed before hungry stomachs, what is to think about except appetite? But enthusiastically desire that one day they also can go to the *shimmering soil,* dreaming about other new planets which are more prosperous, opulent and delightful, since mankind has no life except the shade of expectation.

****

Chapter 2

Danger Comes

The space-craft has just landed in the hill side of the new planet. Mr. K'iche is the first person to get down from the cabin. He is received by a melodious song meaning, 'the last name evanesced from here has come at last; welcome to this precious and prominent prosperity...'! One by one the passengers are coming down. With an expression of surprise...?

Commander in Chief explained:
The first astonishment is the difference in time. Here one day is equal to two hundred and forty three days in the planet you left. That is why life is longer here. Since this situation is mingled with uniform celestial climate and the peculiar diet system, prime and health of persons will last almost throughout life.

Mr. K'iche! have you read that?

"Yea! but not digested!"

It reads:
tzuhtzo: m uy-u:xlaju:n pik
chan ajaw u: x uni: w
uhto:m il[?]
ye'ni/ye:n bolon yokte'
ta chak joyaj

(Thirteenth calendar cycle will end on the fourth day of Ahu. Darkness will blot before Univ. Bolon yookte, god of nine will descend from the sky into red.)

The wonderful sight of the earth appeared on a large screen, placed in the entrance of the Space-Centre! If needed, anyone can select and see any part, any terrain as per their wish, but normally it is showing the places that come in the direction of the satellite-station. From this heaven dweller has got a chance to see a planet namely earth. There everything seems so strange and beyond meaning.

Now it is showing a remote hamlet of *Land of the Ganges*[10] known as, *Kalpam*[11] which is quite unknown to all passengers. Everyone is looking eagerly on the screen as if seeing an imaginary place:

....

....

Few strangers are coming to the poor village by holding the Holy Bible in one hand and the Holy Cross in other. They are smiling sympathetically towards dirty slim naked children who are playing hither and thither forgetting their bleed dry stomach's burning cry. They are pouring blessings by putting hands on the poor innocent people's panic head and touching the Cross on forehead.

"Saviors have come at last to our village...! They are Missionaries of Crosalvism ......," rabble's mumbled words are rising.

Unfamiliar persons abruptly become familiars; go beyond rivers and hills......

Certain persons pointed out their viewpoint by looking at the strangers with sharp eyes:

"Beginning of all hazards is amusing..."

Strangers are squinting against the serene place with amazement since such a locus is quite unfamiliar to them and had not heard before from their land or even from tales of their holy books.

By observing their long sleeved feet-touching jacket, tribal farmers are coming from the field after stopping work and kneeling down before their feet. Since many children orphaned by famine became dependent of the Mission, farmers

---

[10] & 11Imaginary name for India an imaginary hamlet in India

[11] https://en.wikipedia.org/wiki/Kalpa_(aeon)

feel that same may happen to all families. Moreover, families converted to *Crosalvism*, are getting food and shelter from missionaries.

"Before a hungry man poison will also be palatable...," One man observes.

One of the farmers asks the missionaries that "I had cut my tuft and put pendant with rosary in neck to become a Crosalvanist and what else has to do, to get entry permit to *State of freedom*[12]?"

Newly baptized are marching towards them with bowed head as obedient sheep as they have no place to go but to the mission, since they are pulled out of their own communities and culture. They put a name for their celebration. Christmas carols and religious dance troops are wandering in the streets praising Jesus and uttering loudly, "Merry Xmas...Merry Xmas". Coloured star-lamps are jiggle in the breeze in front of houses and decorated road junctions as a sign of acceptance ....!!

While reading, Poorvapunya slipped into small somnolence and slowly fell into deep sleep. The book was still lying opened in her lap. Time crept out silently like a small cat into darkness of night. Nightingales flew over her, singing unknown songs. At last, the moon paled, faded and disappeared in the western horizon.

"Poorva....where are you...? Wake up....; do you forget the routine of the dawn...?" mother scolded but wept in heart knowing that her poor house has no routine except starvation. Her voice trembled like a tall tree in tempest because of motherly compassion towards her only daughter, Poorvapunya.

Leaves of Eternal tranquility were kept apart. She came down from fantasy to facts now!

Poorvapunya looked at the rising Sun with contempt and asked: "Oh! Lord; you come every morning with smiling face but with empty hands for the poor. So we can see you only with unpleasant eyes filled with tears, the true symbol of sorrows. Can it be called destiny...?"

Her thought gradually plunged into the celestial beauty of the village, perceived by ancestors:

This hamlet, named '**Kalpam**' (means *eon*), is a dale of oddness. North-East boundary is a snow-white mountain with a high peak. It is not running on the riddle of development or juvenile gust of lust, like other regions. There are lines of old ramshackle huts on both sides of bare muddy deflected roads

---

[12] Imaginary name for USA.

filled with stones and withered leaves, along with roofless carts laying under lonely *Gul-Mohar* trees to welcome new visitors.

The river flowing into the middle of the village, is very thin in summer and in certain places drift is about to break. Ridged paddy-fields on both the banks are prepared for next farming. Innocent kids are playing along the causeways near. Distant snow clad high mountain tops looked like a black elephant due to the heat of the summer. In the sides of cliff cows and sheep are seeking for grass, not fully dried up. Towards north the road reaches up to the wide embankment beyond a pandemonium, where one of the oldest temple's spires is standing high. Behind the temple, in the corner of a small moor, dry leaves are falling on the small abode of Poorvapunya, which is directed towards East......!

Her Grand-father, Narayan swamy was a respected Brahmin Priest in the nearby temple, adorned with the idol of Sree Krishna.
He had told earlier to Ambal:

"Before the arrival of activist-missionaries of various fanatic religious transformations as *Berithism, Crosalvism, Al-Taqwa* so on in the village, people of different classes were living in harmony without any discrimination except caste system, among the poor and the rich. Christians, Muslims, Jews, Jains etc. were there. But religions never came to their thoughts. No outraging elements existed in the society. No religious splits, chaos or clashes. Pleasure and peace prevailed everywhere as each person was willing to render any help to others as far as possible by him discarding community or class.

Almost all religions have become flowers devastated by the corroding of maggots – the activist groups formatted from and scrabbling on them – growing inside the tender petals.

When Missionaries of Crosalvism arrived, they sowed gospels among the mass and those gospels sowed the seeds of racial discriminations along with belief in Jesus only. Crosalvism divided the world into believers and non believers. It taught that the only extreme believer will go to heaven and the latter will go to hell, where one is eternally barbecued.

Someone engaged in looting, forceful proselytizing and killing of other religious followers. They engaged in killing those who were not strictly following their thoughts. The same reflection occurred in other sects in this village also and then the people began to look at each other with contempt, prejudice and hatred. It ultimately unleashed a reign of violence and destruction unparalleled in history. All temples, cultural centres, libraries etc. were destroyed and brutal attacks followed on resistors.....

Among those artificial calamities Narayan swamy's temple was totally demolished; he was thrown to the street along with his aged mother, paralysed wife and two year old daughter Ambal. Their unsecured life was attacked again and again by spies of missionaries. So Ambal, mother of Poorvapunya, has an incurable wound of enmity even towards Christianity and Apostles.

Her mind turned to the terrible story heard from her mother about those childhood days:

One day, holding the hands of Grandfather Ambal was going the temple on the zenith of the mount in the morning. They got to the top of the hill through a red-stone paved narrow sloppy way.

A lonely banyan tree with stretched branches seemed to be totally separated from this world...

Under its shade, different kinds of serpents' idols were present around the stub .....!

In that small plain land, a little temple made up of *Krishnasila*[13], the blue petro, as a tribute of pre-historic period stood...!

Bell rang before opening the door of the temple. A few devotees were standing with folded hands to venerate in front of the door...

Abruptly, an angry gang carrying weapons came and attacked the worshipers; destroyed the idols, outraged against ritual articles and threw grandfather out of the temple...!!

They turned towards the idols of *Nag* (serpent) under the banyan tree and threw them into nearby bush.....

Unexpectedly king-cobras and other serpents rushed towards the aggressors......!

While telling those kinds of stories her mother's glittering face rose in her memory. Mother used to laugh at those reprobates by telling olden tales with different facial expressions.

"But these types of prodigious tales do not serve the necessity of avoidance of religious clashes, which may befall in this hamlet also..," Poorvapunya's mind agitated.

On the way to the factory, Mary asked:

"Tell me Poorva, how can people hate each other because they belong to different religions...?"

"I think nobody can hate neighbours in the name of religion or caste...," Poorvapunya replied.

---

[13] A black rock used to make statue of God for adoration in temple

"Nay, my friend… that is what happens now everywhere……," Mary's words were full of hopelessness.

"It is nothing but imprudence of activist religious groups as *Crosalvism*……," Poorvapunya nodded her head angrily.

"New reports are coming from different parts of the world about communal riots. Main matters of talks among the factory workers yesterday, were about those cruelties related with riots. Now you are going to join as a trainee in the factory. So you can hear all news from there every day…," Mary reminded.

"Yea Mary, I think this work will fetch me at least a few coins, though not enough to save my family from starvation but can have food at least once in a day to hold our life in a dipped poverty. Most of the families in this village are like ours and how can they hate each other while struggling for existence except hostility against their famine…," Poorvapunya revealed her opinion.

"Can you execrate me or my family as we belong to different religions…?" Mary asked.

"God promise… I think I can't miss you whatever may happen. If water is in the pot, it will reflect on the outside also like affection and belief…"

"But did you hear yesterday's news from *Soil of the Wine-yards*[14] and …… It was bloodshed in the office of a magazine which published some cartoons.,"!

Mary began to tell the news from her memory.

Poorvapunya kept mum.

In the street of Royal empire indigenous dwellers looted shops that belonged to the other nations and targeted their life and in the land of Kangaroo students were immolated to ashes and bust their head with planks.

Poorvapunya intervened with a trembling voice, remembering the story, she read a week before:

"Atrocities like this just described in the book *Eternal tranquility*. Twelfth chapter, which I read last night, is a story about the complete eradication of human society from a region by a religious clash…"

"It may happen anywhere…," Mary hushed for a while.

Remembering the vague bewailing of the people, heard during the live commentary, she continued:

"Today religious clash will break out! Oh! Then all of this village would be annihilated. Then it would be the last one; poor villagers were lamenting all over the place and hence the commentaries were not clear. Here we also are

---

[14] Imaginary name for France

sitting above such secret explosives. The surreptitious discussions of activists reveal this…"

Some persons are in the doldrums, thinking about the disaster that is going to happen. A few are pleasant because today is their Deity's birthday.

In the evening a new inspiration haunted the village because the famous great festival of the temple is on this day. Every year there will be Dramas, pageantry of elephants etc. This year also all arrangements are made by the temple-authorities for the celebration, and that can be read from the pleasant face of the villagers.

"Are you coming with us ..…? We are going early; otherwise yard will be filled………," they walked faster.

The people are gathering in the light of flamboyance and traditional lamps, spread over the open yard of the temple.……

In one corner mahouts are caparisoning elephants by putting golden nets on forehead, locking handles on coloured parasols………

Nearby, a big Stage is being built, though temporary but seems to be permanent and modern .……!

All sides of the entrances, east, west, north and south are filled with footpath-sellers of gilt-rings, puppets, balloons and so on……….!

Trumpet begun…….. Festival has started.… Pomp and jauntiness at the eastern tower as a mark of celebrations.

In the middle of the festooned yard, a few gangs of drum-beaters and flutists in colour-dress are gathered. According to the rising sounds of quickly vibrating cymbals, cadence of large ears of embellished tuskers and gleam of other golden pendants enhance the beauty of the scene. *Alavattom*[15] made up of peacocks' feather, is being swayed according to large sound of accompaniments and rhymes.……!

Exchange of adorned colourful parasols; seem to be glassy in the luminary, between mahouts who are standing on elephants, gives interesting scenery to people! All are standing as in a wonder world.……!
Before waking up to reality, arises a group-wail; some people fall down, some run away, some shout for help………!

"Alas…! What happens…?" – People unaware of the incident but fell down within minutes……….!

The yard becomes a red-fort with blood-stained bodies. The spectators are trodden by a rutting elephant.……!!!

---

[15] https://en.wikipedia.org/wiki/Thrissur_Pooram

Thus the festival lasts in a dire pitiable episode. At last the most stupid declaration comes from the temple:

"The event is due to the anger of Deity...."

Seeing pyres of friends and relatives as first sight, the villagers woke up to next morning with sad and tired face........!!

The atmosphere was covered everywhere including the neighboring house of Lilly, the small child of Mahout Marcus.

Lilly looks and goes towards the first flower which is blooming on her favourite rose plant.

Plucking it she asks her father:

"Papa...... shall I give this flower to my mate...? While lying in pyre, she might have been looking at it. She was too much fascinated by it, when I offered yesterday; but......," her voice trembles.

Hearing her daughter's words, Marcus looks with a shock at his next house, where in the southern corner of the quad, fire-flame has not yet ceased from pyre of his neighbor's little child.....

"No, We will not go there........"

"Why? Papa........; I think, death is not only for them. It was not different for us because mother died just like them. Was it? Can any religion control it? We were Hindus like them till last year. No change occurred to us except some beliefs and names........"

"Yea..., do as you like...," his careless consent is hurdled and hampered in throat.

But even before the approval, she has moved towards the neighbour's house holding the flower in her folded hands....!

She is approaching and slowly entering into the rising pile-fire.....

"Don't..., my dear child...., don't....Lilly...don't.....," Marcus cries and covering eyes with shivering palms.

"Don't be afraid, father....; fire will not burn truthful love....; her soul will cool this fire for me, her comrade....."

Walking with wavering feet, he reaches near the funeral-pyre and kneels down and begins to weep.

"Forgive me.....; I have done that transgression......; I have done the felony......; I was that sinner who killed those innocent people yesterday in the temple yard......; I was that mahout who made the elephant violent and rode it over the mass......; I was that activist who acted for the mission to turmoil and tarnish the temple and Deity.......; I am responsible for those religious deaths......," his confession continues.

"Dear Marcus, if you realise your mistake, you are forgiven........." –hears the words as a new commandment. Marcus gets frightened and gets up!

Lamenting Parents sitting near their child's heap of ash console him further:

"God will forgive everyone; so everyone will have to forgive one another."

Marcus returns with quick steps and waves head and hands in the air as if he has taken some firm determination while his other neighbours are cursing and looking at him with contempt and hostility.

****

Chapter 3

Girl in the Kingdom of Day Dream

Remembering nightmare that happened in the village, Poorvapunya completed her daily routine. Mean while her buddy Mary reached and asked by showing front roof's shadow of the house, slowly creeping down from veranda to the foreground:

"It is half past ten now; are you still flying in the realm of fantasy...?

Please come down to reality; stop your work and come with me...; I have been searching for you from the Christmas-eve...."

"I am only a little fly there, accept; but you are the queen in the land of fantasy. Tiger hasn't the right to blame cat's tail...," Poorvapunya looked at Mary in jest.

Mary is the eldest daughter of a converted Christians, not having hard core religious thoughts. Their forefathers were Hindus. Nowadays, several people are coming to their houses, where priests of Crosalvism do healing and try to turn them to their way.

There is a rumour in the village:

"There are several magical performances like curative the sick by which missionaries of Crosalvism are persuading people for proselytizing........."

They repeat the same words of Francis Xavier that, "wherever you find this type of idolatry, you find a grinding poverty has been cursed."*1

They are ironically spreading the historical event that happened during the middle of twentieth century by picking up the words of Francis Xavier, who was one of the missionaries to north-eastern side of *Land of the Ganges*:

"When I had finished conversion process, I force them to burn the huts in which they kept their idols of numerous gods and goddesses, and I have seen them break the statues into tiny pieces, since they are now Christians. I could never come to an end describing the great happiness which fills my heart when I see idols being destroyed by the hands of those who are its followers.........."

Poorvapunya went to the neighbour's house with Mary. There, an amazing prize was awaiting her!

When she entered in the yard, a stranger came out of the room and wished her:

"Good morning Poorvapunya......, very glad to see you....."

She kept mum, but was looking surprisingly at him as he called her name.

Mary introduced him to Poorvapunya:

"My friend, this is Mr. Michael, came from *Royal empire*[16] after ordination. Now he is doing missionary and charity works here for the Crosalvists' Sabha....."

For half an hour, Michael continued talks with Poorvapunya about the village and the poor families. Due to his eagerness and compassion against the poor, she was attracted to his character.

When she was about to leave the house in the afternoon, he gave one set of Pyjama and said:

"Dear Poorvapunya let me give these clothes to you in the name of God. I am deeply happy to see and get you as a good comrade in this earthly life, like a valuable treasure bequeathed by God..."

She returned home immediately with delight. By seeing the Pyjama, her mother asked:

"From where did you get these jackets....?"

"Yes... Ma...it is given by God...."

"From God....?" Mother wondered.

Poorvapunya laughed and said:

"One, Mr. Michael, of Crosalvists' Sabha gave me in the name of God....",

Mother advised with a groan:

"Dear daughter, you must be aware of the fact that in the name of God, Satan may come first."

Poorvapunya told herself: **God in deep silence But Satan works** ???!!!

"Missionaries, working for the Crosalvists' Sabha, are not Satans, but Saints like holy Angeles because they are serving people to eradicate poverty as well as interceding between man and God. That means, the request for forgiveness of any sin that is committed by them can be conveyed only through the priest, who has a tremendous amount of influence over the laity; since a believer does not go to heaven on his own merit...," Poorvapunya explained.

---

[16] Imaginary name for U.K

Mother thought for a while and replied remembering her old learning from her ancestors:

"My punya, do you think that Crosalvists' Sabha is the patron in these pathetic situations? Crosalvism is not real Christianity as you think.

It believes in exclusiveness and says that Christ alone can lead people towards God and through Him only as He is the only son of God. After the death of Christ, churches were set up in the name of Him. Popes, the Cardinals, the Bishops, the priests etc., became his inheritors, who supposed to be believed that, they can guide people towards Jesus. But how is it possible since they themselves are not following Christ and his words, 'true love and sacrifice'.......?" And even Crosalvanism is the extreme in Christianity. As in an argument manner she continued:

"For us, religion is not a mere ritual, but a philosophy of life. It has no specific religious books exclusively for them but for all, a prophet or a centralised hierarchy. The correct description of Hinduism is '*Sanatana Dharma*'[17] which means true routine of life; if it is sustained; there will not be any poverty or discrimination in the society. Service for upliftment of the poor becomes necessary only if poverty exists. Hence the social discrepancies are artificially created by the upper classes, who are the real exploiters of natural resources on which every one have equal right according to real world concept of *Dharma*. Poverty is not a spontaneously generating one. If one is tempted to accept a religion to get over his poverty, it is not his real belief but failure or surrender before the dearth. Dear, you are very young; you are unable to think the religious squeezing......."

Mother continued her speech like a celebrant on religion depicting several stories and visions. At last she said:

"When I was about to deliver you, Poorva, the hospitals owned by the Crosalvist' *Sabha* were not willing to admit and treat me. Your father begged for mercy before them seeing my critical stage. Finally, I was lying unconscious under that tree, when you were born and cried...," Pointing towards the Gulmohar tree standing with beautiful spreading branches in the small yard she continued, "Later the same Sabha asked me to baptize you as a Christian at least!......."

Poorvapunya thought: showing humanity as a way to convert. Oh god! What a shame to even god!

But they started a Hospital and small factory in our hamlet, at least!!

---

[17] https://en.wikipedia.org/wiki/San%C4%81tan%C4%AB

On hearing the stories, Poorvapunya began to think about her past and sat under the Gul-mohar tree. The sun was creeping behind the gliding clouds in the sky. Gradually shadow of the tree began to stretch its arms towards the East. She went to good old days of child-hood memories:

Wearing a small green jacket and holding the hand of her mother, Poorvapunya is walking along the pathway. A smiling, long-bearded man, seemed to be a priest, gives her a puppy-toy and a small Cross from his pocket pretending affection.

Then she remembered about another old man who had told earlier about her past and future prophetically. He had told her that later she would become a Christian! She had replied surprisingly that it was impossible as she was a Brahmin. Then the forecaster laughed and explained again that it is easily possible because conversion happens where there were neither our own thoughts nor belief. Poor people are the puppets in the hands of aggressive proselytising religious groups, such as Hindus; since they face serious threats from the greatest war made in their past and everything that linked them to their own earth, because the aggressors seek an article of the faith to erase the past.

Before the old man's memory slowly fades away from thought, he approaches and says as a shocking narration:

"Did you hear about the pre-historic days of mankind…? Our fore fathers were man-eaters…! To overcome the sins, they bequeathed and pray to God. If blessing to be receive then, you must believe in Christianity and Jesus. He will save you from all sins."

She looks anxiously and asks:

"Then what would be the results and their evidences …?"

"Surely there will be some miracles like escaping from accidents, supernatural skills etc., as Moses changed the water of the Nile to blood…," Priest answers.

Mother questions about conversion procedure:

"Then how conversion changes a human being? What will be the consequence of conversion?"

Priest reveals thus:

"Conversion means a total change to a human being. His name will change with a new surname. By this, he escapes from the past family links. His language will change gradually. His dress will change. Ultimately changes will come even to life style and thus he becomes a new man. …….."

Her mother asks a doubt:

"Then how can we attain salvation without changing other aspects of life or if all other aspects of life remain the same?"

"Oh that is......," the Priest tries to flee from the matter.

"That is why at the time of setting up a conversion centre, protest comes. It is proved that the cultured, educated and perspective converts and even Christian society may also protest and hence the Crosalvism centres may have to cease their conversion efforts.......," sharp words of mother continue.

In the illusionary imagination, the debate on religious dilemmas entwined like octopus, while the world of dreams was spreading a magical spell over her.......!

Dropping of flowers from the tree along with mighty rain drop and wind waked her up. It was about to get dark. Folks were returning to their house along the country road towards the north western hill from the fields with sheaves on head. Canopy was calmly clearing. Array of clouds began to flow away. In the evening twilight, the farmers with their mow cluster seemed to be the mob with life burdens going towards the end of this world through the gate way of the mountain.

Lanterns began to lighten houses everywhere. Poorvapunya lit the lamp before the sweet basil in the court with devotion. People began to gather in nearby temples and churches, showing their vanity-dresses and ornaments, each other. In poor houses, half naked old women started evening prayers by sitting in small verandas in sparkling flash of little lamps, as they don't have enough cloths to go outside. Spread everywhere loud noises of ringing bells from Temples and Churches like competition in calling God's attention!!

Then, Poorvapunya engaged in the preparatory works for the next day because she has to go to a small factory to join as a trainee.

Early in the morning she got ready to go to the working place with Mary; entered the foreground and plucked crisp flowers from crysanthus and adorned her long flourished hair.

Mary admired the beauty of Poorvapunya:

"Oh! Now the flower on your hair looks like a sparkling ringlet of surfed water in a dark water-fall. How rosy is your face, like a blooming Lotus in the morning. Look, butterflies are flying around your feet with delight! You are an Angel of this poor land. Lords may come with golden chariots to receive you to Heaven. And you are like a celestial nymph...," she continued comments but Poorvapunya kept heedlessness and smiled. Moon-lash flashed everywhere.

While going, they overheard a preaching sound near the cross road. It was a philosopher.

He was trying to purge all blind beliefs and religious debaucheries as well as the futility of hostile attacks on Eastern religions by Western religions, with his words of Wisdom. He said:

"Ignorance rules all minds and hatred prevails their hearts. Basic issues, confronting these places such as poverty and education remain unanswered….."

Crowded people, clapping hands, admired him. But he calmly clarified the reality of life and the deceptions of various religions in the name of God.

Poorvapunya looked into the gap of the crowd. She saw an old man standing among them. A picture of one face rose from her memory to mind:

One day when she was a young child, her Grandfather and his brother were coming to her house; she ran towards them laughing and calling, but the younger brother of her grandfather told her not to call him as a relative since he had already denounced all family relations. He advised her to call him *"Swami"**. That time she was weeping with eyes full of tears, timidity and doubts…….!

Mary was surprised when Poorvapunya told that story and stopped there for a while to hear his speech.

They identified Mahout Marcus among the audience, who was attending the old man's speech.

The philosopher says:

"A true believer is not betrayed by illusionism or miracles. He accepts all ways used for God-realization. Even though annihilated several cultures and social setups, why couldn't the pacifying religious activism like *Al-Taqwa,* find a path of eternal, unquestionable religious civilization and disclosure of life and death, Heaven, Hell etc?   They are not pacifying but making the mankind cruel and unkind by giving misleading statements about the olden stories like Bible or Qur'an as gospels………." The philosopher asked about the reality of religion and faith. The curious audience became silent for a while.

He began to describe 'What would be a religion':

"A religion must be a true path which can direct one to the ultimate Truth. Truth is the reality of life which means the equality of soul in all organisms. Here it is clear that discriminations, whatever may be, are misrepresentations which are veiling the truth. Instead of compassion, killing and eating of animals denote irrational distinction. Wise animals like human beings are tied with Dharma or consequences of all actions in life. Thus a true religion is nothing but virtue, which other animals do not have…….."

"Killing of animals is like cutting of plants as they also have life; then how can we live…..?" One among the audience asked loudly.

Smiling with a deep thought, the old man replied:

"If the top of a tree is cut, another sprout will spring up again; but in the case of an animal …….? This means life of plants is not bust after cutting.

Animals are experiencing all pain and feelings at the time of killing but plants are out of pain as it has no central nervous sytem for feelings. But obliteration of parts of plants which contains jeeva or life must be avoided. No one has the right to efface jeeva by destroying the things. which holds life. Hence, don't eat rudiment of a plant, which possesses jeeva or life in that part, for next genesis. You may forward a feeble argument that when one potato is cut, its life is not lost.

Really, if we cut sprout, its life in that area will be destroyed.

All other parts can be eaten. This rule of aliment is applicable only to those species of animals which have wisdom or intelligence. Others have no binding on their action or consequence of their deeds. Miff and merit are measured in the case of animals having discernment, like human being. Animals which are unable to realise transgression and virtue would be able to attain salvation without following morals….." He concluded:

Which food is good to us? vegetarian or ?

"when you see a dead sheep on the way whether saliva come out from your tongue? Saint asked.

No! Not at all? One of the person replied

"But for a carnivorous it is a good feast to see a dead animal and to smell it and we can't think of killing a cow with our hands and mouth to drink it's hot blood but they do… That is why we are herbivorous and we are known as human beings" he answered. And our intestine is very long and we have no long claws and we are more alkaline like our mother earth.

"In a nutshell, morality is the obligation of wise ones."

The big drops of knowledge dripped again from the old man towards the listeners soaking the soil of their ignorance:

"The Cosmic Soul is the eternal basic ultimate and radical energy which is the combination of physical energy and non-physical energy. Non-physical energy is the negative energy. In other words physical and non-physical energy are generated from the Cosmic Soul or the Basic Energy due to the division process. Physical energy is called as Prakrithi or physical world. The Cosmic Soul which exists in an organism in the Physical world is called Jivatma or individual self. When specific form of physical energy and non-physical energies are combined together, individual self or Jivatma is formed, which is the transferred motion effect from the non-physical energy to the physical energy. This is flowing through generations as a life-river towards the eternal sea, the Cosmic Soul."

"What would be a faith…?" He turned to another point:

"Faith must be the realisation of the real self from illusion."

His speech continued to flow like a gush to the muddled brain of the audience. The gathering trembled with a new inspiration of wisdom as trees in a tempest!

"Does religion make a man's life full of sanctity?" One asked from the crowd.

Another question rose from next corner: "What is sanctity? Who is a saint?"

While they were silently waiting for the reply, the philosopher explained:

"Sanctity is the consequence of merits or the actions which imparts goodness to other living beings. Saint is one who possesses sanctity. A true religion must advise to follow these merits. In a nutshell, a true Religion is only a social concept of 'Dharma' or office. All others are examples of illusionism........."

Another man asked:

"What actually religions are doing now in the name of God?"

"Now destined for selfishness, religions are becoming rotten and muddy because of diversion from the path and aim for which they are created. Basic concept of all religions is ethical integrity more or less leads to social equality. Social egalitarianism roots in love and generosity along with all human virtues and we are doing and acting to do things in the name of God but god is not interested in anything. Just seeing things as neutral observer only and he is deep silence ...."

It was a thunder reverberation: **God in deep silence But...**

He spoke about the necessity of cardinal virtues in a true human being, to be generous, cultured and wise. His words as dart pierced through the triads of hostile religions. The reflections were seen as long sighs, bowed heads and murmurings in the assemblage. Further he particularized the futility of conversion ironically, "as the Pope is unhappy with other sectors of Christians, then there will be unhappiness among other religions against Christians or Muslims........"

"Then why people are coming to Sanadhana Dharma......," another person asked:

"A few are coming not by means of temptations but on the basis of their identities and visualization...," he replied.

Could we ask more questions? One of the persons asked

Swami's eyebrows curved.

Who makes my mind think? Who fills my body with vitality? Who causes my tongue to speak words? What I can see through my eyes are only thing visible to me and same thing is true for my ears also. but truth is beyond to this.

Swami replies through Kena Upanishad

Self is in the ear of the ears, the eye of the eyes, the mind of the minds. The word of words and the life of the lives.

We don't know, we cannot understand, because he is different from the known and he is different from the un-known.

What is the meaning of self?

Swami replies through Mandukya Upanishad

Self is bright but hidden and it is the goal of life to know self

What is our body?

It is the blend of panchabhootha which lives due to prana and is the Holding energy of panchabhootha.

What is self realization?

Swami replies through Brihadaranyaka upanishad

Centered in to the peace that brings complete self control and perfect patience. They see themselves in every one and every one in themselves

How can we realize self?

Swami replied:

Conscious spirit and unconscious matter both have existed since the dawn of time with Maya(illusion) appearing to connect them mis- representing joy as outside us.

What is the meaning of death? Does a person live after death?

Swami replies through Kena Upanishad

All knowing self was never born nor will it die. Beyond cause and effect this self is eternal and immutable. When body dies the self does not die. Of those not aware of the self, some are born as embodied creatures while others remain in a lower stage of evolution, as determined by their own need for growth.

What happens at the time of death?

Swami replies

When body and mind became weak, self gathers in all the power of life and descends to heart and finally to brain and go out through brahmarandra and finally to God. By the light of the heart the self leaves the body by one of its gates when it leaves prana(life energy) follows, and with it all the vital powers of the body. He who is dying merges in consciousness and thus consciousness accompanies him when he departs, along with the impressions of all that he has done, experienced and known

Suddenly an unexpected wave arose in the corner of the session.

An arrow-like object abruptly darted towards the philosopher!

It was a long knife that a fanatic man had hurled at him in the speed of a whirl-wind.

Hearing the clutter, a lady stood up in haste from the front! an open knife penetrated on her back.....; identifying her cry, the fanatic rushed towards her and pulled the knife out of her shoulder. It was his wife...........!

People assembled around him like herd of wolf but the philosopher dissuaded them saying that 'let him study the lesson of truth from the fanatic deeds and their precepts'.

The man surrendered and bowed his head while the philosopher was trying to piece his shawl to bind the wound of the lady and the wounded finger of the fanatic as an elder brother. The place was filled with echoes of the scolding and revilements which rose from the gathering. Words of the philosopher were heard as follows:

"Life is to be considered as individual part of the whole society. When we think about the activities of all organisms or heavenly bodies, it is obvious to see that everybody is doing their duties or routines of life individually. In case human being is also carrying on his own life which is apart from others as society; in general nature, there may have some resemblance in life but it is always different. This shows that the salvation decides individual process. Some religions are putting axe on the root of this truth by injecting fanatics in men. They are the real rivals of mankind and makers of this gorgeous globe to graveyard from which rises the horrific smoke of religious deaths. Actual antagonist will come as an acquaintance....."

Like a drizzle in the summer, the words out-poured down to thought-draught mind of the people.

After hearing the speech, people dispersed seeking their daily routine, but everyone's heart was filled with several rational doubts and arguments about the idiocy of many of the religions transformed into various fanatic groups as Judaism into *Berithism*, Christianity into *Crosalvism*, Islam into *Al-Taqwa* and Hinduism into *Saindhava* etc. Farmers turned to fields, Merchants to shops, students to schools, Workers to only factory in the village.

Day long quietly those qualms were lying in their mind as indigested food. Some insoluble and excruciating substances of them were emitted unexpectedly even during their working time in between ordinary parleys:

"If in the day of judgment, body and soul will rejoin and start a second life, that life should be a worldly one like earthly born man. Then it means that there is one more physical life after death………."

Although religious rites were followed by the people blindly, they used to think, as if mankind is doubtful about itself!

****

Chapter 4

Mystifying Fade Away

Though informal, debates revealed plentiful timely realities, theories, theologies, tongue's talents; tears-soaked sympathetic tales were among the dialect! With a long sigh, someone dragged others' attention to the pathetic story of Julia:

"Do you memorize Julia's chronicle..........."

"Nay; how was that?" The whisper rose from lips of others amazingly.

"Destruction of scientific and cultural developments due to the induction of religious cannons and laws and their communal cautious attempts to capture the neck and dam the last breath of civilization occurred by introducing religious futilities and thoughts. The memorable instance is of Julia's story. Julia was the last scientist, mathematician, astronomer, physicist and the head of the School of philosophy - an extraordinary range of accomplishments for any individual in any age, who worked in the library. The place Syrodia – by then long under Patrician rule – was a city under grave strain. Slavery had sapped classical civilization of its vitality. Julia stood at the epicentre of these mighty social forces. In great personal danger, she continued to teach and publish her books of wisdom........!

One day, on her way to work, she was set upon by a fanatical mob of Daron's parishioners. They dragged her from her chariot, tore off her clothes, and, armed with abalone shells, flayed her flesh from her bones. Her remains were burned; her work obliterated; her name forgotten. Alas! At last, Daron was made a saint...!"

"No surprise; in the Hell who will get the diadem except the Devil...?" Everyone laughed and cared to listen more.

"Tell..., what was her misdemeanor......?" Their curiosity increased.

"She might have prayed for equality.....; might have revealed the truth that Prayers, Drums and Bells of a church won't guide a man to Heaven or salvation.....; might have spoken loudly that real heaven or salvation means the ultimate realisation of God ....; might have taught that realisation can be attained not through Sunday-mass or confession before a priest but through human goodness or Dharma......."

"Oh! My friends; have the sense of hearing about her last day....," listeners' impatience hurried up.

"At last, the obsessive mobs tacked the last sting down in her coffin and carried it to cemetery with victorious gladness. They rollicked round her sarcophagus uttering various slogans to slander her....."

"Did they burry or eat her in such a rivalry and rage...," some one asked suspiciously.

"Should have eaten but nothing might have remained except some pieces of bones and broken skull...," commended by another.

"But, what was her fate...? The woeful ambience arranged an unprecedented farewell to her!! Swiftly vicinity became depressing; Sun veiled his face with clouds; tears began to fall down from horizon's cloudy eyes...; As Godly willful pat, a tender breeze caressed lightly on her coffin. Perhaps it was the sign that her eternal Self was sitting on swinging cot in the eternal peace...! Dear comrades, hear the real conclusion – Can destroy anyone; not the will of destiny"

Little by little, power of permeating day light began to lessen. Languished leaves of little plants lashed to life again, as awakening of small kids after sweltered sleep in the midday's mighty thermo.

Glows entered into clouds in the evening sky. Crows returned to grown up trees seeking nests. Canaille, child and old, were going with serious face apart from other common days because that was the 'Day of God', the day in which God comes on Earth to bring the devotees of newly born religion called, 'Men of God' !!

"In this village, famous for folkways, today is the 'Day of God' for us; don't you know?" The old man belongs to the religion, 'Men of God', continued the tale to his anxious grand-son, Yanov.

Yanov is a five year old boy studying in the Julia Memorial Nursery School. He always asked unanswerable questions to his grand-father while hearing tales related with religions since teachers had taught him the folly of religious tales.

While going to the sacred place with mother and grand-father, he asked:

"My teacher has said that death is not following us, but waiting for us. Is it true...?"

His mother pretended to be unheard. He asked again:

"Mammy, can I meet my father at the paradise.......?"

"Sure my son, tonight, we all will go to the Heaven. Archangel will come to Earth to bring us according to God's command. Today is the last day of this world and people on earth....," Mother replied

"Then how long we can live there?"

"For ever..."

"Then why we are born here? God should have kept all of us there......"

"We are born to teach others, our godly given religion and to obey His gospels......"

"Mummy, why couldn't have given to others also directly by God if this is His own?"

"Yanov, it's too much; no further questions. God will not receive unbelievers to Paradise, you remember......"

Hiding suspicions and sarcasms in mind, Yanov walks with them looking around and narrating to him what he sees.

"At last the fable is filling to fetch...," flush on face of Yanov, while thinking about the scene when the God comes before them to bless all and to carry them to Heaven.

Seemed to be earlier than any day, the full-moon is entering in the eastern horizon in celestial silvery chariot! Gathering people belong to the religion, 'Men of God', with folded hands are bowing then heads in piety. Everyone recognize, this is the last chance to pray on Earth. Restless hearts reckon swiftly the moments, one...., two....., three....! They can't realise real time.

It is past midnight now. See 'Falling stars' in the sky. Nature is quiet. Even the waves of the ferocious sea seemed to be sleeping sheep. What then? Trigger of tempest is tied up in tranquility.

Heart-beat can be heard in the silence. They are talking heart to heart and looking forward the gleaming infinite expanse of the sky. They are expecting for the opening of the eternal entry of enduring Paradise!

Suddenly it happens! The sky begins to shine more and more bully! Something appears in the middle of the sky. It is like a burning fire-ball with mysterious long shape with wings on both sides!

"Wonderful....! Wonderful.......! Angel is coming........., Angel is coming....," folks are crying with joy. Prayers and songs paralyze on their tongue for a while! Eye-lids forget to stir!

It is coming down through the expanse. Brightness is increasing and turns into red! People throw hands in the air and jump with happiness.......!

But, Alas! No one remembers, 'happiness always ends in calamity'

They hear big noises like falling sound of big stars. The startled rabble is running and scattering. Resonance of lamentation fills everywhere. Trembled villagers are rolling down as in deep eddy of a spinning gale. All begin to curse themselves and spread legends as lasting of world is now happening and fire rain will follow soon!

Abruptly, the place became as devastated as a battle field. Rose groaning sounds from different sides; half-dead bodies strangled for last breath; lay motionless corpses torn out while others ran over them! All those seemed as the remains of religious deaths due to superstitions and foolishness. Little Yanov cried loudly clasping his mother's body, but there was none to hear. No Angel came to listen his mourning or to save his mother. At last, sound became low and hurdled in throat; he fell down and fell in to doze!

When he woke up, in that land of fanatic people's self created calamity, some strangers were searching in the dawn, for parts of the satellite which collapsed previous night.

It was not the last day of the world, but of the newly born religion in that village. The disaster spread as last whistle of those beliefs and gospels. But self-declared persons, who act as apostles of God, could not sit idle. They came again in new guise.

That day while walking into the city, Marcus saw a group of people performing a religious dance in the yard of a Prayer Hall under the direction of some apostles, a customs that existed in olden days among some tribes. He thought:

"Are we going to enter into another aeon? Are we in the dale of decade of damnation? This is just like the dances conducted in olden days in Hawaii Islands. There were Cultural as well as religious dances. Cultural dances were revived. But religious dances were destroyed forever ever........"

Common folks were not interested in understanding the reality but very eager to follow the apostles as sheep behind butcher, who is in the guise of shepherd, bearing beard to hide cruelty but to show as sign of affection and glimmering garbs to dazzle the eyes of the poor. Thus the catastrophe became the compost to the conversion techniques of Crosalvism, even though those who trust holly spirit couldn't believe that.

Thereafter, yards of churches were filled with Christians. Copies of holy books were sold as hot cakes. Size and number of holy Crosses, increased and street renamed as holy cross road.

Long speeches were heard from loud-speakers:

"Dear friends, do you know how to believe in Christianity? If not, study what is the real religion for man's salvation.

Christianity is at least three things; A set of beliefs, a way of life, and a community of people. Different Christian groups place different weights on these three aspects. But they always involve all three. All the three aspects are based on the life and teaching of Jesus of Nazareth, who is also known as the Christ...."

Against the pompous arguments of Crosalvists, Berithists tried to tread it by explaining the origin:

"At first its appeal was almost confined to the adherents of Judaism though it presented itself as 'new'. Christianity shares a number of beliefs and practice with other religions, particularly Judaism and Islam. Like them, Christians believe in one God, who created the universe and all that is in it. All believe that this God is active in history, guiding and teaching his people. All three religions including Christianity have been called ethical monotheism. This term emphasizes the belief in one God and the fact that following this God commits us to a number of specific ethical rules or principles.

Christianity originally developed as a part of Judaism. *Jesus* was a Jew. He lived from about 3 BC to 30 AD. He lived and taught in primarily among fellow Jews. Christianity is separated from the main body of Judaism for two major reasons:

Christianity came to regard Jesus as in some sense God's presence in human form. This was unacceptable to Jews.

Judaism is defined by a covenant made between God and the Jewish people. Part of this covenant is the law, a set of religious and ethical rules and principles. Most Christians came to regard both this covenant and law as in some sense superseded by Jesus' teaching and community that he established.

There are several branches of Christianity whose belief varies in detail. However one standard that is accepted by most of them is the 'Apostles' creed'.

Christians believe in God, the father almighty, creator of Heaven and earth.

Human beings are created in the image of God. Obviously there are differences, since we are physical and God is not. What we share with God is the fact that we are rational beings, capable of making responsible decisions, and capable of relationships with each other and with Him.

The other thing to note is that the Christ is seen as "pre-existent". That is, creation was done through him. While he was born sometime around 3 BC, there was also a sense in which that human being embodies something that was around before the world was created. The best known treatment of this is the beginning of John's Gospel.

"In the beginning, was the Word, and the word was with God and the word was God. He was in the beginning with God. All things came into being through him, and without him nothing came into being... And the word became flesh and lived among us; we have seen his glory, the glory as of father's only son, full of grace and truth." (John 1:1-3a, 14)

Sound of those gathered became louder and louder than the loud speaker.

After wandering through the streets, Marcus was returning home in the evening. He saw a strange scene:

His wife and daughter are going with folded mats and a bag containing vessels into the church road...!

"Where are you going with these vessels...," he asked astonishingly.

His wife answered in a shivering low voice, remembering his peevishness:

"Don't be angry please; our priest had sent a messenger ...."

"What was the message...?"

"To attend two days prayer for..."

"For what..."

"To bring you back to belief and way of Christ..."

"Oh my dear, no need of such a prayer. You must return to home. I shall go to the church and attend the prayer..."

"Sure..."

"Promise..."

He stood for a while looking at his puzzled wife's returning as if got an unexpected valuable gift. Then he turned towards the church-road with a secret smile.

Late at night door-bell of the church rang! The priest got down with surprise and opened the door.

"Father...; Prays to Lord...Praise the Lord...," Marcus moved his left hand in the shape of Cross.

"Why are you coming at this odd hour, Marcus? Don't you know that, to delineate Cross with right hand...?" The Priest tried to look at the right hand of Marcus, which he was holding behind.

"Father, I am coming for confession and to receive your sermon..."

"Confession at midnight...? What a sin and deliration this is...?" Sound of the priest hardened.

"Am I a mad man and sinner, Father...?" Marcus looked sharply at the priest.

"Otherwise how can you tell these types of foolish words…?" The priest ridiculously remarked.

"I agree, Father…; but why can't have a confession and prayer …." Marcus moved his right hand slightly towards front side from back.

Seeing the glittering edge of the dagger in Marcus's right hand, the priest suddenly replied by trying to have an artificial pleasing smile:

"But Marcus, you can have confession or prayer at any time. I am happy to see a wise man like you. Moreover, we were classmates…"

"Father, I have a serious doubt. Can a sinner act as mediator between God and another sinner…?"

"No, it is impossible…"

"Then try to remember your past…" Marcus twanged.

"All sins can be forgiven by confession before God…," the priest tried to hide timidity and shame, remembering the old sin he had committed. But the real and mixed reflection of peculiar panic, which was same as to that appeared when Marcus witnessed his sin – pushing a girl's half-dead body into the river after brutal attack – and two days later when the dead body was discovered and declared as suicide, while he was in Matriculation class.

"If sins can be forgiven by confession, I am going to kill you, Father. Then I shall confess my sin as well as yours…" Marcus abruptly moved forward with the dagger.

"Marcus….please……..Marcus………….," the priest waved his shivering hands as if sign of begging for mercy.

Marcus laughed loudly like a mad man and said:

"Father…, what was the name of your grandfather…?""John…," though the priest was totally agitated and annoyed with the actions and words of Marcus, he said calmly remembering the harsh and rude nature of mahouts as a whole.

"Father of grandfather…?"

"Anthony…"

"And his …?"

"Don't know; sometimes a Christian…," the priest waved his head

"Don't know; then how can you claim that he was a Christian? Perhaps was a Jew or …"

"What do you mean …?"

"if you are not sure then why and why you compel to believe?"

Priest kept silence

"I tell you father" Marcus was happy to shed his thought.

"Before Judaism and Christianity there remain Pagans and we looted everything from them. Their God, Adonis and all to built ours"

Priest has no answer and Marcus was maddened to speak

"Even as we observe Sunday as holy let pagan's Sun god is now happy that on our observation of Sunday for Sunday mass. But remember father! History is repeating even today in the form of mass killing in sub Sahara against Christians."

Marcus cried bitterly to a wall nearby:

"Oh God! What a shame and pain to vanish God and Goddess of their belief"

He turned to priest and said

"Lesser importance that one man to be a Christian or Jew or other..." Marcus widened his look as an observatory pause.

"Marcus my son! Don't move away from historical facts and live in the present" Priest was about to shed anger and tears.

"Father now nobody spread Pagans view as there is no pagans and more than that history always written in the name of winners"

"But Christianity...," the priest made a futile attempt to object. But interrupting his words Marcus said:

"Father let us have a discussion on Christianity first. 'Christianity, a missionary religion by nature, was first spread by the biblical apostles based on the Bible, which is only an Epic. Early it reached in the *Plateau of Hijaz &Nejd*[18], and in the 7th century it came to the *Elegy of Yellow River*[19] and Land of the Ganges'. Is it correct...?"

"Yes, it is true. All the information about early Christianity and Jesus comes from his followers. They wrote everything to persuade believers rather than to satisfy historical curiosity. No one could harmonies all the chronological events.

Thus it is impossible to distinguish original teachings of Jesus, prevailed in early Christian communities...," words of the priest wavered and he shocked on the knowledge of Marcus.

"Prophecy is the significance of Judaism, Christianity and Islam. According to Judaism, God selects an individual to reveal his intentions to people. That chosen man, called Prophet receives the strength to impart God's will and plans to the people even if he has to suffer many persecutions. Christianity got

---

[18] https://en.wikipedia.org/wiki/Kingdom_of_Hejaz_and_Nejd
[19] Imaginary name for China

the idea of prophecy from Judaism. In apostolic times prophecy was considered as a gift....," Marcus said in one breath.

"The three religions rooted in the biblical tradition, Judaism, Christianity and Islam are based on the concept of God's transcendence, personality and unity. The Hebrew scriptures opened the idea of transcendence...," twisting the concept, the priest turned to Islamic views to avoid criticism on Christianity.

"Islam approves the concept of prophecy from Adam through Christ and regards Muhammad as the final prophet. Followers of Sufism, the Islamic mystical movement, also have assumed a prophetic role. All these religions and thoughts are the sons of other parent religions such as Christianity was emerged from Judaism...," Marcus deeply sighed when the priest kept mum as if conceded defeat.

The priest on the other hand, was more eager to turn back Marcus from peevishness and to escape from him. So he pretended too much politeness, acclamation and affection.

"Father I strongly denotes once again that all religions are originates from human visions and imaginations. All are destined to have a good society with moralities, since morality is the sign of wisdom. Therefore no need of argument for supremacy, religious conflicts, proselytism and so on, except humanity and natural love. Just as the milky rays of moon light glance through the dark clouds, love certainly glitters among the hostility of different communities and classes...," pointing to the scintillating moon, Marcus turned back.

While walking along the road, he looked at the moon and crooned slowly:

'Thy light, lassie moon – so bright
Welkin-lantern – Charming white;
Is it heart's own love-beam, right?
Or dying bone's leaving life-light?

Chilliness of it –calmness flows,
As thine modest mann'r reflects
Or the drifting dampness – blows
Out of ending temple – neglects!

Elegant gleaming by endless smile
On your beauteous face; or high
Mockery at the mankind's style
Of marring lovely Land, so nigh?

Walking you westwards blandly; yon
Weird castle built yore on eyrie,
To that zenith of glory! Or treads on
Fearing man, mark of blood and gore.
See some blots, akin, on your cheek!
As belle's beauty spots; but these
Perchance, fallen drops of eyes, seek
Help of God for the cosmic peace.'

I am Mad... Am mad...Ha...Hahhahha....hoooooooooooooooo.....

He looked around. Everything was glittering in splendid milky light. All organisms seemed to be enjoying the calmness emerging out of mankind's inactivity in sleeping! Even the creatures, moving for preys, are also very careful in keeping the night's tranquility! This caution can be seen in all animals and birds as if they are particularly vigilant in others' serene life, just contrary to human nature! He scrutinized the behavioral difference of man and animal:

"Human species, which has more power and wisdom, uses its ability to disturb and destroy all other species in order to achieve selfish ends, while other poor living things are always keeping the world in peace..."

He laughed at himself and said:

"Animals are obeying nature and so no need of prayers for escape from consequences; but human being is acting against natural justice and crying for rescue from results of his actions. If actions are of animals, no prominences in having a human face...!"

He was still continuing his walk, viewing the human world, while the moon had disappeared in the western horizon.

****

Chapter 5

In the Chariot of Venus

One day while Poorvapunya and Mary were walking towards Mary's house one day. When they entered in the yard, Michael was coming from the other corner holding a bag as a sign of journey. He came near Poorvapunya and asked in low voice while giving her a beautiful picture of Venus, the Greek goddess of love and beauty:

"May I have to take your leave from our L…?"

"Then my heart would have been dead…," her eyes filled with tears.

"Dear Poorva, I have to go to *Royal empire*[20] now. My aunt is ill. I was seeking you to say 'good-bye'…". With an intension he use that good –bye.

Poorvapunya was bewildered and stood still.

"It is a long journey. You know, journey has become more risky nowadays…," Michael continued.

"Don't say like that, Michael; Life may be short or long. But true love is long for life-time…," emitting love through eye-shot, she said.

"Then tell me Poorva, what are the assignments entrusted with me to do there for you; what is to be brought for you when I return…?" he waved his hands and walked away into the narrow crinkled path.

Just before the last curve, Michael turned back and looked at her as the glace between departing clouds. She didn't stop looking until he disappeared from sight. She covered her face with palms, feeling the unbearable pain of separation.

"Depth of love is revealed at the time of departure…," she thought.

goddess of rain has poured heavy drops from heaven.

---

[20] Imaginary name for Rome

The following days were too monotonous until she received a message from Royal Empire through another missionary who had come.

"How can I send a reply to him…?" She asked.

"If you give your reply before Sunday, I shall hand over it to him when I return home next week…"

She wouldn't understand his English intonation… but she can feel unspoken word of love at that moment!

She replied next day itself, in which she wrote:

"Here once again, from monotonous monastery of monad, Monsoon has come –

'Not to wave hands as symbol of farewell
Not to say gloomy goodbye
Not to pour drops of lamenting sunder
Not to look far off, for vanishing pals

But,

To join with emotional ecstasy of union
To sing choral hymns about grandeur
To've pleasure together in splendor
To greet all brothers and sisters…'

'Ha..! Likewise if all left jewels were returned yet again…"

Clouds in the sky never claim thunderbolt in yesterday's dusk. Nevertheless they also seemed to be trembling like me, as if echoing for days in ears your heart breaking words 'goodbye', heard at the time of departure.

Perhaps, like me, ability might have been lost to bear parting, since mind had already broken while saying goodbye to others in the pavement of life; or weary shiver from hands might have entered into heart, putting them unconscious and waved towards disappearing dearer ones.

It is true; there is not even a single tear remains in weep-drained eyes to pour out…

Hence the only one assignment to be put before you is –probably the biggest and hardest of all – "comeback"

While returning after giving the letter her eyes peeped towards the new neighbour's house hearing a heated talks about the small dog, which she knew well. But she couldn't see the pet dog there, as usual.

Though she listened carefully their talks while walking, was not able to understand because they were firing in a language strange to her.

She acted to be careless while walking. now –a- days lot of persons from all walks and places now stay in their village.

The milky-white puppy bought from the land of wine yard was so fondly Welcomed-One in the entire village. That pet was the most common guest for all kitchens there except the house of Dirk Wiedmann.

Unfortunately that day the puppy came to that house. Love and affection radiated from its slight bluish eyes towards Dirk's father. It licked his feet and wagged its tale. As a thunder in winter, an idea flashed in his mind and animosity engraved. With a hand gesture he invited that pet animal to back side of his kitchen. Poor dog couldn't realise the man's gilded love. He gently massaged over its head and took a wooden plank to smash on its legs!

The poor animal made a low groaning sound and ran away as a cripple with broken leg. Its leg was bleeding. In the evening twilight its deep cry seemed to have disturbed the entire village except the cruelty of mankind.

It knelt down before its mistress, Miss. Lore.

With cursing and scolding words Lore walked towards the gate:

"Oh! Mon pauvre chouchou (chien!) qui vous a inflige cette cruyaute! De dieu ils recevront surement chatiment. Allemands[21] vous etes de K'iche maintenant les plus nuisibles du monde…" (*Oh my poor pet dog, who had done this cruelty to you? He will soon get punishment from God. Now, you people why like this…*)

The groaning dog slowly crept towards her and licked on her leg. Somehow managing to control tears she cursed:

"Au, dialme, vous tous, au diable vous, allemandes…," (*Dam you all…Dam you all ……..*) she looked at the neighbour's house.

Hearing her words Dirk Wiedmann crouched and came silently out of his house towards the fence. Seeing the angry face of his beloved girl-friend, he commended:

"Jetzet ist dien Gesicht schoener geworden…" (*Now your face is more beautiful than ever had seen….*)

"Hola, ne soyez pas idiot! Tous les allemands sont plus mechants que les fantomes. Regardez ce chouchou. Helas!

Qui peut faire cette grande cruyaute sauf un allemand comment pourrais… Je esperer affections de telles…?" (*Don't be silly. All of your country men are nasty*

---

[21] Germany

and cruel in history. Look at this pet dog. Alas! Who can do this much cruelty except like you? How can I expect love from such...)

"Nein Lor'e. Sei nicht so emotional und dumm. Mein Deutshland* kann es nicht ertragen..." (*No, Lore... Don't be so emotional and unwise. My land can't bear the expense of this ruthlessness...*)

"Dirk, cela peut etre juste filou corrompu, qui a fait ceci. Bien sur dirais-je, quequ un de votre famille pour se venger de nous, pas vrai...?" (*It may be right, Dirk, But who is the bastard rogue did this? Indeed I say someone from your side to revenge against my family, right...*)

"Es koennte richtig sein.... Aber treue Liebe soll den Hass ueberwinden..." (*It may be correct. But we have to melt that hostility with our true love...*)

"Indigne, vous et votre pays n ont pas meme bouge d un pouce, ces cinquante dernieres annees et n ont rien appris de l histoire..." (*It's shameful that you and your Country have not moved even an inch from past fifty years and not learned a line from the history...*) –She argued with a serious look.

"Fuenfzig Jahren....? Was denken sie mein Schatz...?" (*Fifty years...? What do you mean, my darling...*)

"Fuhrer la celebrite de cetle chambre a gaz comme vous le savez, dans un examen de la. France, notre pays a remaruqe que la personne ne la plus. haissable abattu avec toutes ces.............." (*Fuhrer, that Gas-chamber Celebrity. As you know, we made a survey and opined that the most hated person to us who dejected all with that ...*)

Spiel nich.t mit deine franzoesische Sachen! Schatz, warum sprichst du jetzt von der Geschichte? Es ist wahr, dass der krieg 30 jahre daverte und jetzt ist es Geschichte. Als die franzozen den Rhein ueberquerte, gewann den 30 jaerigen krieg die ruhe..." (*Don't play with your French poll and French cap. Dear, why are you pulling out those rotten histories now? It is true that there was a war which lasted thirty years. But now it is only a story of past. Remember the reality. When French troops crossed The Rine, the Thirty Years War crossed the line to peace...*)

"Aussi, notre amour........," (*So our love*) her sound became mild and moist.

"Unsere liebe ist wie den flus Rhein immortal..." (*Our love is like that river Rine. It will remain forever...*)

Even though they were no botheration on what they spelt out, it was only the deep and upswept love that helped both to understand their different language each other. It was only that love, which remained in their heart, blotted outrage of their anger. Not it became a religious war fought for thirty years. Nothing in this world was ungraspable before their crossing looks filled with fine rays of love.

The deep love within their heart, melted their rage and frustration. They looked at moving clouds, as dark and grey clusters. Her blue eyes looked like a lustrous lake where he saw flowers of love in abundance. He felt her eyes in tears. Now it looked like a serene pond with gentle ripples around. Small ripples caressing buds to bloom...her long hands felt like stem of lotus...her lips be fond of petals carry water droplet... border line has moved away...body lines and curves are more visible now. he immersed in to her lake of love and dug up pleasure from her tenderness. Her wine bottles crushed. His black forest got fire. They took wings to ecstasy and to heaven!

To increase the splendor, pored drops of emotions from the clouds as drizzle. Falling drops flowed down slowly and slowly from their forehead through their body wetting hairs and dresses from head to foot as if melting all hatred between the two nations by the Attribute's magic wand, the true unselfish love!

Road became muddy and slippery. Filthy water flew over the pavement with gurgling sound. New small waterfalls formed from steep ridges of roadsides. Small fishes moved across the turbid water-flows seeking new ponds. Frogs croaked loudly as if trying to imitate the sound of waterfalls. Grass-tops bowed to the ground when water flew over suddenly.

To protect from cool drops of drizzling rain, Poorvapunya plucked a Taro-leaf and held as an umbrella. But the naughty breeze came frequently to pull off the leaf and she wet through. The rain or the chill zephyr couldn't break her thought until she reaches home, noticing the new developments happening in her village:

Crosalvists have tempted all its followers to adorn front walls of all Christain houses with pictures of Jesus Christ, holy cross and Saints. Clergymen are going with quire-groups to houses of devotees for special prayers and healings. Certain sects beat on drums, claps and make sounds, ample to break eardrums of the nearby dwellers, as part of their prayers. Al-Taqwiites have persuaded all from child to old, to take care in wearing white caps and tires even in their houses. Pictures of Central Mosque are hanging in front of all Muslim houses. Newly built terraced houses' ventilators are in the form of minarets. In almost all Hindu houses, due to extravagance and erosion of old aristocracy, even the usual lanterns of the dusk are also slaked.sandal paste and saffron seem in most of the Saindhavittes' forehead. New battle ground is ready.

Everywhere religious faiths and their comparisons and criticisms are becoming the common subject of talks among the poor and the rich as well.

Hence everyone in the village is trying to study more about his religion as he has to engage in conversations and discussions during the walks, works and even waiting at the dining table!

"None could escape from this nefarious circle…," Poorvapunya smiled to herself thinking that she also tried to learn from her mother about Hinduism.

She saw people coming out of the church after the mass.

Loud discussions of the people returning from churches were mainly comparisons of Christianity and Hinduism based on the pamphlets issued from Biblonic Society. Poorvapunya noticed the attractive coloured printing style and costly papers used for making the pamphlet glossier.

"Poorva, take this. You read and tell me what is written in it…" –Molly, the milkmaid holding one copy of the pamphlet, said while trying to walk speedily together with Poorvapunya.

She glanced at the letters. It started thus with truths, half-truths and tale-bearings:

"There are two basic kinds of religions in the world Eastern and Western and their typical differences can be seen in Hinduism & Christianity.

Hinduism is pantheistic, not theistic. The doctrine that God created the world out of nothing rather than emanating it out of his own substance or merely shaping some pre-existing materials is an idea that simply never occurred to anyone but the Jews and those who learned it from them. Everyone else either thought of the Gods as part of the world (*Paganism*) or the world as a part of God (pantheism).

If God is in everything, God is in both good and evil. But then there is no absolute morality, no divine law, no divine will discriminating good and evils. In Hinduism morality is practical; its end is to purify the soul from desires so that it can attain mystical consciousness. Again, the Jews are unique in identifying the source of morality with the object of religion. Everyone has two innate senses, the religious sense to worship and the moral sense of conscience; but only the Jewish God is the focus of both.

Eastern religions come from private mystical experiences; and western religions come from public revelation recorded in a book and summarised in a creed. In East, human experience validates the scriptures; in the West scripture judges experience.

Eastern religions are esoteric understandable only from within which and few who share the experience. Western religions are non-esoteric, public, democratic and open to all. In Hinduism there are many levels of truth: Polytheism, sacred cows and reincarnation for the masses. Monotheism (monism) for the mystics, who declare the individual soul one with Brahman (god) and beyond reincarnation. Truth is relative to the level of experience.

Individuality is illusion according to Eastern mysticism. Not that we are not real, but that we are not distinct from God or each other. Christianity tells you to love neighbours; Hinduism tells you that you are your neighbours. The word spoken by God himself as his own essential name, the world is the illusion, not the ultimate reality, according to the East. There is no separate ego. And all are one and part of Param-bhrahma[22].

Since individuality is illusion, so is free will. If free will is illusion, so is sin. And if sin is illusion, so is hell. Perhaps the strongest attraction of Eastern religion is that clergy men cannot take you out from guilt and hell.

Thus the two essential points of Christianity – sin and salvation – are both missing in the East. If there is no sin, no salvation is needed, only enlightenment. We need not be born again; rather we must merely wake up to innate divinity. If we are part of God, then we can never really be alienated from God by sin.

Body, Matter, history and time itself are not independently real, according to Hinduism. A mystical experience lifts the spirit out of time and the world, in contrast Judaism and Christianity are essentially news, events in time: Creation, providence, Prophets, Messiah, incarnation, death and resurrection, second coming. Incarnation and new birth are eternity dramatically entering time. Eastern religions are not dramatic.

The ultimate Hindu ideal is not sanctity but mysticism. Sanctity is fundamentally a matter of the will: Willing God's will, loving God and neighbour. Mysticism is fundamentally a matter of intellect, intuition and consciousness. This fits the Eastern picture of God as consciousness –not will, not law giver.

Hinduism claims that all other religions are Yogas: ways, deed and paths. Christianity is a form of Bhakthi yoga only. There is also jnana yoga, Raja yoga, Karma yoga and Hada yoga.

For Hindus, religions are human roads up the divine mountain to enlightenment-religion is relative to human need; there is no one way or single objective for truth.

The summit of Hinduism is the mystical experience, called Mukthi or Moksha.

---

[22] https://en.wikipedia.org/wiki/Para_Brahman

Martin Buber[23], in "*I and Thou*" suggests that Hinduism - mysticism is the profound experience of the Original pre-biographical unity of the self, beneath all forms and contents brought to it by experience, but confused with God. Even Aristotle said that "the soul is, in a way, all things."

"Molly…, in it observation and analysis about Hinduism is made with closed eyes. Hinduism is not based on Polytheism. It says about the Ultimate Power, which is the basic of all. As my mother said, it is wisdom with which we can understand that physical world is illusion in the sense that everything or this physical world is originating from the Basic Power or God and is ending in it as its own dream of happiness. Life is also one of the streams of this cyclical material world flowing through the generation of living beings. Since we, human beings, have wisdom, we have to follow Dharma, because this physical world is based in Dharma of time. Hinduism is only depicts full laws of Nature, which includes all organisms and stresses the importance of following them as described in *Vedas*[24] and *Upanishads*[25] while other religions say only about some human conducts discarding all other organisms' equal right to live. Instead, other creatures are supposed to be for the use of man. Then can we accept this rule if another species come from another part of the cosmos with more ability than man?

Suppose, if you are your neighbour, there is no need to say further, to love your neighbour as it is your Dharma.

Another thing, intellect is the speciality of man. Only with this, man can claim difference from other animals and so he is obliged to follow Dharma. By following Dharma and realizing the meaning of the universe or life, by using wisdom he can attain salvation or Moksha.

Dear Molly…, you should have read following verses in Bible : 'After baptism in the Jordan River, by John the Baptist, Jesus retired to the neighbouring wilderness for a 40 days period of fasting and meditation' (Mathew 4:3-9 ; Luke 4:3-12) Thus Jesus also attained realization and enlightenment through meditation, the way and view of Hinduism. Fasting was to understand the specialities of organic life and, a way to achieve control over wishes, a method of Hinduism…"

Molly put hands on head and said with fear:

"Oh Messiah, it may be sin to hear these words…" her mouth turned dry.

---

[23] https://en.wikipedia.org/wiki/I_and_Thou

[24] https://en.wikipedia.org/wiki/Vedas

[25] https://en.wikipedia.org/wiki/Upanishads

"No, dear Molly; Ancient Greek religion has been the subject of speculation and research from classic times to the present. Herodotus believed that the rites of many of the Gods had been derived from the Egyptians. Prodicus of Ceos[26], a sophist philosopher, seems to have taught that the Gods were simply personifications of natural phenomena, such as the sun, moon, wind and water. Euhemerus, a mythographer in his Sacred History, gave expression to ideas which prevalent when he interpreted the myths as distortions of history and the gods as idealized heroes of the past. Etymological and Anthropological lines have produced that Greek religion resulted from the synthesis of the Indo-European believes with ideas and customs native to the Mediterranean countries, the original inhabitants of those lands having been conquered by Indo-European invaders.

Primitive cultures in the West have no religious concepts except the feeing of Spirit, rather than an idea. Hence myths or complex stories about heavenly bodies, elements, and natural forces, handed down from generation to generation. Main mythical themes were parables of timeless philosophy. Complex of these was the soil in which religious concepts originated later. Thus, there religion involves belief in a personal, living and Spiritual God…'

"I am as a buffalo. I can't understand what you are saying. Really no need for me to have this kind of knowledge, as I am only a poor milkmaid. Every day starts with milking of cows and washing of cow-shed. Day ends with returning home with cows after grazing and feeding some wild birds and wandering children who come everyday as evening guests. Between these, I can understand only the laws of cows with hunger…," said Molly, shamefully covering face with both hands while stepping towards her house.

"As you can recognize the cry of those poor hungry animals and others, you hold the greatest wisdom rather than merely reciting the meaning of certain mystical and mythological words like these…," Poorvapunya waved hands at the milk maid.

Main talks of youngsters sitting on culverts, centered round, how did the conversion to Christianity effect personal life.

"Explanations could be heard even from children……..," one exclaimed with anxiety and continued, "Besides a change in religious affiliation, they also assumed the surnames of the priests who baptised them or the sponsor. Usually the converts of the particular hamlets adopted a common surname. However

---

[26] http://plato-dialogues.org/tools/char/prodicus.htm

it must be emphasised that some families retained their original Sir- names. Most of the other aspects of their life remained the same........"

Some ridiculed it by borrowing the words of Jomo Kenyatta. Once he said: "when the Colonisers came to the *Dark Continent*[27] we had the land and they had the Bible. They asked us to close our eyes and pray. When we opened our eyes, we found that they had the land and we had the Bible......."

Apostles forgot the cardinal fact that while members of all native dweller groups have a collective right to preserve and practise their own culture and religion, they must also acquaint themselves with and show respect to the culture and traditions of the majority. Group rights cannot prejudice the enjoyment by all persons of universal human rights and fundamental freedoms.

Many scholars have advised:

"Group-rights must not be used to engage in ethnic discrimination or incitement or to hate other groups. No group-rights must be used to challenge the territorial integrity, sovereign equality or political independence of any region......"

In that topsy-turvy stage, days went by. Rosaries encircled many necks. Scarcity of long trousers reflected in shops.

Seeing the attraction of people towards conversion, priests and Crosalvists dared to argue with the Philosopher. At the same time they planned to eradicate his nuisance. Some of them intruded in the audience while speaking and asked him several questions:

"Can anyone attain salvation without Jesus?" the sound stridently echoed in the air.

"Before Jesus there were prophets who were led to heaven, realised God and attained the salvation. There were ways for the rescue. So the argument that salvation can be attained only through Christ is quite baseless......"

He explained again:

"According to belief, Christ was crucified for taking all sins of human beings. It was one of the true ways for goodness that Jesus showed through the crucifixion. He told his disciples spread his gospels not as a means to convert others to Christianity but to spread the light of goodness as the way of truth among the people everywhere. The meaning of the way of truth, which Jesus showed, is the way of service up to ultimate sacrifice for fellow-beings. Really, "undertake sins" means sins can't be cured by the doer but by healers and hence He was victimised as a result of the cruelties of mankind.

---

[27] https://en.wikipedia.org/wiki/Dark_Continent

Christianity involves two ways- Baptism and belief in Christ. The meaning of the words of Jesus reveals that 'Christ' means the truth and way and everyone has to follow the truth and way to attain salvation. Baptism is only a symbol of starting the truthful way of life or Dharma. It is clear that Jesus showed the path of dharma which was existed before him.

Those who sin purposefully and pray to God to forgive are the believers that they can befool God.

Life of Jesus also depicts this view point, as Christ said, "I am the truth and way." Christ represents the truth and the way to ultimate life path. He shows through life that man has to follow the concept of goodness.

Certain Christian groups are preaching that 'after Christ there is no sins as he has taken all......', to clear that if only the light of goodness exists in the society then only there will be separation from sins..."

"Thoughts are to be shared; that is good culture. Religious centres are doing the same. River will flow if there is no hindrance. Thought is also like that...," others expressed their objection.

"Anything which grows by feeding on money-power will possess all malice...," some other groups criticised.

"Those who make desert will be destined to die in it...," one man judged indirectly with contempt.

Chain of calamities catered ladleful porridge of new belief. By the bye face of the village has been changing miraculously. Main modifications were in mind and manners of the people. Accordingly humanity gave way to harshness and hostility. Meanwhile, as if to catch fish in the muddled water, claim was put forward by Al-Taqwiites to build a mosque at the place where one Muslim-merchant died in the Temple-yard accident.

Incident pictured...Went to various parts...Money flown... half went to pocket...remaining shown to believers.

By using the tinkling of money-bag and religious hostility, the construction work of mosque immediately started in the place while one piquant thing to them was happening in another place.

****

Chapter 6

An Opening to Sacret Shroud

Both sides of the streets and pavements including ghats all over the village are adorned with Festoons as beginning of the carnival and first Holy-mass related with it, of the Church   have begun the prominent functions with all glories.

After the Cross-procession, time has come to go to the feast-hall…..

"Welcome to the Shamiana……; Here delicious foods are waiting for you as in the heaven………," announcement is being heard through the loud-speaker.

People are chasing children, who are the first participants in the Holly-mass, into the hall through an entrance on the left side while others are coming out one by one through another door on the right side after feast.

Faces of the people, coming out of the hall are pleased with the memory of the items they had eaten. Children are chewing tongue even after they washed their chops……!

Before long, some ran to the side of trees; some felt unconscious and fell down; some vomited on others' dress also……!!

Finally a clamor began to rise from the swarm. Everyone knew that people were underwent venomousness in the feast…….!

Revenge was carried out by the mahout Marcus successfully. The people heard about the secret of poison that Marcus had for food. After the temple-yard incident he was suppressed with frustration, guilt-feeling and confession.

"This is not my victory; only a little remuneration for my defeat. Dear my friends, I will not be the last man to do these kinds of deeds. Now I can see faces of the people who died in the temple-yard. Many children were among the dead. Alas! Who can regain their ever-lost jasmine-white sparkled smiles from hands of the Lord of death? Now I realised the folly of man-made beliefs beveling by selfishness to barbarism…….," Marcus babbled like a maniac.

Maniac Marcus and the venom flows through veins of hamlet is now more maniac than that of Crosalvism, Berithism, Al-Taqwa and Saindhavas etc.

One day he disseminated the story of a girl who became nun, People thronged to hear and expressed curiosity as well as objection about it like milk-food mixed with poison. Believers and supporters of church, at first stood like warriors without weapons. But before long, they fell on him like elephant on a rat, with hacking arguments. Some persons attempted to bark against dog.

Prologue of the story was continued thus:

The thought of social status, usually vest with families from a pastor or nun comes, persuades a newly converted family to take that determination.

So the elder daughter Alamelu was selected for wearing veil. There were no main obstacles except her unwillingness and beauty. But those were not mounts before the river of their firm decision. One idea, though a little cruelty, came to their head.

Next day at midnight a small furnace filled with burning woods fell on Alamelu. Her legs, hands and part of her face were burned by embers and hot ash. She became gritty and ugly because of black rough scars. The incident was described as 'godly blessing' in order to domesticate her brain to accept veil and to conceal purposefully their spiteful action.

Then she was directed to Mission head quarters to receive veil. After some days and months her half-decayed body was covered with a holy veil colored in white pall.

So Alamelu became Sister Alice, emphasising the anecdote that 'saints are created, not born'

"Each veil may have such unveiled story to tell…!" People of other religions tried to wrap their scoffing face with palms.

Another day Marcus came with a new story of two love marriages that took place in a rich Crosalvist family of next village:

One day two brothers entered in the front-yard of their house with their brides. One bride was wearing sandal paste on her forehead as the last part of her caste's symbol that is to be set aside after inter-religious marriage. The other bride was wearing rosary and customary Christian dress as usual.

The fascinating thing was that the marriage of the converted elder brother received all support of parents since heavy ornament boxes bigger than bride, were carried to the house. Over and above the groom and bride were getting down from bride's own new decorated horse-cart. But on the other side, of the younger brother, the groom had been secret lover for several years of that protestant girl that belong to an ancient well-bred orthodox family. At last they got married discarding parents' protests.

"Who are you to come here? Get lost and dam……," parents and relatives cursed the younger bride and drew away their second son. They argued:

"We are only throwing you out from our family. If you were in a other faiths' house you would have been killed by throwing into fire or by bullets of pistol….."

Outcome of anger compelled the parents to go to police station complaining against the couples by forwarding pros-petition.

At that time parents of the bride were sitting in the police station discussing about their lost family reputation and the way of pros-petition by which it can be regained. They forcefully presented their opinion:

"Crusade is must against fundamentalist and Crosalvist religious sects, those offer false mirages and mass healings as inducements which have no spiritual merits. This marriage is nothing but inducement……."

Since it was a matter of religion, the police officer also nodded head as support.

As a storm, the true history of the bride from the upper caste flew to the police station in the form of a petition by her parents. In the petition it was written thus:

"She is not our daughter. Really we had been looking after that Christian orphan girl due to suicide of her parents after being expelled from Catholic group when she was only eight months old.

All the ornaments, she brought to her groom's house are stolen by the groom and are now tinged imitations. The horse-cart was already sold yesterday to a merchant…"

Veils of ruses began to disappear and sprout of religious comparisons and criticisms appeared. Class rooms of each religion tried to attain domination in this regard in the beginning. So the analyses of opposite religions were only blind attacks instead of correct or proper evaluation.

While the creator of intra-religious conflicts fumes and ended as flowing volcano. Like oil to fire, fundamentalism began to kindle revolts between castes of Saindhava.

Before long, Hindu youth movements of saindhavites were formed to stimulate activism among Hindus to promote inter-religious comparisons and criticisms.

While hearing some classes and debates Islamic youth movements also did the same to claim their supremacy of Islamic religion:

"Hinduism believes in the worship of god in every conceivable way, both as supreme, formless and universal self and also as individual gods and goddesses. Islam believes in one and only god who have 99 names, but is most popularly called by name, Allah. Islam is based on the sayings of the almighty Allah that have been conveyed to mankind through the many prophets; Muhammad (P.B.U.H) being the last one. Hinduism based upon the teachings of God in the form of His incarnations and manifestations, the Vedas, Upanishads and the Bhagavath Geetha[28]."

"Hindus believe that Divine powers complement one another and that all religions are merely different paths of reaching the same goal –the 'Parham Brahman...," taught in opposite classes by fanatic teachers of Saindhava with passivity about Hinduism while telling about the Resistance of Islam to change ideology.

"If Islam religion originated before Christianity then it will be clear that Christianity has ridden over Islam due to its vacuity." –argument came from Crosalvists' class rooms and audience.

One tried to safe guard the stand of Islam in his class:

"At the begining Islam was far less objectionable and more civilized than Christianity, but whereas Christianity has, gradually become more dishonest, Islam has tended to stand still, and has thus been left behind. This is partly because of Islamic values, laid down to avoid the sort of corruption that had beset religions like Judaism and Christianity. Islam religion must never accept any change of any kind. And to this day, the true Muslims continue to obey this religious instruction and resist anything new in social morals."

The opposite group whirled their words like sword by telling about true face of Al-Taqwa where majority exists:

"The extreme act of violence in the name of Islam has created a horror throughout Chittagong Realm[29]. It is beyond all imaginations how many millions of lives this dreadful and wicked act has affected. It is certain that not even an era will ever give proper curing. No one can bring back the earlier peaceful situation. Everybody's distress and concern have reached the extreme level for the safety of their family members, friends and relatives left behind. People have been observing the situation with disappointment and anxiety that the administration and law enforcement authorities are acting as silent spectators. Moreover, in most of the cases the head of State and Muslim authorities, who are authorized to carry out law and order, are persuading to commit such atrocities against Hindu and Christian minorities..."

---

[28] https://en.wikipedia.org/wiki/Bhagavad_Gita

[29] Part of present Bangladesh

On the other side, preacher of Al-Taqwa pointed out the carnages that existed among Hindu realms in olden days, which were sanctified by epics and stories. In addition, almost all Hindu Deities are adorned with weapons:

"Since weapons are synonyms with violence and war, how can they be treated as orators of wisdom and virtues...?

According to Hindu belief, *Kaliyuga*[30] the fourth aeon is the continuation of *Dwaparayuga*[31] the third epoch which was also an era of Deities, in which wars occurred as per stories of epics...!"

During the celebration of *Vijayadasami*[32], a new obeisance started in the *Durga*[33] *Temple* along with feast on every day. Long array of poor people started to appear before the temple. The fanatic administrators began to feed the people not only with food but also with religious hostility through criticisms and drollery.

People also showed interest in the discussions to pass time up to the lunch time and to get attention of the administrators thinking that it may help them to get more food and seat in the first raw. One man said:

"Islam itself is strongly opposed to any change to its original form. Is it a non adaptable religion? Whether a way of life suggested 1400 years back is still be fit enough for today...?"

"Hinduism is ready to accept any school of thought to any extent. Profound thinking may come from any part be accepted by Hinduism...," another man observed.

"Semitic religions say that there is only one god and it has created the world. Hence direct pray to the sole god is appropriate and the worship of creation is wrong. As in the case of Christianity, Christ is the son of god or its creation. Worship of Christ thus becomes worship of creation. Christianity says that Salvation can be attained through Jesus only. −God's creation can give salvation or can act as an intermediary for getting salvation. Thus they accept that worship of creation is correct and can give salvation...," next man commented.

"Many Semitic religions put forward the argument that Hinduism believes in polytheism. But when we think on Gospel and teachings of these Semitic religions, it is clear that they are based on teachings considered to be imparted through human beings, though they are not treated as incarnation of God.

---

[30] https://en.wikipedia.org/wiki/Kali_Yuga

[31] https://en.wikipedia.org/wiki/Dvapara_Yuga

[32] Hindu festival of Victory over evil

[33] Hindu god of Power

Some kinds of greatness are levied upon them. Moreover they are representatives for implementing Gospels conveyed by God...," pointed out by another man with a laugh of victory.

"According to Islamic belief, to give His teachings, God selects perfect man from society...," one of the fanatic administrators joined the talks.

"Islam Accepts several ancestors as prophets and says that Muhammad is the last prophet. As a lay man's argument though it is accepted, they give no reasonable reason for the argument. Some say that Qur'an is complete and enough for ever. Then comes another question comes, if Islam was given by Allah himself to Adam, why couldn't he give one proper and adequate religion at that time especially when Adam was considered as the first man. If so mankind should have followed a good way of life, then what would have been the real future...?" Another comment came from a critic.

"As per Hinduism there is one ultimate soul or God that is Brahma. The teachings of Brahma are implemented by incarnations just like prophets who are implementing gospels like Semitic religions. Here also creation is acting for the creator...," discussions suddenly stopped when the plates were placed before them for dinner as if food is the panacea to put down one's tongue.

Al-Taqwiites argued to defend their faiths against Berithisem: "In the imperium named *Daughter of Phoenix*[34], Jews had been undergoing severe persecution from Catholics. The conquest of Muslims brought freedom to them..."

Among these hot arguments and blaming, real positive inter faith relationship or better religious dialogues did not get attention. One of the debaters viewed:

"The encounter of religions must be a true spiritual one. If one Christian, Hindu, Muslim or Buddhist approaches another religious person for a debate with the prior idea of defending his religion by all means, there shall have a valuable defense of that religion and certainly exciting discussion. But there will not be any religious conversation, understanding, evaluation or real comparison..."

One of them observed the clashes of modern ideologies:

"Clashes of ideologies happened in several places and in many ways. Half a century ago, the great ideological divide in the world was between capitalist and communist system. The debates were not curtailed not only within the compartment of centrally controlled economies and free markets but also

---

[34] Imaginary name for Jerusalem

between the concepts of single party and multiple party Governments and various types of social setups. Religions were kept away from entering into the debate directly because capitalism and communism were in agreement in this matter. Communism found religion as an obstacle to the progress of a nation. Capitalism excuses religious beliefs but its involvement in modern life is not much encouraged. Hence one may ask, 'Can religious faith save modern society?'

Modern life, through the progress made in all segments of life and life-style, has made life longer, more comfortable and more satisfying for many people. The social services rendered by Rulers if they function correctly, the benefits of all technological developments and inventions can be extended to all common populace. Every one of every religion will agree that life is better if we have enough food, shelter and prosperous opportunities for development, safety and social protection for all family members. Apart from this modernist's argument, one can see a basic urge in human being on spirituality repealing the above view point, otherwise how can we distinguish men and animals..?"

Modernists laughed at them :

"The superstitions of human society decided Galileo to be stone death, is in the expectation of future preys. All these criticisms, arguments and blaming will form into an explosive, which will be enough to destroy the calmness of this village in near future ..."

Thenceforth face of streets in many places began to glow like florid cloud in twilight.

****

Chapter 7

Problems Problems Every Where

Invasion of various fanatic religious transformations as Berithism, Al-Taqwa, Crosalvism etc., to the integration of the village, was continued. Almost all religious activism stepped in and rooted.

Atmosphere of the world began to fade while religious discriminations paved way to all immoralities including destroying of prayer halls and other religious centers by opposite groups, dacoity and brutal butchering in the name of God all over.

A tragic story came to Poorva punya's mind.

It was an early morning in the winter. People in the Volvo village were much hesitating to wake up for their routine. Sleeping under blanket as a puppy in the cold season was a great comfort to them.

But the unexpected wail of neighbors woke them up bitter earlier.

"Oh! God, they looted our houses. We lost everything. All of our prosperities washed away in water...," a mob is bitterly crying in the street.

People are rushing here and there. Peter's father opened the door slightly and peeped at his neighbour's shop, adjacent to house:

Fume was spreading from Dany's shop, set fire in the night. His bullock was crying from manger bitterly. Blood was oozing from its tail, which was cut off.

"What madness happened to the society...? He exclaimed with regret and closed the door with a noise.

He was trembling with fear.

"What happened...?" Peter's mother entered the room with astonishment.

"Nothing...," he murmured in a shivering voice.

"What was the noise outside...?"

"I have already told you; nothing...," anger reflected in his answer.

Suddenly heard a knocking on their door.

"Who...? Who is outside...?" He asked?

"We...... we are; Open the door before they trespass and loot your house too..."

"How can we afford these attacks? We have to retreat and revenge up on. Come with us...," visitors explained about the attack of a Taqwiite group last night.

"If they are attacking in nights, we are daring to butcher them all in the noon...," seeing the bravery of the visitors, Peter's father also got courage.

Within half an hour, Peter's father and others summoned all of their religious members and marched towards Al-Taqwiites' colony. They slaughtered the opposite group in an easy way like cutting of weeds.

"Where is your God...? Peter's father roared before making wound to a Taqwiite follower.

They did not hesitate to grab the modesty of women seen in an isolated house!

One group entered a house with venomous accents. They saw a shivering young woman hiding behind a door plank, covering face with her veil. When they were tearing her veil and throwing it away, she was crying loudly. They ridiculously mimicked her cry and said:

"Cry more vociferously; we like it very much as it will be a good stimulant to us..."

When they threw her scattered corpse into a well after some time, one of them imitated her cry.

Throwing of small children to mud and pond seemed to be their hobby. Even pet animals could not escape from their attack. Till sunset ther work was continued and all of them were very tired when returned with smile of satisfaction.

At that time in other part of the town the oldest church was burning down along with the hundreds of devotees gathered inside for special evening prayer. Smell of blazing human bodies was not irritating but pleasing to the opposite group that surrounded the church holding flambeaus. That much they were maddened not to realize the meaning of slogans written on the fence of that church:

'To kill is not the job of man but of time...'

'Who have the ability to create, only can have the right to destroy...'

"Since most of the fanatic religious transformations have attained considerable strength in many places, they had to involve and play their own part in clashes and became prey to all blames of all religious fights...," religious debates continued everywhere.

Tide of unbelievable tidings began to spread strongly from various places: "In the *Vale of Peace*[35], Saindhavas and Al-Taqwiites are still in conflict. It is a chronically unstable region of the world, claimed by both at *Mohenjo-Daro*[36] and *Land of the Ganges*. The availability of dangerous weapons and the eagerness to use them are destabilising the region further. Moreover, thirty to sixty thousand people have died during last four decades...," the news followed on. "In *Queen of Isles*[37], in one of the province, conflict between Crosalvists and Al-Taqwiites caused uncountable damages. Hundreds of people were killed and thousands of Crosalvists were driven out. Homes and Prayer Halls were destroyed...," another report continued. "In the *Semitic Land*[38], Berithists, Al-Taqwiites and Crosalvists are in continuous war. The peace process between the *Realm of Hebrew*[39] and its neighbouring lands suffered a complete breakdown. This has resulted in the deaths of thousands in the ratio of three dead for each Berithist. The major strike that broke out earlier is still continuing...," heard the next news.

"In Mohenjo-Daro different groups of Al-Taqwiites are in combat. Not low level mutual attacks are going on throughout...," another news-flash.

"In the *Roof of the world*[40] confrontation is going on between Buddhists and communists. Country was annexed to the *Elegy of Yellow River* in the middle of twentieth century. Brutal suppression of Buddhism continues...," repeated headlines.

"Where ever fanatic religious transformations comes across with real religions, then instability starts. Take the case of the *Vale of Peace, Realm of Hebrew, Roof of the world,* and *Perl of Adriatic*[41] or where ever...," social observers remarked with regret.

All news from all parts of the world is becoming more and more horrible and they resembled each other. Arguments, opposing and supporting religions had unity in disclosing the fact that all parts of the Earth are disturbed and undergoing religious conflicts.

---

[35] Imaginary name for Kashmir

[36] Imaginary name for Pakisthan

[37] Imaginary name for Indonesia

[38] Imaginary name for Middle East

[39] Imaginary name for Israel

[40] Imaginary name for Pamir

[41] Imaginary name for Croatia

By utilising these opportunities, religions began to stretch arms into political and administrative sectors in several places such as *Royal Empire*:

"Many of those who had already come to oppose capital punishment in Royal Empire in early decades of the twentieth century were Reformed Nonconformists who saw it as non-Christian. However, the Nonconformist's support for abolition, in contrast with the support for capital punishment on the part of Church-group, reflected in the ideological and institutional, as well as the theological, divisions between the two groups.

The Church-group, the upholders of the established Church of Royal Empire one of the hierarchies of the State, had a corporate view of society and religion, the state could and should execute. The protest of Nonconformists, by contrast, was not part of the establishment and saw themselves as outsiders. They tended to affiliate with the anti-establishment liberal and Labour parties. Those who were supposed to be traditional holders and wielders of Dominion opposed the use of power of the State to take life, whether it was the life of a murderer or military deserter..."

"On the other hand, when people of the same religion's persuasion had immigrated to the *State of Freedom*, their social position changed and had become the dominant culture. There execution could be regarded as the will of the people and the voice of democracy and not the mere exercise of power by traditional elite...," critics noticed the difference of their attitude.

Many members of the Church-group felt that the toleration of heresy in their midst was like a disease in the body of Christ that threatened the very contract between God and his people. There was an increasing rhetoric among the popular preachers to purge this infection to restore God's favour and with it, social stability. To increase this feeling many incidents happened. One of them was too peculiar:

"Henri slept in his bridal suite with an entourage of 40 gentlemen, all of whom were killed. Henri and his cousin were dragged before the king and threatened with death if they did not convert. They did and Henri became a prisoner of the court for the next four years, living in constant fear of his life....," another man described another story.

Everywhere people gave a good reception to almost all religious and social workers who came to Land of the Ganges just like welcoming a folk-dance group. It was clear from their attitude:

"The approach of various fanatic religious transformations as Berithism from Judaism, Crosalvism from Christianity, Al-Taqwa from Islam etc., from western world to Land of the Ganges was nothing but a mock. In the matter of religion and in the spirit, the western mind has not reached by the ancient mind of the East".

Supporters of western religious transformations put forward many hot statements of famous Personalities to oppose the above said ideas.

Horizons of religions in many places were becoming deep red. Stories of conflicts and deaths started to hear frequently. One of them was in Volvo nation:

In 'Volvodys', the famous new capital of Volvo nation, by dusk of Friday the streets were deserted. Inside high-rise apartments and the strong cottages on the out skirts of Volvodys, residents waited for the explosions and the sirens to begin.

"Last night I thought I was in the Suriyah and through old *Mesopotamia*[42] battle field, not somewhere in Volvo...," said Nabila chabi, a twenty two year old sales clerk. Her angular face was swathed with a white head-scarf. Her eyes displayed the fatigue of a sleepless night.

Volvodys is at the epicentre of violence. That has exasperated many of the poor immigrant areas in Volvo's northern suburb for nine days. On the tenth day, after the sun set violence resumed, with youths setting fire to two buildings including a bakery and ten cars in the northern suburb of Volvodys.

Nights after nights youths, armed with rocks, sticks and the gas-line box, have confronted with official force, and set cars, business and government buildings and schools on fire. The worst unrest in Volvo in recent years has paralysed the government, setting senior officials bickering over how to curb the violence.

The attacks have underscored anger and frustration among immigrants and their Volvodic born children who inhabit in the country's largest and the poorest slum areas. A large percentage of this population was migrants. Attacks and fires were triggered when two teenagers were electrocuted after they intruded into a power sub-station in an attempt to evade a guard who had set up an identity check post.

"The previous two nights, there was panic everywhere...," said Sadique, a leader of the religious organisation in Volvodys.

"People didn't know what was happening outride their own building. When they left a car out; they didn't know what they would find in the morning...," another man explained with regret.

---

[42] Olden name of Iraq

"No matter what the group, if it is deviant vis-à-vis in the larger society, most people will raise the question, 'how is it possible for someone to believe something that is ridiculous?'. If you are converted to Berithism being a Crosalvist, other Baptists will scratch their heads and wonder that how couldn't you become a Roman catholic! A Baptist believes in Virgin Mary, and her son. In another context if you are converted to the Baptist church they are perplexed, whereas, people will think that you are worried. Throughout the world the new religious movements are considered deviant. So the perplexing question that how is it possible for someone to change something so odd and so peculiar…?" Religious conversations and arguments went on while fables of miracles and stories of saints were spreading to strengthen believes of each sect.

People were not able to understand the uproar and its use and stayed like calm calves with a girdle of bell.

Clashes between religious groups increased. believers of each religions start digging inside their belief as an attempt to get more gold and diamonds. Animosity increased in the village so as in other part of the world. One such story happened recently in *the Plateau of deserts*[43].

---

[43] Arabian desert

Chapter 8

Fire of Greediness

One night Poorva punya's mother told a story to her daughter. Telling fable was her passion even though Poorva punya is now grown up.

'In another small monarchy there is a primitive man, who has been living for ages because he has supposedly taken an aromatic medicinal drug, prepared from a peculiar plant!'

The hearsay at last reached the castle of the Emperor, famous for his inequitable and stupid governance. He had heard several fables about magical powers of witches to reform olds to youths, give life to dead persons etc. Hence he believed the chitchat easily and decided to collect more information about it. That night he saw an odd dream:

An angel pours a gleaming sweet liquid into his mouth, whispering divine but strange words in his ears! He becomes a youth adorning with all heavenly made royal dress and crown! His loud cry with exhilaration and excitement has enough strength to wake him up!

He thought about his celestial state if he had the Elixir and decided to gain it.

But it was not possible to send combatants to another kingdom. So the Suzerain became sad with the dreams of long indefinite life, which can be attained by the elixir.

One day he asked his intelligent Minister:

"What can we do to search for the elixir…? Any how I want to get it…"

"Drastic cravings will lead to disasters…," the Minister tried to advise and dissuade him from his desires. But seeing the gloomy face of the Suzerain, the clever Minister replied quickly:

"Lord, we can do one Horse-sacrifice. While going with the horses, soldiers can also seek out that herbal plant and herbalists…"

"Yea, that's true. Then do the needful…," the Suzerain nodded his head as consent.   The next day itself the warriors went to all sides with sacrificial-horses. They went on journey even without food and sleep day and night since they had been given the command by the Suzerain that if anyone returns without information, will be sacrificed along with horse in the sacrificial fire.

After several months, the soldiers who had gone towards Eastern side, returned with news about the elixir and a strange tribesman.

They revealed the secret story in detail:

"There is a remote country side forest covered by blue hills. Some tribal families are settled in nearby hillside. Several herbal plants are seen there. The tribesmen believe that the divine plants like Elixir are among the flourishing plants…!

Many fables are prevailing about such plants. Someone said that certain plants will glitter like precious stones in the night! Some plants have ability to produce sounds like animals and birds! Some herbs will transplant themselves from one place to another! Certain plants can be seen only at midday. It sleeps in day-time!

Most important among these divine plants is the species of Elixir. It is supposed to be four plants in the category Elixir. The essence of one species is capable to give life to the dead persons and is the panacea for all diseases. It can capable to prolong life indefinitely. Next one is able to change all other metals into gold. Another one gives extreme wisdom to any goon. The fourth one is the supreme among these and possesses all elements and abilities of other three herbs!!

There is a tribesman who said to have seen the effectiveness of the herbs. But he doesn't know about it. He says that he is living on leaves. One day while cleaning the leaves in a river, he saw some strange leaves moving against the very strong gush! Before his tries to take back, it went into a deep vortex…!

He searched for that plant but couldn't find anywhere in the wilderness. But once he saw another wonderful sight. When he was walking near a thorny bush, on the other side one monkey, emaciated by age, was eating a small plant-leaf. Suddenly that ape became stronger and bigger as earlier. On noticing this he ran towards it but the monkey had eaten the whole plant by that time…"

"How can we believe that the man is telling the truth…?" The Suzerain asked with astonishment.

The combatants continued the story:

"The man looks at the age of thirty or thirty five but can say about the events that happened centuries before! He narrates about the species of birds and animals which were seen in that place and had already been obliterated from earth. He describes about the tribal growth for last three centuries...!

"Any way we have to get that Elixir before the completion of Horse-Sacrifice...," the Emperor said persistently like a child.

AT that another group of soldiers arrived with another story about the Elixir! They had the tale of identifying those divine herbs.

They said:

"Like other plants, Elixir has its own peculiarities to identify easily. One plant of the Elixir family, which has the power to cure all diseases and prolong life indefinitely, will not be burnt by fire. Another species, which is able to transform all other metals into gold, will move against the flow of water. This plant is the most poisonous in the world. Next one makes divine noises during night and it sleeps in day-time. This is the plant which teaches songs to birds. The fourth one is supreme and is unknown to every organism because of its mysterious nature...!"

Entered another group of warriors, with information about the techniques to collect the divine herbs easily!

They began to explain:

"Certain birds can be used to gather these plants. In order to get the plant, which has the capability to change other metals into gold, the bird named *crow-pheasant*[44] can be used. At first, locate the bushes where these birds make their nests. When their eggs are hatched, tie legs of chicks to branches with iron-wire. To release their young ones from chains, crow-pheasants will collect the plant, belongs to Elixir family and put in their nests. Then the iron-cords will be broken to become gold and the free small birds will fly away with their mothers. They put the nests in flowing river and take back the parts moving against the flow. These remains will be the parts of Elixir plant.

To collect other type of plant, which prolongs life indefinitely, we can make use of phoenix birds. Set fire to some bushes of forests where nests of phoenix birds are usually seen. Thinking that the whole forest and their nests will be burned in the jungle-fire, phoenix birds will collect the Elixir plants and place them below their nests. After some days when the young birds are fly-away, take all nests and put in fire. The unburned remains will be parts of the Elixir plant..." Getting the other type of plant, which is able to grant wisdom, is a Herculean task. First we have to domesticate the bird, Blue Cuckoo of Nightingale family, which is the most untamable bird. After making it homely, arrange the nests within our premise. Blue Cuckoo has a hereditary character

---

[44] The greater coucal / *Centropus sinensis*

that, they don't make its own nest. But when it becomes a domestic bird, it will use the nest, which we make for it. Then find and mark the first egg, since it has an ancestral malediction that first chick will be a dumb one! To overcome this curse, usually Mother-Cuckoo brings the young one at midnight to the branch of the Elixir, which grants efficiency to sing. From the branch of which plant, such small bird sings first, will be the Elixir..."

"How these divine pants came to our Earth...?" The Minister pressed his fingers thoughtfully.

The last group of soldiers, who were waiting for their turn, narrated the story:

"These plants came to earth from heaven. It is a puzzling tale. During the period when Truth and Justice were prevailing on earth, it was usual hobby of angels to come here. One day an Angel came here with Athena, the goddess of wisdom. To greet her Persephone, wife of Hades, ruler of the underworld, presented a small combination of quintessence, the fundamental five elements – Fire, Air, water, soil and sky. While seeing and enjoying the wildlife and landscapes, Athena put it in a place, marked with a stone over it. At the time of return, she searched for it but failed to find. At last she noticed a very small strange plant beneath the stone. She blessed the plant by evoking all qualities of the mixture of quintessence and said:

"You will be invisible to all..."

The plant appealed:

"You put the combination on the earth knowing that it is a seed of life. So..., Ma, you gave birth to me. If I am invisible, my life will be futile since other organisms are living on plants..."

By seeing its view of justice and supremacy of virtues – even willing to sacrifice for the benefit of others – the goddess blessed with other boon:

"Each plant will sprout from your stem, leaf and flower and grow with each of your qualities and they will serve other organisms apart from your own germ from the root..."

Thus the plant sprang from its stem got the power to prolong life indefinitely and to cure all diseases. More over this is able to resurrect dead persons. Other plant germinated from its leaf which attained the ability to transform all other metals into gold! The next one originated from its flower gained capability to grant extreme wisdom to anyone. This plant is supposedly taught sounds to birds and animals!

The Suzerain ordered the Minister to set fire to the jungle. He was not ready to endure to follow the methods to gather the herbs or to think about the pathetic situation of wild animals and birds if the forest is burned. Fearing his peevishness, his command was immediately executed. When animals were wailing with pain while burning down to ashes, the Emperor was laughing madly by dreaming about his celestial stage after taking the Elixir.

Within a few days fire ceased and the entire wilderness burned out. Then in front of all, the Suzerain himself went out in search of the Elixir. Rolls of smoke were still going up from smoldering bodies of animals and plants. From smoky atmosphere stink of burning flesh was penetrating into nose with enough strength to hinder breath! Suffering all these, the Suzerain entered the place, filled with ashes, in greed of getting the Elixir.

In the middle of that place he saw a marvelous sight! On the mount of ashes, green leaves of a very small twig are sparkling! He ran towards it with a jubilant cry. Before prevention, he walked on the ash hill with stretched arms and took the twig suddenly. Alas! It was a deep crater-like hollow filled with embers. In front of his soldiers and Minister, he sank with all his longings.

When they were looking with bewildered eyes, another twig was falling from the beak of a pigeon, flying over their head!

****

Chapter 9

Halcon Days of Spring

With melodious songs of dreams, dragonflies flew everywhere in meadows and moorlands on either sides of the road reaching to the factory compound. The pairs of yellow butterflies flying into the road by mistake flew away suddenly seeing the workers passing by.

When Poorvapunya and Mary entered the factory ground it felt that the siren rang more loudly.

They started work as usual. On the other side, the night-shift workers were about to stop work and the lowering sound of the siren made notice in a leaping manner as a tired man's sigh after a long work.

Faces of the outgoing workers were pale and indifferent apart from the natural human feelings and expressions.

"Yea..., Man is machine of life...," she thought.

Slowly one lady, swathed face with a scarf, came there soothing on her belly and said with less flourishing face:

"Dear Poorva, you are blessed....."

"Why, Rhabhia....?"

"Because we have to follow the five pillars..

"what pillers"?

"One pillar or practice is fasting. Even a pregnant lady like me cannot be exempted from that and other like Salah, zakah, Sawn and Haj"

"I think that is the greatness of your religions and heard that it is not necessary to take the fasting while pregnancy, but can complete when it is possible instant...."

"As you know..., the contradictory statement is that Preachers seek support of Science in the case of conciseness to speech about its merits, but the same science tells about the demerits of fasting during pregnancy. Really who can follow utter absurdities?"

Another man objected:

"You can complete fasting even after the delivery and if women fears as it effect her baby"

Some others also came and joined and the conversation became a disordered chit-chat.

One man said:

"All religions have their own customs and rules. One can't be blamed alone..."

"By the foolish customs all religions are seeking marketability in others ...," another person waved head.

"If man has God in his hand, it will be the first thing that he sells..." another person supported him.

"Yes......we find some scope of our religion in Al-Taqwiites' world...," Paster Nainan Nambudiri smiled.

"How is it ...?"

"It is by practising Crosalvists' approach"

"Crosalvists' approach......?"

"Yes my friends; look, it is tough to observe fast and pray. Am I right...? But in our religion there is no such painful fire-testing practise and of course more or less our taste-buds are lucky enough to enjoy all sorts of foods throughout the year"

"In our religion there are no hard and fast rules to be followed and that flexibility is surely our advantage...but... hhuuuum 40 days fasting we also observe," Anthony supported the newly converted Nainan Nambudiri, who is now a Pastor.

"Then why are you retaining this dress code and name, Nambudiri...? One enquired with contempt.

"It is to make them feel that we don't have much difference in style but only in path..."

"Why your missionaries are interested in certain populous countries only...?"

"There are two reasons. Mainly number matters"

"Number matters...? What Number?

"large numbers...!" he put his lips like elastic.

"But here we are more than that...?"

"Yes my friend; here great large number of people who believes in Hinduism are still remaining in darkness and we, Crosalvists are praying for them in Sunday masses throughout in the State of Freedom..."

"If number is the matter, then why not throwing eyes to the Elegy of Yellow River......?

"Hindus are much flexible. More over Land of the Ganges is good and here race is more pure in perception. So getting them is a matter of pride to entire Crosalvists' mission globally..."

The debate ended in arguments, curses and challenges. It sowed new seeds of hostility among them. Some faces were red with anger. Some were frustrated and suggested:

"God Don't divides anyone but glazier of fanaticism divides hill of social unity causing damnation of all organisms..."

Days went one by one through the hamlet providing the villagers, new leaves of life.

Corners of the firmament began to gloom and darken with clouds and shiver with thunder-bolts. High peaks of mountains were seen covered with mist. Streets filled with opened umbrellas in the dawn and dusk while children and elders were walking hither and thither in a hurry to their home.

One Sunday, Michel met Poorvapunya near the temple and invited her to Mary's house.

It was a cold Wednesday evening. Poorvapunya was welcomed to attend the Birthday function of Mary at her residence.

When Poorvapunya entered, the prayer was going on in the room. Only countable numbers of invitees were gathered there. Mary looked like a Princess of stars. She was dressed in white top. Her hair was decorated with arched lace beautifully.

She heard the preaching based on cannons of Christianity:

"Pray for the mighty people of our village to live as god fearing and true lovers of Jesus. It's our responsibility to bring them into light. Dear believers, you work deeply among others to reach out the message of Holy Bible and it is time for Christ's blessings to come in this village very soon and open them for gospel.

After that prayer one of the family members distributed some pamphlets among the audience. While Poorvapunya was standing away from the hall, Michel put some pamphlets in her hand one by one.

Michael was in a brown suit. The embossing black mole on left cheek made him a separate easily identifiable man from others. Birth day cake was dissected by Mary and her mother put a slice to her mouth as well as to Poorvapunya. Michael gave another piece to Poorvapunya and smiled.

The sun was about to set. Setting sun's leaning rays were entering in to the house through opened lattice.

When Poorvapunya returned, Michael also started walking to her house.

"How was the cake Poorva, wasn't it sweet...," Michael broke the silence while walking.

She smiled and kept mum for a while. Actually she was in thought and wondered that how come Michael call her pet name. Only her dear relatives and Marry used to call her 'Poorva'. She was about to ask him but withdrawn.

"Look, Poorva....; those glorious clouds? They are looking at you. Perhaps they may be aspiring to be born in this land to see you near...," he pointed at a glittering cloud-cluster.

"It would be quite okay, if I were a cloud to look at......."

"Really, Poorva" he hold her hands and said "your cheeks are like snow white petals" ..... to walk in this evening with you, is very nice. My mind is overwhelming with joy.....," he romantically smiled at her.

"God has given this eve for me to remember grace...," she replied.

They slowly walked along the vermilion-rays paved way, chit-chatting, like naughty butterflies with golden wings in the new spring.

Her gleaming smile flashed. Cheeks were lushes with bountiful dimples and eyes sparkled. Poorvapunya glanced at warmed face of Michael.

Setting sun filled beautiful hues on spreading clouds. It seemed golden tapestries are unfolded in the western horizon.

Even after entering the house, the event spelled in her mind like new drops of summer rain.

She yearned for new spring's footsteps. A fresh affection filled in her mind towards the whole world and all creatures in it. Hours seemed to be longer than sixty minutes. Everything appeared to be new...! Then the adage has become true in her case:

'Good frame of mind is making life colourful and vice versa. World will set and rise. Man has no prominence in it, unless and otherwise makes his own life prominent'.

As usual, the following day also the street near the temple was bustled. Bearing mundane burdens of life momentous-faced folks were passing and gathering while little sparrows were taking pleasure in the day break thanking God for granting them once more......! Morning Sun's narrow rays extended yellowish streaks on top of the banyan tree which is standing as nature's inn with bloated branch-roof....... !

While the routine of that hamlet was progressing, the day time also moved forward inch by inch. The flowers which bloomed in the morning became paled, drooped and fell down. Even-flowers began to wake up and peep from their bud-green petal-veils when the bell rang from schools at four o'clock.

Children came out of the Primary school-gate like flooding of water while shutter opens at dam. Unni, the youngest musician of the village, studying in the school also returned home. An unexpected small rain had already begun.

In the evening, even while looking at the falling and withering raindrops in the foreground, the burden of learning lessons troubled in the class room on that day, has not yet disappeared from mind. Unni, the only child of the house, peeped into kitchen door.

"Mother is busy with cooking...," he said to himself as if confirming avoidance of mother's interruption to his intention.

Slowly and stealthily he got down to the front yard and began to bathe in the rain. While the chill drops cooled his body, he capered like a lamb, with enjoyment.

As a call from heart, mother ran to the yard and caught him suddenly:

"You, naughty boy, what are you doing here...? If rain drops fall on head and dip, fever will come. go inside..."

"Ma...; please look at those flying birds; they are enjoying the rain. They have no shelters like ours. They don't have thought of fever...?"

"Unni, don't ask such silly questions. Go inside otherwise you will get beaten up by me..."

"Ma..., let me free. I want to join with those birds and to fly through clouds in the sky."

"Birds have wings to fly, my dear; your hands are not enough to flap in the sky. Please come inside and learn your lessons..."

Even if he turned to portico holding hands of mother, was not satisfied with mother's advice.

"Why can't we fly...Ma...?" He desperately looked into the sky again and again.

The poor child clung to his mother's hands with anxiety and doubts. She slowly desiccated his head with her raiment's edge. He offered to sing the poem, which he had studied on that day from school. Pointing to the rain falling like beveled arrows, he sang in mellow voice:

> 'Yonder, drips of drizzle effuse tear
> And true fondness of this World ev'r;
> Little drops, though high dazzling! ere
> Be'tle of death, can dash it nev'r!

Autumn and odds of winter-dews' chill
Not only reflect, tear of Thine;
But the malaise of maggots and all,
Naughty creatures' manoeuvre-mine.

Splendid and speckles life Thou gifted,
Albeit Oh! Kids as skylark's tales,
Slide from truth of the Cosmos; gilded
Glimpse of selfishness betrays fools.

Thy romping pets are fretting to death
In furtive fryer of their own vice;
Yet Ma...! Thee absolve; they requite with
Memoirs, lasting than vows and lives...'

"Well my child, you have studied the song full. I am making sweet butter balls for you. Sit here and study. Shall bring it quickly...," mother turned towards kitchen using the food-trick to turn his attention to learning. But he was also looking for time to skylark his mother.

"Yea... Ma...," he sat down and nodded.

When mother had gone, he slowly stepped into the yard. Looking at skylark, he asked:

Dear little bird, you are blessed with wings. Hence you can fly along the sky and see all amusing things there. You may be singing songs about those sceneries; perhaps,

'May be a gift, thine charming sound
By the mystic murmuring plants
Of that sky —evergreen and grand;
Ye, to chant about their fine bands'

"Lend me your wings for a while. Then I shall bring that lotus for you from the sky...," he looked at the lotus that bloomed in the garden lake.

Swaying in the breeze seemed to be the call of the lotus. Small wavelets created by scattering rain-drops in the lake were reaching to the feet of the flower from all sides. He saw the beautiful Lotus in the stank hailing him with a divine smile. Slowly moving towards the bank with stretching his hands and he walked into the pond. While holding the flower he began to descend little by little in it!

Mother came to veranda holding sweet butter balls in a plate, calling her son.

"Unni, where are you my child; these butter balls are for you, come…"

Seeking him, mother was coming to front of the house. The drowning hand of her child was the scene that welcomed her.

"Unni…, Oh…!" She loped and jumped into the lake, covered with green leaves of lotus and water lilies…

Somehow she entered on the shore holding the cold body of her son. Seeing the wet flower between the frigid folded fingers, she threw it away angrily. There it was written on the soaked soil:

"Ma…..my… buss"

In frantic mood when she entered the house, the melted sweet butter balls were flowing from vestibule to yard through steps…!

Laments rose from her:

"My child…, wakeup…; see, not only these sweet butter balls but also my heart is melting …," drops of hot tears fell down from her eyes.

That time, eyes of her child had shut, become cold and chill….!!

Among the other atrocities and burdens in addition to the stormy changes due to the flourishing and spreading religious works, all other disasters were discarded by people. But Unni's death broke the heart of the hamlet. All of a sudden people became sad and began to rethink about the folly of man's snootiness and selfishness, setting aside their religious discriminations emphasising the maxim:

'Bitter experiences will make everyone virtually good at least for some time.'

****

Chapter 10

Forever Unlock the Immense Doorway

Attention of all people turned towards the nearby hermitage, which was sustained as unaffected by any of the recent social evils, recollecting historical events:

"The oldest and pellucid pavilions of human culture and philosophical visions originated and prevailed in immaculate hermitages."

As its last link, the familiar wayfarer was sitting under the tree looking at the jolting leaves seemed to be murmuring primes. Seeing the reality of life in those gleaming leaves and hearing the jingling sound, his lips groused, half as rumination and half as question to the people who were eager to hear his words:

"What is the meaning of this life?"

"Simply to say, life is to know self. In deep meaning, life is the running of physical world, which originated from the eternal basic world, and has been flowing towards that basic world. Thus the physical world is mortal and perishing. On the other hand, the basic world is the Basic Energy which never ends or begins."

"What is basic world and how it differs from physical world?"

"The basic eternal energy is called the basic world which includes the whole universe. This is inactive or stagnant in nature. When it attains activeness, basic energy divides into positive energy and negative energy. Positive energy combines and transforms into different forms, and that is called physical world. The transformation takes place because of the self combination and influence of negative energy.

Really the negative energy might have been called physical energy but we name it as positive energy because of our usual familiarity is only with this physical energy or physical world.

If any part of physical energy combination attains a certain stage, capable of holding negative energy which passes through all physical things; with attracting force-field in it, can unite with negative energy. Then it becomes the basic energy. The basic energy thus produced, will be held in the force-field until that field exists. More over it attains an effect of activeness though inactive in nature since it is within the active field of positive energy and clubbed with it. Hence this basic energy particle is called jeeva or life while staying in the field. The part of physical world which holds this jeeva is called living being or jeevi.

"Where I came from and where to go...?" Questions began to rise from the audience one by one.

"Not only you but also each and every organism and all inorganic substances are not coming or going elsewhere. All are the transformed part or form of the physical world. Physical world is the transformed physical energy which originates from the basic eternal energy. The basic energy particles will be divided into positive and negative energy at the time of death. Death is the failure due to cessation or disorder of the force-field or magnetic field to hold the basic energy particle or jeeva.

"What happens after our death...?"

"At the time of death the negative or invisible energy will go to the infinitum and the positive energy will be disbursed to cells of the body and ultimately dissolves in the physical world itself.

"Please explain about invisibility of basic energy and negative energy...," people became curious.

Basic energy particles have no positive or negative value because of its inertia nature. The existence in neutral state makes it invisible. The negative energy particles have the higher speed than positive energy or light about several times. Above all, it has the features just opposite to light. So our all equipments made up of physical energy, are not able to detect negative energy particles."

"What is god and what is faith...?"

"God is the eternal inactive Basic Energy or the Base which involves the whole universe. The universe has two physical parts and one invisible base. Physical parts are positive physical world and negative physical world. Positive physical world involves the whole moving and physically realizable world which includes all heavenly bodies having different forms of various galaxies, their attractive forces, movements etc. This part comes only a minute percentage of the whole universe. Negative physical part involves the area filled with negative energy as darkness. This part involves the positive physical world. So due to the full-filled travel of the particles of negative energy, positive physical world contains darkness. Positive physical part comes only up to twelve percentage of the Negative physical part. The third part or Base contains both the positive and negative physical worlds. Physical world is only an illusion of the Base or God as a dream of man. It is enjoying the extreme happiness of movement in its inertia stage, through that illusion.

"Why can't we see God...?"

"We are made up of physical energy but there is invisible basic energy particle in its force-field or magnetic field. So we have the physical ability as well as non-physical ability. By that non-physical ability we have the capability to realise invisible negative energy and basic energy. Realisation of the basic energy or ultimate Soul which is called God, is known as self realization.

"Is there any difference between the death of a believer and non-believer...?

"No difference. But the difference in death occurs to persons who have realised God. Belief and non-belief are not matters in the way of realisation."

"Is the transfer of life from one to another like lighting one lamp from another...?"

Life or jeeva is not multiplying and increasing as flame from one lamp to another. Jeeva is formed by the union of positive and negative energy particles in the force-field of an organism.

"Is there any supremo to human beings over other animals...?"

"No supremacy in physical status. But wisdom differentiates man from other animals. Animals having wisdom have to follow Dharma in all actions. In other words man is obliged to follow the rules of Dharma and has to suffer all consequences of his actions. The advantage is that, man can attain self realisation and moksha (emancipation).

"Whether all other creatures are created for human beings...?"

"No. Mankind is only one type of species among other creatures. Since man has wisdom, he has to preserve all creatures and their environments"

"Is there any living being in any other place than Earth...?"

"The word 'Life' is only a conventional name of Soul. There are so many forms for the Soul. Hence there may many places where life exists in other places also."

"Where is the boundary of this universe...?"

"The whole Universe consists of three parts –The moving positive physical world, the moving negative physical world, and the neutral basic energy world. The positive moving world includes all galaxies and all of their transformed various forms. It is called moving part because all its contents are moving. The movement can be described as, when one part is moving from its place to outer side another part is moving to first one's place. At the same time, another third part is moving to the second's place. This type of movement results convergence and divergence or swirls, attractions and expulsions. Over and above collisions and breakages also occur. Another result is that when one inner part becomes outer part, another outer part becomes inner part. So there is no permanent outside or boundary. However, this positive moving world exists inside of the negative physical world.

The negative world consists of negative energy filled area. Even though negative energy particles are passing through all positive world areas, it passes longer area than positive world limits. Hence there is a vast area covered by this negative energy only as full darkness. This part is covered by the neutral part, the basic energy area. Therefore the negative energy area is inside the basic energy area. But the basic energy has no positive or negative value due to its inactiveness. Therefore, this area cannot be detected or measured and can say it has no beginning middle or end. Really this means everything comes from the basic energy and ends in it. Thus the basic energy is the only eternal one or God."

"Why can't we see God...?"

"Just as your eyes can't see yourself; since eyes is situated in you as your part. Suppose a drop of water among other drops in a beaker, if it looks at it can't see the shape or boundary of the beaker until it stays inside the beaker. If the drop gets out of the beaker and looks, it can see the shape of the beaker. Likewise if you go out of the macrocosm you can see what you are seeking. Self-Realization is the way to have this knowledge..." He added: Likewise, with true knowledge all sorrows and happiness can be known; no need to realise."

"What is incarnation...?"

"Various aspects of the macrocosm are depicted and described in personified forms, in order to understand those aspects more clearly, by self realised geniuses or Sages from olden times. Since the aspects are more difficult to grasp by common people, they can recognise only the outward picture of the actual matter and misunderstand them as incarnations.

Description of matters in the form of narrative picturesque model was the specialty of olden days especially destined to teach others easily, to make it easy to remember, to impart easily from generation to generation as stories without leakage of its central theme. More over the usual method prevailed in those days to transfer and keep knowledge was oral teaching. In this case, the matters to be taught must be very impressive and easy to study and recollect. Most of the ancient knowledge and thoughts were not only story based but also in the form of ballads or stanzas."

"What for numerous Gods and Goddesses…?"

"There are no several Gods or Goddesses. Various aspects of the universe are personified and called by a range of names."

"What is ultimate supreme…?"

"The eternal Basic energy is the ultimate supreme. It involves the whole universe. So everything is it and it is everything."

"What is salvation and way to attain it…?"

"Salvation is the self rescue or refrains from future sins of worldly life. To understand about salvation, first have to analyse the different stages of various species. All species of organisms, those have no ability to analyse the value of consequences of their actions, are not coming under the purview of salvation. This is because they can't recognize the value of good and evil actions and therefore cannot abstain from sins purposefully. On the other hand, the species, those have the ability to divide actions into sins and merits, can desist from evil actions. Avoidance of evil actions makes one competent to have powerful positive energy force-field which will hold negative energy particles and to transform into basic energy particles, essential for salvation. These types of species are bounded by the value of consequences of all actions such as sins or merits. Since life is running as a river through generations, value of all the consequences are to be suffered not only by the doer but also by his following generations. But by using wisdom, through avoidance of evils and self realization one can attain salvation and thus can escape from worldly sufferings in future.

"Can a human become God…?"

Since God is the Basic energy, through salvation one can become God like but not God. Salvation is the returning of one's jeeva or life to the Basic energy."

"What is sorrow and happiness…?"

"Sorrows are the consequences of sins and happiness is the consequence of merit."

"Whether praying will heal our sins…?"

"Praying will not heal our sins, but realising the consequence of our sins can divert us from future misdeeds…"

"What is divinity…?"

"Divinity denotes the self realized stage of one person."

"What is blessing of God…?"

"In macro sense the whole universe or macrocosm is the blessing of God. In micro sense life is His blessing. In genetic sense wisdom is his blessing."

"What is the main difference in thinking power between Human and Animal...?"

"Man has the wisdom or ability to think without information through organs. Animals have thinking power only limited to and related to the information received through organs. If a dog while going before its master, sees one person picking a stone, will think that he will throw the stone and will run away. But it cannot imagine that he will not throw the stone in front of its master. Means there is no intellect they have"

"How the universe will end...?"

"End and origin is always taking place in the case of all positive energy based articles and world. This can also be called change. Change or end and origin are the specialties of the positive energy. Now the cluster of galaxies which includes our solar system is diverging from one swirl. So it may be treated as expansion. After this it will converge to another swirl. This type of end will affect only that cluster of galaxies. Though these types of convergence or divergence are occurring always, it does not mean the end of the whole moving world. The whole moving world will end when its positive energy content loses the value of equilibrium due to changes or self combinations to various forms. Ultimately Positive energy world will combine with negative energy world and become the basic energy world. This may be called the dissolution of physical world. Then as usual the basic energy particles will divide into positive and negative energy particles and thus new physical world will originate. This process is cyclical...".

"Why there is different species on earth...?"

"Interaction among positive energy particles caused the origin of combined organic physical substance capable to hold life. After life is originated due to the combination of positive energy and negative energy particles in the force-field or magnetic field of the organic physical substance; that life has been flowing through generations. During this flow, due to the multiplication of the physical substance into various forms called evolution caused various species of organisms. There may be similar branches or sub-branches to a river or a tree among other several branches. Likewise life-river also has several similar branches or species of organisms, which are undergoing changes..."

"Why disaster and calamities are happening...?"

"All disasters and calamities are the part of ever changing phenomena of the physical world..."

"Is there any God on earth...?"

"Yes. Because, Earth is the essence of God. Not only Earth but everything here is a part of God..."

"Is there any relationship between God, Inorganic substances, organisms and Man…?"

"Like man, inorganic substances are also part of God since they are also made up of physical energy or positive energy which is basic energy's division. But organism, while it is a part of God since it is made up of positive energy, holds particle of God in its original form i.e., Basic energy particle itself."

"What is Ghost…?"

"Not such a thing. All immoral aspects are characterised by that name."

"What is a sin and how it differs from sacredness…?"

"Any action, by an organism having wisdom, which causes any agitation to any other organism, is a sin. Any action which causes goodness is sacredness."

"Which is the supreme religion…?"

"All religions are supreme if they persuade men to do the good. Unfortunately nowadays almost all are transformed filling with selfishness, hatred, cruelties and all other immoralities in men which are the cardinal evils. Therefore they are not at all supreme but most dreadful poisons able to annihilate mankind and all organisms from the world."

"What are the main differences among various religions…?"

"Most of the religions came into existence with a view to rescue men from the prevailing social injustice through individual moral practice. That is why all religious teachings criticise social unfairness that existed in the society when those religions originated. In the depth of all religions the common factor of human virtues are seen. Because the persons caused formation of all religions were social reformers, wise and well wishers of mankind. They all tried to reform society by their own methods. So religions have difference in methods of practice to attain the same goal."

"How become analytical vibrations of religious gospels and teachings…?"

"Misunderstanding of meanings and misinterpretation for misuse and other prescriptions caused many vibrations to gospels. More over all gospels and teachings are man-made; hence several mistakes were included. The difference of social setups occurred after the formation of various gospels; caused deterioration, inapplicability, need of suitable revisions, and necessity of new teachings."

"What is the holiness of religious books and how they state the cardinal factors of human life…?"

"All religious books are written by great authors having good imagination and wisdom. Since the central themes are various aspects of human life, all such books have impact on all eras. As they implicate human life and virtues by triggering eagerness to follow goodness, with narrations of consequences of all kinds of actions, possess holiness."

"How mistakes remain in the religious books…?"

"Fingers of a writer can make readers to be in tears by feelings. But a noble writer can make   readers to be in tears by extreme happiness of truth. In this attempt there may have some exaggerations, misleading guys, purposeful hiding of facts or human-mistakes. Religious books cannot be set apart from this because they are also literary creations of various periods."

"How is the survival of Atheism…?"

"Atheism is one kind of thought which consider only physical nature. Even though it is an incomplete thought, it can question many foolish customs followed by religions. Such customs make religions also incomplete. Thus atheism has equal status and becomes good when compel to follow Attribute's justice in natural way."

"Why even small kids die before getting a chance of realisation though they are innocent…?"

"In wide sense death is a natural process to all physical things. Kids are equal to other animals having no wisdom. So self realization is not possible but salvation is natural. All organisms without wisdom are not bounded by the value of consequences of their actions.

"How can science be compared with religion…?"

"Science deals in physical analysis of things while religion deals in moral analysis."

"Why fate is commonly shared in calamities…?"

"Sudden natural changes which cause loss to living beings are termed as calamities. Since all organisms are equal before environment, it affects all without any prejudice."

"What is vital force and difference with inertia…?"

"Attraction or vital force is the consequence of movement. Repulsion is the negative process of attraction and hence it is also related with movement.

"Is series of life, a circling legend…?"

"In macro sense life circle is not a myth but true."

"Is faith in God a necessity…?"

"It is necessary to follow human virtues or Dharma as actual God-belief denotes goodness."

"Where god lives…?"

"God is not a living creature but the entire macrocosm can be named as God in common sense."

"Is there any Satan…?"

"There is no supernatural Satan but all immoral human beings can be termed as Satan"

"What is basic objective of this life…?"

"The whole world, as in its inertia state, through self motivated dreamily action enjoying the movement or 'Brahmananda'. In that enjoyment this physical world which involves all galaxies, swirls and negative energy covered parts are only acting as mere dices. When compared to this, man has zero value. But, man has wisdom and hence can enjoy 'Brahmananda' by realising self, simultaneously while acting only as one of the links of Life-river. When we look through the angle of common parlance, can see that physical achievements such as wealth is not an object of life as no one can go with it while dying. So it is clear that self realisation is the basic aim of human life."

"Is there any rebirth…?"

"There is no rebirth in the sense of one dying organism has to take birth as another creature. Division of one creature to increase its species or the process of giving birth to next generation can be called rebirth. Thus the Life-river has been passing through generations. So, all subsequent links of generations have to suffer the consequences of actions done by ancestors.

"What is 'Moksha'?"

Everyman has to follow Dharma in order to impart joy to his own life as well as to his successors and to avoid sufferings of consequences of his evil deeds in his life and his followers. The value of merits out of Dharma or sacred actions makes one able to hold more basic energy particles or ultimate Soul and to dissolve into it. This dissolution is called 'Moksha'.

Claud applauded for the speechless words!

Like hornbills got wet in a summer-rain, quickly the perplexity of audience paved way to intellectual happiness and looked at each other with joy of wisdom. And the night died.

****

Chapter 11

Devotees of Satan

Poorvapunya and Mary were on their way to the factory as usual.

As in an endearment-shore's sprouting grass, Poorvapunya's mind danced in a breeze coming with blooming Lilly's sequel brace.

Alas! A hindrance occurred to that gentle gust of air...?

On the way, she saw a funeral procession comprising of a few persons across the road.

She became astonished and afraid! She tried to divert attention and suddenly moved to opposite side.

The rhythmic prayers entered into her ears as piercing arrows.

Unwillingly, but due to anonyms fear she made an eye view over the coffin. On its dark top some artificial flowers where glittering. The dead body was lying inside the coffin as a sleeping man.

With fear and beating heart, she looked over the procession.

She was shocked to see familiar faces among the crowd. Face of the dead man came to memory all of a sudden as a lightning. The poor farmer who had been living near the place was lying in the coffin! She had seen him some days back in the market place.

Even then a mysterious abhorrence conquered her mind against that corpse. The last journey of everyone from this earth may be in real aversion. She tried to justify her thought.

Behind the procession, the last person following the coffin was his tired and suppressed widow, trying to make her weeping silent.

The street became empty as the persons suddenly disappeared seeing the funeral procession since the man died due to epidemic which was spreading unexpectedly in the village.

Thousands of questions entered into her mind.

"What is an epidemic? Is it a punishment of God...? How is the same fate of calamities to a group of people who undergo the epidemic?" Are they the same sinners in the view of God? Are we the escapers, like earth-bits under the dry leaves while raining? Or else who are dying for religions only have value of death?

Though Poorvapunya and Mary were walking together, both of them were in their own world of imagination. So they walked as if strangers. At last Mary broke the silence:

"Travel to the town, nowadays, along the road, is very agitating because of the peeping of tramping leaches, who think that girls of upper caste and converted families have no strict moralities ..."

To rescue herself, she handed over the Rosary to Poorvapunya. When they were about to cross the second turning point, one Van stopped near them and a gigantic man got down chucking on his whiskers, roughly looking towards Mary with a deep risus. Suddenly he caught hold of her and threw her like a grass sheaf into the vehicle and closed the door. Poorvapunya was standing astonished and frightened even helpless to cry. Darkness crept into her eyes, breath ceased and seemed the surroundings to be whirling around her.

After a while she got up to reality seeing that the van evanesces from view. She cried loudly seeking help. Gathering swarm also could see the swiftly running vehicle at a distance but were helpless to follow.

"*Hoorah...Hoorah....Hoorah........*!" They uttered with disappointment and anger. They diverted to different ways. Some turned to follow the cab, some went to call others and some ran for collecting weapons.

At that time, in the vehicle, the terrorists were enjoying themselves in thought of getting an upper caste Hindu girl as their religious victim.

The vehicle enters into an isolated grassy ground surrounded by deserted mounts. Behind there is a cavern like old building. The unconscious Mary is being carried to the cavern, just as flock of wolfs carry one rare prey to their lair.

There inside, one Taqwiite Clergyman is waiting for them. Seeing her, he asks slowly:

"Did anyone see you?..... Or..... tried to prevent......?" He stretches himself and relieves of numbness.

"No; if anyone had done so, that village would have been kindled alive......," answers a long bearded man among the activists.

"Not only is that little village, but also this whole world itself is on the point of our dagger..........," one of them commends with a brave action.

Discussions continue till the time of prayer.

The Priest and others clap hands with joy. After locking her in a room another man comes out and nods head towards the others. All are going according to the finger-gesture of their Boss.

Hill tops are covered with gloaming in the dusk, a queer and mysterious deliberation starts in the rendezvous by the gang. All members are very eager and thrilled to assimilate.

"A new assignment but sign of ancient significance attributed to our great Al-Taqwa, will be coming true.........," looking at Mary another man busses himself.

Mary wakes up hearing a terrible sound. Trembling like an antelope, she looks around.

Footfalls are coming nearer and nearer.......! The sound seems to be tramp of Yama, the God of Death.

One of the beard squabs entered and asked her to move out. She was taken to a mud-spattered van, filmed in thick black, seemed to be the carriage of Hell.

Two persons were sitting in its back seat. She was thrown to a corner space. Her stir eyes filled with fear. Masked with thick green cloths, activists sharply looked at her with yellowish eyes.

Van began to roll through deserted land following the tracks of vehicles covered with whirling dust.

She looked around. In the long distance it could see mounts of sand cumulated here and there. One of the stout persons who seem like a beef cake suddenly tied her eyes with a black ribbon.

"It is over; what is the use of eyes to one, who has nothing to see...," remarked the tall man with a head cap.

She felt deep darkness spreading around. Deafening engine sound and murmurings disturbed her thought. A journey to unknown destination........!

Waiting for the last minute, her mind was plunged into past days' memory:

Uncovered pavements and line of hutments glimmer before her. Everywhere tearful eyes are gleaming in search-lights of small lanterns moving through streets and catwalks; brought up home and its sandy yard, which keeps the glory of childhood days are gloomy in her absence.

"Mary.......Dear child........Mary.........," rising the whisper. The entire village is weeping.

Realising the true love of natives her mind filled with a daring thought:

"Yes; my people, I can see a hearty homage from you. I am not afraid but bold to die in the name of folly religious militancy............"

"Even though, how can I desist mother....; my dear friend Poorvapunya......," flow of her notion broke!

The cab was dashing through an intriguing path, cutting through middle cliffs of a high mountain fringe......!

Van turns and struggles to balance......

"Oh...! Boss, steering is out of my control. Which ghoul is hiding here to control it..........," words of the driver quaked.

Just in the blink of eye it happened!

Concussion of the van, tremor and screaming cry of activists made her feel that she is falling into fully opened mouth of a Dragon as in olden tales. Before she could guess anything she felt that the van was rolling down like a ball. Hit her head on the top, sides and finally was thrown out over rolling stones.

"Alas! We have damned.......," sob heard from one activist.

While crowing down from rolling rocks, somehow her face was free from tied ribbon. But darkness in the environment concealed everything from vision. Even though it was noon, she couldn't have seen surroundings. That much she was seriously shocked and injured.

By gathering all her strength she crept and felt a new celestial stimulation. Slowly light entered her eyes........!

"Oh! I am lying on curvy rocks.......," sweeping bloodstained face she cried. The solo sound penetrated into environs her without any replay. It resounded like twang of a bowstring.

Hurdled brook, due to the fallen Van in its way, turned and spilled in another way solacing her with immaculate cool drip. Ears were disturbed by weeping cry from nearby crevices. She looked around. Trees were seen as towering devils spread hairs in the sky. Slowly, she tried to stand up but couldn't.

Suddenly the Van caught fire. The burning Van flooded like a flambeau. In the blaze, one of the militants crept out of it with a loud cry for help:

"Help me ... Yea Allah.......water....Allah....Ho........"

Slowly his cry became feeble and shabby. Cry of his heart captured her commiseration.

"Help our fellow beings. That is our duty ....," Mary recollected the words of Jesus.

She crawled towards him with handful of water. Slowly and slowly poured it to his face and lips. His half closed eye-lids opened. Tearing eyes turned towards her. Casting was paled but deep deplorable looking as if a ruffian kneeling at last before an angel. Closing eyes forever, he whispered:

"We are dead; you flow away, the true bird of humanity.........."

"Yea, escaping………," showing the drifting blood from forehead she murmured.

Mary trailed to a rock. Her body was crushed with agony and rankle.

"Oh Jesus…., I am dying…….my mother…I am going……Ah………!" She stretched shivering hands and looked up.

A bird was flown into the infinitum.

Thunderbolts of all religious climatic changes throughout the world began to reflect in *Kalpam* also. While the Soul of the village was showing enough boldness to resist all types of invasions in the beginning, kidnapping of Mary spoiled the courage and inflamed fanaticism over cowardice.

Religious conversion-tactics of Crosalvism, Al-Taqwa, Berithism etc., were also changed according to the development of sector-wise conventions and classes.

"As per the figures, the population of our religion is going down in the village, while that of others are increasing. This is a result of conversions carried out by the members of their religious activists. There must be workshops across the country, focused on plans and methods to fight against conversions of our people to Crosalvism and Al-Taqwa.

Religious conversion became very much popular and a burning issue of today and these two religious sects very much moved ahead with multidimensional agenda. In the name of missionary works, crores of dollars are flowing into many poor countries, especially to our nation.

Some extremists are trying to make impurity in other religions in the name of love marriages, abduction, pulling girls of different castes especially upper-castes to sex markets and distorting entire family structure of all castes. If the scenario continues, then all other true religions will become minority within one decade…"

In counter Saindawites targets to demolish mosques and churches all over.

Communalists continued campaigns against conversions while secret proselytizations were going on according to the different religious customs even in interior places of the *Kalpam* village.

As the increasing heat of atmosphere, people are seen going to prayer halls according to their religions and fractions. The speed of their moving feet seemed to be saying:

"To believe is easier than disbelief because skepticism needs thinking."

Different voices were also heard from another corner among the chaotic conversations:

"Blind beliefs not yet lead mankind to any goodness or progress. On the other hand, creative thoughts are the ladders of all human developments. Hence thoughts and beliefs are to be connected together in such a manner that beliefs must be on the basis of thoughts and analysis. Thus all religious beliefs and canons must be reviewed and revised according to the geographical and periodical changes…"

Beginning of summer holidays triggered the heat of religious arguments; and conversion techniques turned to forceful actions and threatening. According to the changing face, mind of the village also distorted into rigid and brutal. People began to realize the changes happening to the village due to the invasion heat of fanatic religious groups:

Someone has changed name of *Kalpam*. Few People now call it '**Gape Dome**' which means wonderful cupola. Name of the small but beautiful market place of the village, '*Shree Rangam*' became '**Shoe Town**'. Changing of names was not happened un-expected but due to the invasion of foreign languages through migration and due to scrupulous religious conversions. All these changes are purposefully made to evacuate historical relations and heritages, with an objective to start new culture based on *Adamic beliefs*.

Among the changes, erection of various Al-Taqwa-mosques, Crosalvist-churches and other monuments got special attention since almost all of them were located in populated public places and on roadsides. In the middle platform of cross roads, new cupolas sprang up, where beautiful trees and its hangings were seen before. Religious schools became more important than public educational centres. Social up-gradations and degradations began based on religions. Verdict of Justice and injustice started to come from religious headquarters. In some places old huts were dismantled and modern concrete houses were built up with the cash earned from conversion, to show blessings of God to particular religion and its devotees. Sound of Prayers flew like wail through loud-speakers and bells echoed in atmosphere as if competing with chain-crackers.

Even the approach of teaching about religions was also not in order but chaotic in the beginning. Most of the preachers criticized other religions and showed eagerness for conversion before teaching about their own faith. This method ignited the hostility as well as religious clashes instead of understanding among people.

****

Chapter 12

In the Lunatic School

Thirst of new religious gestalts also opened their mouths, in the form of new summer camps for theological studies at almost all populated areas. Ephemeral campaigns' long tongues stretched as far as possible against children to quench the thirst by swallowing their little brains.

One of such news came from the State of Freedom:

On a holiday, Ronald and Julia sent their 11 year old son to Mishall's camp; they expected the boy's summer stay would be a positive religious experience in Christianity. In fact, the camp itself notes that 'Jesus for All' and it operates as a section of the local church in which a Bible-centered programme is used to develop spirituality.

Third day's oration was on 'The developments originated in *Land of the Ganges*, stretching from *Gandharam*[45] to *Mahavamsadesam*[46] and *The Vijaya Kingdom*[47] to *Lydia* manifesting ancient civilization. Vedic tradition of Land the of Ganges was the remarkable advancement, the parent of humanity and original ancestry of all religions. Its influences are seen in the Elegy of Yellow River, Queen of Isles, *Flank of Palms*[48], Soil of the Wine yards, *Sheen of Wisdom*[49], *Scandinavian Dawn of Letters*[50], Semitic Land, Plateau of Deserts and the State of Freedom.

---

[45] Imaginary name for Afghanistan
[46] Imaginary name for Srilanka
[47] Imaginary name for Sumatra & Bali
[48] Imaginary name for Iran
[49] Imaginary name for Norway
[50] Imaginary name for Sweden

The camp started with the description of past and present predominant matters of Vedic tradition of the Land of the Ganges, memorable for ever: An attempt to arouse their superiority on their land

The largest civilized and the biggest free society of the mankind is the Land of the Ganges.

Inhabitants of this land have invented the number system and zero.

The world's first university was established in Takshasila in 700 B.C.

Ayurveda is the earliest school of medicine known to the world.

The art of navigation was born in the river Sindh 6000 years ago. The very word 'Navigation' is derived from Sanskrit word 'Navgatih'.

Bhaskaracharya calculated the time taken, by the earth to orbit around the sun in an year (5th centaury) as 365.259756484 days.

The value of *Pi* was calculated by Budhyana in the 6th Century and also propounded the Pythagorean Theorem.

Chess was invented in this land.

The place value system or the decimal system was developed in Land of the Ganges in 100 B.C.

There are thousands of Religious Monuments and hundreds of Theological Centres in this land.

Thus the class continued with analysis of various merits and demerits of the land and its religions.

But no one awakened.

But, for young Joseph, the class didn't work out in that good way. Instead, the boy's parents alleged in their complaint that he was subjected to an assortment of "inhumane punishments, degrading and criminal conduct" during ten days stay in the summer camp. Among eighteen various indignities cited in the petition, had his dress spoiled, tied tightly to an iron rough-edged pillar, got dipped headfirst in an ugly pond, and was laid on ice. As a result of the camp's negligence, the Julia's charge, Joseph had suffered hurt, ill feelings, mentally severe anguish, and disorder of his faith in Jesus and Christianity.

On a Sabbath day, appeared devotees in a *Synagogue* in the heart of *Shoe Town*. It was written in front of it:

"I keep the Lord always before me"

When the quorum filled, started prayers. Liturgical Torah reading took place. It was an attraction to the people passing by, to hear *Torah* in *Hebrew:*

אַהֲבַת עוֹלָם בֵּית יִשְׂרָאֵל עַמְּךָ אָהָבְתָּ: תּוֹרָה
וּמִצְוֹת. חֻקִּים וּמִשְׁפָּטִים. אוֹתָנוּ לִמַּדְתָּ: עַל־כֵּן יְיָ
אֱלֹהֵינוּ. בְּשָׁכְבֵנוּ וּבְקוּמֵנוּ נָשִׂיחַ בְּחֻקֶּיךָ. וְנִשְׂמַח וְנַעֲלֹז
בְּדִבְרֵי תַלְמוּד תּוֹרָתֶךָ. וּמִצְוֹתֶיךָ וְחֻקּוֹתֶיךָ לְעוֹלָם
וָעֶד: כִּי הֵם חַיֵּינוּ וְאֹרֶךְ יָמֵינוּ. וּבָהֶם נֶהְגֶּה יוֹמָם וָלַיְלָה:
וְאַהֲבָתְךָ לֹא תָסוּר מִמֶּנּוּ לְעוֹלָמִים: בָּרוּךְ אַתָּה יְיָ.
אוֹהֵב אֶת־עַמּוֹ יִשְׂרָאֵל:

It read as:

"With love everlasting Thou hast loved the house of Israel Thy people. Thou hast taught us Thy Torah, its statutes, commandments and judgements; and therefore, Lord our God, when we lie down and when we rise up, for all time we will speak of what Thou hast ordained, rejoicing with fervor in learning the words of Thy Torah, its commandments and statutes. For they are our life and our length of days, and on their we will meditate by day and by night. May Thy love never depart from us. Blessed art Thou, Lord who lovest Thy people Israel.)[i]

"Judaism had shared certain characteristic features such as radical monotheism, the belief that a single transcendent God created the universe and governs it. Through revelation the mind of God is manifest to the traditional Jew. For the Israelites, at Mount Sinai, God, the creator of the world revealed himself a twofold *Torah* to Moses. The content of that revelation was the *Torah* (revealed instruction). In the Hebrew Bible (*Tanach*) which contains three sections –*Torah* (the Pentateuch), *Nebiim* (the prophetic literature) and *Ketubim* (the other writings) –all forms of Judaism are rooted.

Rabbies, the Jewish sages teach *Written Torah* (Sripture) and *Oral Torah*, which is to be transmitted orally from master to disciple.

Individuals must regulate their lives in the interaction with others as well as with God, according to the commandments (*mitzvoth*) in which God's will for mankind is expressed.

There are two ritual requirements to become a Jew. A male convert must undergo circumcision. If they already circumcised, a single drop of blood is drawn as a symbolic circumcision. The converts must undergo immersion in a Jewish ritual bath (*mikveh*) with appropriate prayers. Judaism is not a missionary faith and doesn't actively try to convert people…" One Rabbi said about his religion.

"Conversion to Judaism is not something to be done lightly. The Rabbi will have to make sure that the person really wants to convert, and that they know what they are doing.

Some Rabbis used to test the 'would be converts' by turning them away three times in order to see how sincere and determined they are. This is unusual nowadays.

If a person doesn't know any Rabbis to discuss conversion with, they probably haven't got close enough to Judaism and Jewish life to be thinking of converting. They should start by talking to Jewish people, and attending some synagogue services…."

One day When Marcus was going into the vegetable market, he noticed that a man was fixing a new board in front of a small shed. Words in Arabic language were written on it:

"*Din—E —Elahi*"

"What is this…?" Marcus eagerly asked.

"This is our religion, *'Din—E—Elahi'…,*" the man replied shrinking his shoulders.

"Among the disordered situation these kinds of attempts will also come to create new religions in *Gape Dome*. I have no anxiety in it. You are trying to plant a small seed of the dead religion, *Din—E —Elahi*. It was tried earlier to establish by a Moghul emperor, Akbar, who reigned between 1556 -1605, but did not succeed…," Marcus laughed.

After a week Marcus came that way incidentally. That time the words on the board were changed:

"أَثْمَار" (*'Adhmar'* means Fruits)

"What happened? Didn't thrive…?" Marcus looked at the man, who was squeezing lemon and preparing juice.

"Your bitter tongue became fruitful…"

The man threw lemon-rind away.

"Apart from the reforms of eastern religions, seen as molder of the culture and philosophy of this village, many religious reforms were also established in. In addition to these, one comparatively new religion entered, is Sikhism. Though it was established in the 15th centaury in Land of the Ganges, don't know why has not yet stretched arms into our hamlet…!" Marcus talked to a man wears turban, purchasing fruits.

Another man chewing betel-nut disclosed his awareness:

"Sikhism is an ethical monotheism which combines the elements of Islam and Hinduism. *Nanak,* the founder of Sikhism was a mystic, who was a Hindu in early years..."

Hearing these words, the Sikh said:

"Sikhism stresses the unity, truth and creativity of a personal God and urges union with Him through meditation on His title name and surrender to His will. It advocates active service rather than ascetic withdrawal. It rejects caste system, priesthood, image worship and pilgrimage but admits Karma and transmigration. The spiritual authority is *Adi Granth(holybook of the sikh),* which contains hymns written by Sikh Gurus.

Sikh males are expected to join *Khalsa* ("pure"), a military and religious brotherhood. Initiates are baptized by drinking sweetened water stirred with a dagger and take the surname Singh ("Lion"). They must observe *Kes* (no cutting of the beard or hair), *Kacch* (wearing of soldiers' shorts), *Kara* (iron bangle), *Khanda* (dagger) and a *Khanga* (comb)..."

Marcus left the place not very late when compared with other days. Most of the shops had closed except some small illegal liquor selling stores.

Seeing an unusual gathering in one such store, he entered in. There one senior man was reading one notice and explaining to other members of *Castisem,* another rivulet of *Saindhava* as *Saindhava* itself the fanatic transformation of Hinduism:

"Along with the religions that developed in *Land* of the Ganges, the followers of other religious philosophers also entered in this village as they saw themselves as a separate religion, but did not always get this recognition. For example *Lingayat* in southern part of Land of the Ganges saw themselves as a different religion, while others saw them as a sect of Hinduism. There were also some tribal communities who demanded to be recognised as separate religion from Hinduism. But in the 19th century itself some Hindu reformers had remodelled Hinduism to adjust it to the modern period. The largest non-Indian religion entered here was Islam. Judaism and Christianity might have arrived here before they arrived in Europe! All of these religions have root in our *Gape Dome* without any wars. But now religions have transformed dangerously into various sects all over the world as Crosalvism, Al-Taqwa, Berithism etc., and are flourishing rapidly. Now Al-Taqwiites are about 10 % of this village's population. Crosalvists are not more than 1%. There are also *Zoroastrians* who even though make less than 0.01% of population are known around the village. There are also a few thousand Beritheists in the town. Lighted standing oil-lamps, are becoming common in mosques and churches like temples, as the first spark of big burning fire. Before swallowing our woodland of Hinduism, we have to take quick actions against this jungle fire of other religious invasions..."

"By removing the thistles and dry weeds of Castesism from Hinduism to clear your land for prevention of fire....," Marcus interfered with a laugh.

"Which is the best religion among all" a question was asked by an unknown from the audience

All gathered there kept for a while

"No doubt, its Christianity" one answer came from the audience

"Then where you place my Islam"? That voice was much louder

A young boy questioned. His voice was shivering.

That discussion went un-ending. Claim on each religion wasted their time and energy.

Nobody said the truth. Nobody disclosed that humanity is the best religion in the world. No one argued for that.

But if you are closer to religious thought then you are far away from god. Even if it is the reality then who will hear?

Summons for prayer from the old Mosques became louder now. New style and tune.... Because its newly constructed Masjid.

Sunnite group constructed another mosque near the old one which is under the custody of Shiites group and began to teach about their religion in the orthodox way. To get more attraction from people they introduced another technique.

One day, hot news spread in the street:

"Imam Ali has come from *Gift of the Nile*[51]. He is a famous Muslim Scholar..."

Most of the sand covered area of yard of the new mosque, built in imperialistic style was filled with Muslim families to hear his words in real Arabic language. He started his speech:

"Man was created to worship Allah alone as Allah has explicitly stated in the Qur'an, 'I have only created Jinns and Men, that they may worship me'

The religion, Islam was founded by Prophet Muhammad based on his teachings in Arabia. The Arabic word *Islam* means 'to surrender to the will or law of God'. *Muslim* is one who practices *Islam*. According to Islam, Nature itself is Muslim as it automatically obeys God's will.

The word 'Allah' is a contraction of the Arabic term *al-llah* which means 'the God', the Supreme Being. He is supposed to be eternal, transcendent, exceptional and single. Muslims are forbidden to depict him in any symbolic

---

[51] imaginary name for Egypt

form. Most important faith is that there is no god except Allah and Muhammad is the messenger of Allah. Allah has seven attributes such as life, knowledge, power, will, hearing, seeing and speech. His will is absolute and all that happens depends on it. It includes believers and unbelievers who are predestined to faith or atheism…

The *Qur'an* and the *Sunna* are considered as the two fundamental sources of Islamic doctrine and practice. Qur'an is regarded as the speech of God to Muhammad through the angel of revelation named Gabriel in the Arabian desert in the seventh century. So God is considered as the author and Qur'an is infallible. Hadith, the record of the Prophet Muhammad's actions, precepts and life constitutes *Sunna* or example.

According to Qur'an, God breathed the soul into the first man.

The five cardinal duties as the "pillars of Islam" are Profession of faith (the *Shahadah*), Prayer, Almsgiving, Fasting and Pilgrimage."

"In all words, Imam Ali cared to dart arrows against Jews and Shiites. He said more about Islam but took special care to conceal that, 'The concept of Islam and the word 'Allah' existed in pre-Islamic Arabian tradition. The idea is turning through Babism, Bahai and so on'…," ridiculed Beritheists, who overheard his speech.

Another day high wall of the Mosque of *Al-Taqwiites* was seen as decorated with the words:

'Truth will be far away from human society, in which life is sophisticated with religious selfishness…'

– Marcus

After seeing the pale face of devotees and the Katib waited till dark to erase it. They secretly remarked that the words were not of Marcus but of the philosopher, since his face was common among the audience of the hermit.

From that day Al-Taqwiites' oration, comparing other religions with Islam became more rude and rigid. It continued in the following way to get supremacy over them:

"The religion of Islam is not named after a person as in the case of Christianity which was named after Jesus Christ, Buddhism after Goutama Buddha, and Confucianism after Confucius and Marxism after Karl Marx. Nor was it named after a tribe like Judaism after the tribe of Judah and Hinduism after the Hindus.

Islam is the true religion of Allah and as such, its name represents the central principle of Allah's religion, the total submission to the will of Allah.

Islam is the religion which was given to Adam, the first man and the first prophet of Allah and it was the religion of all the prophets sent by Allah to mankind. The name of God's religion, Islam was not decided upon by later generations of man. In the final book of divine revelation, the Qur'an, Allah states that, "This day have I perfected your religion for you, completed my favour upon you, and have chosen for you Islam as your religion."

If anyone desires a religion other than Islam (submission to Allah (God) never will it be accepted by Him.

Abraham was neither a Jew nor a Christian: but an upright Muslim.

You will find nowhere in the Bible that Allah saying to Prophet *'Moses'* or his people or their descendants that their religion is Judaism; nor to the followers of Christ that their religion is Christianity. In fact, his real name was not *'Christ'* but it was *'Jesus'*! The name *'Christ'* comes from the Greek word *'Christos'* which means the anointed. That is, *Christ* is a Greek translation of the Hebrew title, *"Messiah"*

The name *"Jesus"*, is Latinised version of the Hebrew name, *"Esau"*. Everyone however refers Prophet Esau (PBUH) as Jesus. Like the other prophets were come before him, he asked the people to surrender to the will of Allah (which is Islam) and he warned them to abstain from praying all other creations of God or human beings. So worshiping Jesus is also sin as per Islam since Jesus is a creation of God.

According to the New Testament, he taught his followers to pray as follows: "Yours will be done on earth as it is in Heaven."

Message of Islam and its implication could never agree to worship another human being under any circumstances. God's religion in essence is a clear call to the worship of the creator and to reject the worship of creation in any form. This is the meaning of the motto of Islam:

"Laa Elaaha Illallaah" (There is no god but Allah)

Its repetition automatically brings one within the fold of Islam. Sincere belief in it guarantees one paradise.

Thus the final prophet of Islam is reported to have said, "Any one who says: 'there is no God but Allah' and dies holding that (belief) will enter paradise"

It consists in the submission to Allah as one God, yielding to him by obeying His commandments, and the denial of polytheism.

The message of false religions approaches with baseless philosophical concepts. According to False religions Allah is only a figment of man's imagination. Thus it can be stated that the basic message of false religion is that Allah may be worshiped in the form of his creation.

There are so many cultures, sects, philosophies, religions, and movements in the world. All of them claim to be the true religion and only right way to paradise. How can we determine which one is correct? Or else can we accept that all are correct? We can find answer only by analysing the superficial differences in the teachings of the various religions about the ultimate truth, and recognizing the nature of worship.

False religions invite man to the worship of creation by calling the creation as creator, God. For example, Prophet Jesus invited his followers to worship *Jehovah*, the Supreme or Allah; but today those who claim to be his followers advise people to worship Jesus, claiming that he is the Supreme or Allah....!"

Buddhists ridiculed *Al-Taqwiites* by saying about the rite of circumcision:

"Several islam concepts are taken from Judaism. Then how can it be treated as donated by God afterwards?

Although Qur'an does not mention about circumcision of male or female, Islamic custom demands that Muslim males must be circumcised before marriage. Generally this rite is performed in childhood. Earliest evidence of circumcision was found from ancient Gift of the Nile, it is believed to have been used to mark male slaves..."

If the religion, Islam was given to the first man, Adam by Allah himself surely should have advised the correct Islamic path of life to him. So the ways followed by Adam and his successors can be considered true and correct according to Islam. Then how can it become false today? How God can say later in Qur'an that '*This day have I perfected your religion for you, completed my favour upon you, and have chosen for you Islam as your religion*'...?!"

Adam is considered as the first prophet and Muslim as per Islamic belief. At that time there was no Arabic language. So God should have given messages in the primitive or ancient language. Arabic is the offshoot of South central Semitic language, which came later.

It is considered sacred since it is the language through which the Qur'an is believed to have been revealed. Qur'an is an unedited literature like the Bible or Torah.

In prehistoric times it was commonly assumed that every species of life including human beings had descended from a pair of aboriginal ancestors who had been created directly by God. In this respect the story of Adam and Eve differs only in details from many other similar myths of the ancient Middle East..."

On the other side of the village, behind the board which denotes 'No entry to non-Hindus', hardcore Hindus started to gather safely for retaliation against Crosalvists and Al-Taqwiites. They began to propagate their ideologies through their own way and need and criticisms on other religions:

"Idols in temple represent the qualities and virtues of Universal Self and not the physical body. More over people are coming to Hinduism and Buddhism, rather than these two religions are going to people.

Basic confronting issues such as poverty and education are remaining unanswered. If mission work aims well being of human race then why are they not eying at poor countries like Chittagong Realm, The Mohenjo-Daro and Gandhara Desh, where poverty is much deep rooted…?"

"Due to the profound ignorance about Hinduism, propagators of Crosalvism and Al-Taqwa have been doing great service indirectly to Hinduism. Their vehement disparagements are continuing for getting sympathy from the natives, during the last several centuries. They made all possible attempts to declare Hinduism as a religion of the Brahmins and a religion of satanic cult. In the effort to convert lower casts to their religion they criticised Hinduism in all way ignoring its philosophical depths and its true character. When they set foot on soil of Land of the Ganges in the medieval period, unknowingly they forced Hindus to become more defensive, determined and resolute to safeguard and maintain their own religion.

They earned few converts but fortified and made their own mission more harder and more cumbersome. Their vituperate attacks forced Hindus to shift stress and attention from the external aspects of Hinduism to the inner serious knowledge of the *Vedantha Darshana* (Supreme Insight and ultimate knowledge)[52] culture and practise of Yogic disciplines.

Hinduism underwent marvelous transformations during the past centuries and reforms are still going on due to the selfless efforts of many great souls to meet the aspirations of the coming generations of new centuries and thus make it fit for future. Their efforts resulted in the eradication of contemptible and atrocious practices such as child marriages, caste system, blazing of widows, untouchability etc. These reforms made good to all religions to break the walls of orthodoxy and to come out from the compressed compartments of constricted chauvinism and directed the human world towards creation of a multi-religious secular society.

Hinduism may be the only religion in the world which is surviving all the other religious system and evasions over several centuries and millenniums and emerging constant, strongest, vivacious and most vibrant than ever before…"

"Vision of the ultimate truth makes Hinduism more distinctive and prominent than other religions…," another supporter of Saindhava suggested.

"Mankind must be taught the way of peaceful life, which is one of the basic elements; need to be fulfilled for a cultured life…," motto of modernists stimulated debates on faithful and faithless together.

---

[52] https://en.wikipedia.org/wiki/Vedanta

Chapter 13

Pleasure Without Pain

Serried concrete seats in the public gardens, hurly-burly markets, tree-shades where children used to play and crowded cross-roads paved the way to summer holidays.

Greenish knolls become lurid and gritty in the draconic sunny parching weather. Bark of trees begins to rending, plants are rifting and drying. Pavements are filled with dried leaves and branches. Can see panic-stricken birds and animals wandering and searching for springs and meadows where dry-broken mud-lumps are standing as dazed souls of ponds! Tortoises are creeping to get shelter in thin wood lands from where tigers and tigresses leading by harts and rabbits, pulling out and gyrating tongs as the symbol of thirsting!

Flaggy parrots, may be seeing this, flow descanting the sooth that, 'No one holds any natural umbrage or strife if body is debilitated'.

Squeezing of human race by religious fundamentalism all over the world gave path to modernist thoughts and flakes of those silver-clouds entered in *Gape Dome* also in the form of Higher Education Centre under the management of the Julia Memorial Nursery School.

"None is to object religions. But none is not to object inhumane activism in the name of religions…," Principal of the Julia Memorial Nursery School reminded while addressing audience in the auspicious occasion of inauguration function in the Higher Education Centre.

Another Professor characterized about modernism:

"To begin, we have to review the important features or aspects and aspirations of modernism. Really all betterments and developments of social civilization are the contributions of modernist approach to human life in society. In physical as well as in spiritual views, modernists often see themselves with a scientific approach to life in order to replace traditional outlooks..."

Analysis of various religious roots and developments was done by modernists:

"Religious fundamentalism is a strong, even extreme, reaction to modernity, and must be understood in the context of modernism. The term fundamentalism is not very precise, since it stems from a specific movement in early 20th century. Crosalvist movement is applied today by vague and approximate analogy to indicate all extreme and violent reactions to modernism, as and when people speak of Hindu fundamentalists or Muslim fundamentalists. But it seems that there is no turning back, the term is with us, but we must be with caution..."

Anther modernist orator viewed thus:

"After an in-depth research into religions and world history, I can never understand, what is being achieved by converting a Jew or a Hindu into Christianity. It is true that you can see unpleasant things in Hinduism and Judaism as in Islam and Christianity. All cultures and all religions have the Good, the Bad and the Ugly aspects in them. That mixture is universal. I wonder what the goal of Baptists is to go after Jews and Hindus first and then Catholics...?"

"Hinduism and Judaism are cultures and rest are mere organised religions. If we study world history, we can see that Hinduism and Judaism are two ancient cultures and all organised religions of the world today came from those two "mother cultures". Analysis of all religious history shows that Hinduism is to be considered as mother of all cultures and religions...," debate continued.

"Islam, Christianity, and Bahaism came from Judaism. Buddhism, Sikhism, Zoroastrianism and to some extent Jainism came from Hinduism. Everything that is coming from the West has its roots in Judaism like the Ethics and morality segments of Islam and Christianity...," reality is revealed by one modern analyst.

"Everything you see in the East has its origins in Hinduism. Believe it or not, even the rituals of Christianity that people in the east follow, has close resemblance with Hindu rituals...," supported by next man.

"Every species has separate natal identification. Since man has no such classification marks as Hindu or Christian or Muslim, none can argue for separation...," one modernist argued.

"Sixty six books of the Bible deal with the trails and tribulations of the Jews. Similarly, in the Hindu scriptures one is studying about the culture of Land of the Ganges, the culture of the people who gave up their nomad life style and settled on the banks of the rivers such as Ganges, Brahmaputra, Godavari, Indus etc...," one man pointed out his opinion.

"Sixty six books of the Bible do not mention the prosperous Indian Hindu civilization nor about the Chinese civilization, since Bible was written by Jew and for Jews. According to the Bible, Jews are the chosen people of God. Jesus Christ was a Jew. Jesus did not intend to break away from Judaism. He came to make Judaism better by eradicating the evil things that have crept into it...," another man described.

"Blind belief is more dangerous than skepticism ..." One atheist suggested. Abundance of religious thoughts, abasing resemblance study, upheaval and unending rampages between communal Heads and cultural combatants were increasing rapidly day by day; but ablazing sunrays of the summer were reducing amazingly the amplitude of streams and streamlets!

Queue of damsels and bints with empty urns yearning for water on hips, moving towards the wilting and drying eye-sides of streams seemed to be small brooks because of dwindling rills, became usual sight everywhere from dawn to dusk.

In the draconic draught, the village authorities decided to dig deep wells in different parts. All lakes and lagoons were being cleaned and deepened their beds.

Into one corner of the village, folks flew one day following the flaming news:

"During the digging, saw remains of an old Buddhist temple rising from mud...!!!"

Hearing the reports certain Buddhists came and began to dwell there. Gradually the place became a pilgrim centre. The people came there, could visualize the right views and noble truths from the Budha Kendra, where teaches the concepts of Gautama Budha:

"Buddhism was found by Gautama Buddha, *'Enlightenedone*[53]*'*. His earlier name was Siddhartha Gautama, 'Gautama' being the family name. He attained enlightenment, for which he had been searching, while meditating under a bo-tree. Then he began to preach the noble truths. Four Noble Truths are 'Suffering exists', 'Suffering arises from attachments to desire', 'Suffering ceases when attachment to desire ceases', and 'Freedom from suffering is possible by practising the Eightfold Path', which consists of Right View, Right Thought, Right Speech, Right Action, Right livelihood, Right Effort, Right Mindfulness, and Right Contemplation. Ignorance is the cause of all sufferings.

---

[53] https://en.wikipedia.org/wiki/Gautama_Buddha

These eight fold path is divided into three qualities such as (1) wisdom (Panna) –Right View, Right Thought. (2) Morality (*Sila*) –Right Speech Right Action, Right livelihood. (3) Meditation (*Samadhi*) –Right Effort, Right Mindfulness, Right Contemplation.

Buddhism analyses that a human being is only a temporary combination of five aggregates or bundles (*Skandhas*) namely the material body, feelings, perceptions, predispositions or karmic tendencies, and consciousness. According to the Buddhist doctrine of *Pratityasamutpada* or dependent origination, ignorance in previous life creates a tendency for a combination of *Skandhas*. As a result mind and senses will operate and sensation will be exercised. This will lead to craving and a combination for existence leading to renewed cycle of birth and death. So it is a belief in rebirth without transmigration.

The ultimate goal of Buddhist path is to attain *Parinirvana* or final nirvana which means the release from cyclical existence. To gain this goal one has to achieve *Nirvana*, the enlightened or conscious stage in which there is no greed, hatred, and ignorance. Nirvana is attainable by anyone but those who are unable to pursue, can work for better rebirth by improved Karma and observing the precepts. The precepts prohibit killing, stealing, harmful language, and misbehavior and intoxication. Ethics of Nirvana involves the 'Palaces of Brahma', which involves love, kindness, compassion, sympathetic joy and equanimity..."

Pilgrims, to that Place of Enlightenment, increased in number and accordingly fame began to rise amazingly. The precepts of Ahimsa* and Nirvana* attracted the village as a whole though it was also a concept of Hinduism.

The rapidly growing glory of the Buddhist temple was a pessimistic sight to Saindhava activists. They elaborated campaign on Hinduism from the background of temples in the village, thus describing from its root:

"This religion, Hinduism, the most commonly used name, is called *Sanatana Dharma* (eternal religion) and *Vaidika Dharma* (religion of Vedas). It may be derived from an ancient inscription translated as 'the country lying between the Himalayan Mountain and Bindu sarovara'. It is known as Hindustan by combination of the first letter 'hi' of Himalayas and the last compound letter 'ndu' of the word Bindu. Bindu Sarovara is called Cape Comorin Sea in modern time. It may be derived from the Persian word for Indian. It may be a Persian corruption of the word Sindu (river Indus). It may be a name invented by the British administration in India during colonial times..."

They revealed the theories about early history of Hinduism:

"The classical theory of the origin of Hinduism traces the religion's roots to the Indus valley civilization circa 4000 to 2200 BC. 'The development of Hinduism was influenced by many invasions over thousands of years. The major influences occurred when light-skinned nomadic 'Aryans', indo-European tribes invaded Northern India (circa 1500 BC) from the steppes of central Asia. They brought with them their religion of Vedism. These beliefs mingled with the more advanced, indigenous Indian native beliefs often called the *Indus valley culture.*' – This classical theory was initially proposed by Christian scholars in the 19th century. Their conclusions were biased by their pre-existing belief in Hebrew scripts. The book of Genesis which they interpreted literally appears to place the creation of the earth at circa 4000 BC and Noahic flood at circa 2500 BC.

These dates put severe constrains on the date of the 'Aryan invasion' and the development of four Vedas, Upanishads and Hindu religious texts. A second factor supporting this theory was their lack of appreciation of the sophisticated nature of Vedic culture; they had discounted it as primitive. The classical theory is now being rejected by increasing numbers of archaeologists and religious historians.

The originators of the theory were obviously biased by their prior beliefs about the age of the earth and the biblical story of the flood of Noah. The Noahic flood, supposed to have happened according to the biblical story in the Cradle of Semitic religions lying between the Mediterranean Sea and the Dead-Sea, should not have affected the Indus valley…"

Another introductory address about Hinduism was as follows:

"Later in history, under the Achaemenids, Greeks, Bactrians and Sakas, the Iranians and the Indians were forced to meet as citizens of the same empire; they met as complete strangers, not as cousins or as scions from the same stock. The earliest literary productions of the Aryan settlers in India were Rig-Veda, Sama Veda (consisting of chants), Yajur-Veda and the Atharva Veda (a composite of the religious and magical compilation). The Vedas comprise Mantras (hymns), Brahmanas (ritual and ceremonies) Aranyakas (forest speculations) and philosophical Upanishads. In the context of this commonly accepted interpretation of the Vedas, it may be recalled that European orientalists have too often considered them mainly from the theological, anthropological and sociological points of view. A study of the material in its religious aspects is difficult, since even the great commentary of Sayana is in terms of the ideas of his own age. John Dowson in his Hindu classical Dictionary observed, "The Aryan settlers were a pastoral and agricultural people, and they were keenly alive to those influences which affected their prosperity and comfort. They knew the effects of heat and cold, rain and drought, upon their crops and herds, and they marked the influence of warmth and cold, sunshine and rain, wind and storm, upon their own personal comfort. They invested these benign and evil influences with a personality; and the influence behind the fire, the sun, the cloud, and the other powers of nature, they saw beings, who directed them in their beneficent and the evil operations. To these imaginary beings they addressed their praise and to them they put up their prayers for temporal blessings. They observed also the movements of the sun and moon, the constant succession of day and night, the intervening periods of morn and eve, and to these also they gave personalities, which they invested with poetical clothing and attributes. Thus observant of nature in its various changes and operations, alive to its influence upon themselves, and the perceptive of its beauties, they formed for themselves deities in whose glory and honour they exerted their poetic faculty".

But on a careful analysis of the Vedas, it would be apparent that the Vedic view is more subtle and deeper in concept. The One being whom the sages called by many names (Ekam-sat) is referred to in the neuter gender, signifying divine existence and not a divine individual. The Monotheistic God stands in relation to man as a father and a patriarch, while in a Rig Veda hymn to Agni he is called "my father, my kinsman, my brother and my friend". Monotheism, as it has been aptly stated, contemplates the divine in heaven and polytheism contemplates the divine in the universe. Polytheism believes in the assembly of Gods, each possessing character of his own. 'Assembly of gods' denotes only the personifications or characterisation of different aspects and peculiarities of the Universal self..."

Enthusiastically the Saindhavas used indigenous Temple-Arts and others also to attract people towards their campaign. One day Poorvapunya's family also got an invitation to attend Kathakali[54] show in the temple-yard.

"Today there is Kathakali, an odd and old indigenous dance-drama famous for its colloquial songs and act through hand gestures and facial expressions...," Poorvapunya's mother explained with some expressions as imitating Kathakali.

"Can we understand gesticulations...?" While walking, Poorvapunya asked.

"Story will be told in the form of songs as repeated stanzas until the meaning of each part is expressed by gestures and expressions. So it is easy to grasp the story..."

"Today's story...?"

"It's a famous story about the Decline of Rangarajapuri (an ancient renowned realm of the King, Rangaraja). Rangaraja was a very famous king

---

[54] https://en.wikipedia.org/wiki/Kathakali

for his virtues, good administration and wisdom. His country was enjoying a golden era of all glories in its history. Once an injustice occurred:

A married woman, who was a dance-teacher, well known for her beauty and artistry, was kidnapped by a soldier of neighbouring country in disguise according to the order of his young Ruler. Raja ordered the other country's Ruler to surrender the woman and appear for trial of court immediately. When his order was rejected by the other king, he conquered that country. But before the war, the other King had already married that dance-teacher and she was made his queen. Rangaraja could understand this fact only when the other King and his Queen were brought before him as captives after the war. The young Ruler was the soldier in disguise who abducted the teacher! Suddenly Rangaraja released them and proclaimed that the young Ruler and his queen would be treated as his adopted son and daughter. They were returned with all royal treats to their realm escorted by Raja himself. During the journey into that neighbouring country Rangaraja saw several widows crying on the sepulchres of their husbands, who were soldiers and died in the war. He returned with agitation about the unwanted killings he did.

To overcome these sins, Raja decided to renounce crown and sceptre. Thus Regality was given to his son and he received *Vanaprastha* (vedic ashram system 3rd stage), the last *purushartha* (The four *puruṣārthas* are Dharma (righteousness, Artha (prosperity), Kāma (psychological values) and Moksha (spiritual values) or stage of life according to Eastern culture. Then he went for a pilgrimage on foot to *Kasi (holy city)*. According to custom and as she was a perfect wife, the queen of Raja also accompanied him. During their journey, they had to cross a thick forest.

When they entered the jungle, the sun was in the middle of the sky, but day-light was seldom entering under the thickly spread branches of trees. Fire-moths were flying as if it was dark! Rhythmic chirping sound of cicadas was penetrating into the calmness of the woodland. Birds were flapping and making sounds frequently. In the faint light they tried to continue their walk. When tired, they sat under a tree.

That time, an unexpected misery happened! A serpent bit on the Raja's legs. Suddenly his body sweated and turned into blue! His wife sat near him helpless in that deep wilderness and wept. Then they heard an oracle from above leafage! They saw a thrush over the branch of a tall tree singing,

> "Future is unknown, hence undo weep
> Creature you; calf can't gauge cow-ma's
> Wishes, wise, may come mercy in leap;
> Blest drug, bestowed on bitter mace…"

Raja could understand the inner meaning of the song that everything happens may seem bitter first but may come as good blessing later. That symbolical song of wisdom made them prudent to continue journey. While going into inside, deepness of darkness also increased.

When they reached near a pond, surrounded by reeds, one arrow flew across the reeds in front of them as if to block their way! Before the astonishing Raja and wife, a gigantic form appeared like a cluster of super darkness from behind the reeds! It was a wild man with a bow in hand.

He tied Raja with a climbing-stem and made a laugh! Raja asked him what he was going to do. The jungle-man replied:

"You are my prey now. I am going to eat you..."

"But I am a human being like you. Then how can you eat a fellow-being...?" Raja became curious.

"It becomes invariably vital. I shall eat the first animal which I see each week. Sometimes get only small ones such as rabbit or rat. In order to compensate this deficiency, I eat one man each in every year that I see first in these woods. Now you are the first man who comes this way this year..."

"I am a pilgrim going on foot to *Kasi* with my wife. A poor pilgrim can't be treated as an ordinary man. I am not scared to become your food but it is injustice to make my wife helpless in this jungle and she is unable to complete her journey without me. So I shall return after my pilgrimage at the earliest to give myself as your feeding...," Raja pleaded.

"Compassion or canon is not my policy. If you want to escape from here you have to defeat or kill me...," the wild man roared.

"A person who received Vanaprastha is abstained from arms, ale and animosity..." Raja explained his stand.

"Oh Lord of the jungle, please hear my words. It is the duty of a wife to rescue her husband from crisis. I beg you to eat me instead of Raja and let him go...," the Queen humbly appealed with saluting hands.

"Alas! I don't eat females of any species since they are to be respected for sustaining pedigrees...," the wild man opened hands helplessly.

Raja was lead to a nearby vast meadow with a flat rock in the middle. Blood was still oozing from the wounds of Raja's snake-bitten leg. When the wild man saw Raja, blue coloured in day light, looked at him head to foot and asked astonishingly:

"What's this? I never had seen such a blue man like you! Perhaps your flesh would be more delicious..."

Seeing the blood on Raja's legs, the wild man tasted it with thirst. But suddenly he became unconscious due to poison.

Raja and his wife continued their journey remembering the song of the thrush.

After hearing the tale, Poorvapunya said:

"Only arts and literature give pleasure without pain. That is why beauteous nature is artistic..."

Poorvapunya and her mother entered the temple-yard. Night was descending slowly. Ornamental chandeliers with beautiful pieces of crystal glasses were glittering around. Drum started. Rhythmic drums made an enchanted atmosphere. Convincing spectators concentrated on the lighted standing lamp in the middle of the arena.

All of a sudden a curtain rises behind the standing lamp. It is held by two persons from either side. According to the increase of drums, certain folds and vibrations appear on the gold-coloured curtain as symbols of inception. Slowly and slowly crown of a character appears over the curtain! A lamb is being carried to one side of the stage and the curtain is removes. Thus Kathakali starts with spectacular movements and expressions frequently framing on face, made artistically attractive by special make-ups. Story telling is by symbolic actions of hands and fingers according to background song, poetic version of the story.

As the dance-drama is moving forward through marvelous scenes, all clap their hands to express delight and assent to the lively gestures.

Now the scene on the stage is Raja's departure from palace after receiving Vanaprastha. Veil of sadness is covered everywhere! People are in tears. The Raja makes a gesture by closing all fingers of both hands to simulate a flower bud as if to say:

'A flower blooms today, falls tomorrow!'

Spectators are dipping into emotional intensity of the character's immaculate façade. Some burst into tears seeing that Raja comes down from his throne and puts his crown and sceptre on the step.

When the drama was reached to its climax, midnight had elapsed. But the splendour of specific scenes was filling in the viewers' eyes instead of sleep and slumber. The standing lamp was still burning on one side of the stage.

Even after return from there and while walking through the paddy field, the characters were dancing solemnly in Poorvapunya's mind. Hence when reached home, Poorvapunya took the metal pot from porch and poured water on her foot mechanically and perfunctorily went to bed.

In the following days, atmosphere of the dale was dandled with fabulous fables and panic with tangled tides of tedious talks on tumultuous religious beliefs.

Among those legends, there were returnees from heaven and hell; some went there alive! Among the flood, were toxic serpents and fiery fluids! Some tales were about saviors coming from heaven to rescue the believers and to punish the unbelievers.

Religious heads ordered to castigate the babblers who roared against religious activism.

****

Chapter 14

Fight Between Good and Bad

The church passed a resolution against Marcus, 'He must undergo a trial for his anti-church activities and to bear punishment if found guilty'.

Marcus was summoned for trial by his church authorities. Several times he didn't mind but on repeated persuasion by his neighbours, he decided to appear. When he arrived, the Parish Hall was adorned with a small group of dignitaries to witness the trial and the church authorities.

They saw stern figure with a big nose that appeared on the door steps. Their attention focused on his prominent nose and lower lip and its severe expressions.

By seeing him they stopped chanting and looked at each other with arcane authority and apparent smile.

At one point he turned his head towards the spectators as if to say, 'don't be afraid', imparting them a strange and divine feeling.

Marcus showed no signs of remorse. He was resolute and courageous. Without delay the trial was started. The clergy asked three questions furiously as below.

The clergy: "Do you know the resolving powers of our church...?
Marcus: "It holds all powers, what really it hasn't."

The clergy: "As a Christian, what are you doing...?"
Marcus: "What you ought to have done."

The clergy: "Are you challenging canons of the church...?"
Marcus: "You say so"

The clergy:	"You are guilty, Mr. Marcus…; you will be punished. We give judgment in the name of God, to save you from sins by *garrotte* after one month…"
Marcus:	"In case, show the power of judgment given by God…"
The clergy:	"………………"
Marcus:	"Canon says that clergies are mediators between man and god. Is judgement a mediator's job?"
The clergy:	"………………"
Marcus:	"What is the proof that I m doing the wrong?"
The clergy:	"………………"

When he was coming out of the hall, his face was showing soft traits and eyes were large and bright with a gentler expression.

"Now I look like a man who lives in this world who has my share of bad luck and sorrows. Aren't I…?" Marcus asked frowning at the church authorities.

He turned towards them after stepping forward in a hurry and narrated the story of Randy Island in a nutshell:

"Randy Park Church, you might have heard, is now burning second time in communal violence. If anyone see an instance of victimization, no one can stand without eyes moist by tears.

Robby is one such instance. Now she is a girl of fourteen, belong to a low caste family. Her mother died in the riot before twelve years back. Before death she was brutally attacked by activists on her modesty behind the darkness of drastic conflict. While tearing away her jacket, they had no religious discrimination!

Her father trampled to death in stampede while escaping to nearby Randy Park Church. It was his good luck. Otherwise he had to die by the hands of activists in the church. Her house was smashed and numerous homes were burned along with inhabitants. People ran away from slums to a nearby old church for refuge. But militants surrounded the church with cheer, like wolves as if helpless preys come to their den directly. Alas! Militants had no enough bullets to kill all people. So they finally depended on pestles to crash people's head. Undamaged heads were cut off and bodies were burnt inside the church. Now those thousands of skulls are being kept in a mausoleum!

Robby's daily routines are clinging to her one year old younger brother's growth. Her life revolves around the gloomy household chores. While other girls of her age are pleasantly going to school in the morning every day, she cleans vessels, cooks breakfast and washes clothes near the waiting shed, which abuts on her hovel, without remembering the days in which she was lying unconscious below the staircase of Randy Park Church, before twelve years during the clashes.

"You were alone. Your father and mother died earlier. Then how could you have a younger brother...?" One day an old lady asked humorously.

To Robby, it was a stupid question. She was not a literalist to explain that her younger brother was a residue thrown into dump by the garbage of new civilization of mankind; she happened to see that child among the waste and recognised him, having same human-blood and ancestry. So she humbly replied:

"Pardon me; I am illiterate. I can't define the word 'brotherhood' as you can learn..."

Marcus laughed loudly and continued satire:

"Last riot was due to intra-religious hostility and competition. Some churches allowed low castes to participate in their mass. But other groups objected. That simple contention became the reason to lose thousands of lives. Now intensive inter-religious clashes are going on additionally resulting in brutal carnages. This time number of skulls will not be less than a billion. Hence each religion can build own museums or can erect, not so small, cranial churches, mosque of skulls and so on as remarkable monuments of 'our religious culture' for future generations! Otherwise, you can sell them worldwide as ornamental decoration at lower rates...!!

Really it is impossible to distinguish skulls according to religion but no one will dare to raise such questions until you throw away your ruthless and rude religious canons and weapons..."

While the church authorities were sitting bewildered, Marcus got out, gently walked away and disappeared in the street.

In his way, another tragedy was waiting!

When he was walking near the mosque-street, he happened to hear a deep groaning. He peeped into the fence-door. A man was struggling as he was tied up inside.

Marcus looked around and called loudly:

"Hallow....Hallow......"

Nobody was there to reply.

Somehow he managed to get inside the fence and untied the man. That poor man bowed his head with joy and swept the blood, oozing from wounds on hands and legs, and said with weep:

"My name is Hussein; not a mad man. I am a poor labourer working in a distant place. Yesterday some persons gave me drinks. It wasn't a real alcohol,

I am sure. It worked like a whorl-wind in my stomach and after a while I tried to walk, but unfortunately crawled like a snake and quickly felt unconscious. When I woke up, I was here in chains! They told me that they want one lunatic to be tied in front of the mosque and later I will be released when my lunacy is cured! With unbearable sorrow and anger I roared several times that I am not mad! Hearing my words they laughed at me and went away."

"If a chain is in the neck, it would be an ornament and if locked on leg, it would be symbol of insanity. It means everything is according to viewpoints…," Marcus remarked with a smile.

"All lunatics may not be in chains…," the man replied with eye-gesture.

"You escape immediately before they come…," Marcus threw the chain and urged him to run away.

"Now I am mad enough to give them a punishment. They were only five persons. Even if they were ten, I would not have surrendered if I was not drunk. See my strength. I am a master of martial arts…," the man broke the hard wooden doors and windows with legs! Knocked down thick walls with fist! Within seconds he destroyed the central parts of the mosque!!

As if he was satisfied with his deeds, the man abruptly vanished in the street corner. From surroundings some persons came by hearing the noise of demolition. Marcus hid himself behind wall near the gate and peeped into the half-opened entry.

Devotees mourned over the damaged walls and doors. Some others found that the stranger had escaped miraculously from the chain! They examined the chain, not broken but untied!

"Oh! God has rescued him…!" They said loudly with astonishment.

"He might be a magician or saint…!; otherwise how could unite the chain while his hands were tied together…?" People looked at each other.

"God is compassionate. He destroyed this mosque as a punishment…," some persons judged.

While all of them were running towards the pole, in southern side of the mosque, to which the chain was fastened, Marcus silently crept inside the mosque and hid himself under the ruined roof-side. He sang in a low voice as if an oracle comes from the sky:

> 'Hear the dawn chorus! Wake you soon;
> Yesterday night, Oh, might have done –
> By thine malice, all inhumane sins;
> Bygones let bygones; vow – not hence.'

Hearing the oracle, people turned towards the west, closed their eyes, bowed their head and began to pray as loud as they could. Suddenly Marcus got down into the front yard of the mosque and appeared behind them as if entering through the gate.

Seeing Marcus, they shouted at him:

"Where are you going, mad man..., into our gate...?"

"I heard some bereavement-cry from here. What happened...?" Marcus looked at them curiously.

"Nothing is here just as your madness. You go away, the demented rat...," they cursed him.

"Yea, I am going; but that doors and walls...? I think your god has come..." Marcus pointed towards the damaged mosque in a ridiculing manner.

The people quickly entered in the mosque and closed the door with a piece of damaged door-plank as if it was vain to argue with Marcus.

He said loudly while walking away from there:

"Literature has always succeeded over mankind; good instances are religious books. Poor folks, no prominence is with human life. He also turns to soil like other creatures..."

****

Chapter 15

Wolf in Darkness

Marcus was wandering through the main street on a hot Friday. He uttered his new mottos pointing towards prayer halls, while devotees were coming out:

"Religions were created for justice of life but brought up for injustice of living…"

In the afternoon he saw some people, assembled in nearby ground of a mosque after *Juma* (special prayer).

As a black dot he could see a cab rolling to them from a long distance, through the old thorny bush covered road coming from *Dragon-Cave*. While hoofs of moments were moving speedily, sound of the horse-hoof became more and more clear. Then wheels of the cab stopped with a noisy sound.

A man with rosy cheeks and sharp eyes got down. Two armed guards stood loftily left and right as if protectors of their God and Religion. Golden lace of his turban was flickering in the sun light. Long silver-beard seemed to increase further length to his lengthy face.

People looked at him as if seeing a godly man of mystery, with respect, conjecture and conceit!

"This is the only man who survived from the *Dragon-Cave* because of holiness…," the multitude murmured

He was taken to a small wooden stage. A green flag, hoisted at the top of the platform, was flying in the gentle breeze.

"I greet all of you in the name of Allah. I came here, crossing windy deserts and hills to see you, my brothers. Across *Babylonia*, *Mesopotamia* and far towards East, martyrdoms of your brothers are becoming innumerable. Do you know? In *Golan Heights* situation is much worse than ever before. It is shame to all of us and for past two hundred years we have been fighting to owe our own land there. Eastern Mediterranean soil is soaked in blood. Your nostrils will fill with burned human flesh in dark continent; otherwise we have to fight against the enemies. In *Land of the Ganges* you may be safe. But beware that same may happen to you also in near future. Hence I say that fighting in the name of God is the justice of this eon.

I assure you that in this holy war those who sacrifice their life will surely find a place in heaven. Our holly book says:

٤: ٧٤ فَلْيُقَاتِلْ فِي سَبِيلِ اللَّهِ الَّذِينَ يَشْرُونَ الْحَيَاةَ الدُّنْيَا بِالْآخِرَةِ وَمَنْ يُقَاتِلْ فِي سَبِيلِ اللَّهِ فَيُقْتَلْ أَو يَغْلِبْ فَسَوْفَ نُؤْتِيهِ أَجْرًا عَظِيمًا

(4.74 Let those fight in the way of Allah who sell the life of this world for the other. Whoso fighteth in the way of Allah, be he slain or be he victorious, on him We shall bestow a vast reward.)[ii]

٤: ٧٥ وَمَا لَكُمْ لَا تُقَاتِلُونَ فِي سَبِيلِ اللَّهِ وَالْمُسْتَضْعَفِينَ مِنَ الرِّجَالِ وَالنِّسَاءِ وَالْوِلْدَانِ الَّذِينَ يَقُولُونَ رَبَّنَا أَخْرِجْنَا مِنْ هَذِهِ الْقَرْيَةِ الظَّالِمِ أَهْلُهَا وَاجْعَل لَّنَا مِن لَّدُنْكَ وَلِيًّا وَاجْعَل لَّنَا مِن لَّدُنْكَ نَصِيرًا

(4.75 How should ye not fight for the cause of Allah and of the feeble among men and of the women and the children who are crying: Our Lord! Bring us forth from out this town of which the people are oppressors! Oh, give us from Thy presence some protecting friend! Oh, give us from Thy presence some defender!)

٢: ٢٥ وَبَشِّرِ الَّذِينَ آمَنُوا وَعَمِلُوا الصَّالِحَاتِ أَنَّ لَهُمْ جَنَّاتٍ تَجْرِي مِن تَحْتِهَا الْأَنْهَارُ كُلَّمَا رُزِقُوا مِنْهَا مِن ثَمَرَةٍ رِزْقًا قَالُوا هَذَا الَّذِي رُزِقْنَا مِن قَبْلُ وَأُتُوا بِهِ مُتَشَابِهًا وَلَهُمْ فِيهَا أَزْوَاجٌ مُطَهَّرَةٌ وَهُمْ فِيهَا خَالِدُونَ

(2:25 And give glad tidings (O Muhammad) unto those who believe and do good works; that theirs are Gardens underneath which rivers flow; as often as they are regaled with food of the fruit thereof, they say: This is what was given us aforetime; and it is given to them in resemblance. There for them are pure companions; there forever they abide.) [iii]

The new way of resistance can be achieved only through new thoughts, opinions and determination to offer life to safeguard our ethical belief. This is the new ultimate revelation that you have to follow. For this, we need volunteers to fight unto the last breath…"

The rabble listened his discourse carefully. The thrilling rash words pierced into their mind as double edged swords. They were gazing at the guns which were hanging on shoulders of the guards because, the only thing they had to do was standing ovation to praise the speech.

After the descant, with a new expectation his cab was driven into an old unused sloppy way covered with thorn-bush, towards the hill side, where there is a legendary rock-cavern known as *Dragon-Cave,* which is believed to have been the grotto of Dragons.

All the villagers have heard the story of *Dragon-Cave* since the tale has been transferred from generation to generation. Moreover, on *Dragons' day* in every year, people see fumes curling up into air from the cave!! Whoever dared to go there didn't come back. According to the legend, in olden days Dragons had been visiting the village and curing all diseases and famine on *Dragons' day* every year. Later when people tried to go to the cavern before the day of visit, Dragons angrily killed all of them by spiting fire and stopped their visit forever.

When the cab entered the *Dragon-Cave,* opened and closed the windows of a spooky-looking labyrinthine building on the side of a steep high hill, with a blunt sound like isolated fox-howl.

Thick shabby rose wood walls were covered with some hollowed and frayed blocks. Peeling-down creepers were almost hanging from the roof. Window flakes were dangling in the air and most of its coloured glasses were broken. Combined with blowing wind, hordes of weathercocks were making whistling noise around the bungalow.

A tall black man with white hat slowly entered the front-yard entrance.

The watcher walked towards him and wished with a slim smile.

"Today you have come earlier for duty......," the watcher started talk.

"Why are we keeping all these dead bodies of renegades and sceptics? Can we convert their tombs as *Dargas* or ....? the horse-guard asked.

"These are nothing but precious monument of our religion......," watcher replied, followed by a serious rumbling.

"Yea..., Testaments reveal the nobleness of religious gravity...," the horse-guard agreed.

"Employment will input an implicit character in a man. That is why your smile is a grim one......," the horse-guard commended.

In the stagnant black pond, muddy dark rocks above the clay water level, remained as devils of the dell. A giant eagle remains aloft flapping wings over head of this haunted structure. Major part of this pine paneled building is an abode of black bats and wild cats. Red flowered climbing stem are overhanging in a dry tree. Densely branched sculptural trunks with twisted top having thick foliage around, is darting horrible shades over the Minaret.

A big wolf disappears into the darkness.

In the backyard, in dim-lighted lantern, two shadows are moving around. One dwarf dressed in black trousers is observing their surroundings like a night owl. A tall Stout man is walking around.

Rooms inside are partially covered with spiders' web.

"A real mystery................!" One who sees this place will say.

The dwarf picked a cloth and covered his body and locked the latch of the door and walked around a long hall in which a dozen black boxes were kept inside. A bowl of galipot is fuming in one corner.

As ephemerals, thoughts and attitudes of the people began to change frequently. Most of the mob indulged in religious talks and debates in the mentality of enlightened philosophers only to safeguard their religious ideas with the help of half-spoon granules of knowledge swallowed from classrooms. Atheists also gained a prominent role in that chaotic situation. One man lighted the lamp of argument:

"All religious books have described about heaven and hell with earthly atmosphere because there is no heaven or hell and show the limitation of humanistic power of imagination, and thus all are imaginations..."

"Boat will not rove by itself. So we have to row the society to the shore of the truth ...," modernists came forward.

"Religions are the step mothers of social injustice...," another man observed.

Another sudden development happened was that Atheists crossed hands with the modern approach lighted by the Higher Education Centre of the Julia Memorial School in the analysis and study of different schools of thought about Incarnation, Immortality, Self realisation, various vanished religions etc. They observed:

"Buddhism came as a teacher out of compassion for suffering humanity and not impulsive over incarnation. Jainism says incarnation as a Supernatural being, descended from heaven. Zoroastrianism depicts that Celestial pre-existence came as a body which came from heaven, poured with rain passed to his mother through the milk of heifers. Christianity says about embodiment of god in human face. According to Hinduism incarnation means *Avatar*, especially of Vishnu. God can become incarnate in many places at the same time through partial *avatars* like *Amshas*. Hindu *Avatars* do not fully participate in human suffering or loose the knowledge, power and their divine nature..."

Atheists gave more publicity against idol-worship showing the history that Babylonians, Egyptians, Greeks and Romans were idol worshipers. Until Hebrew prophet teaches, Palestinians were idol worshipers. Christians also have several reverences of images, in which separate, divine personality is addressed through images.

Higher Education Centre of the Julia Memorial School taught about various vanished religions: Their class followed.

Zoroastrianism came from ancient Persia, the prophet Zoroaster found the religion. All doctrines of the prophet are preserved in his Gathas (psalms). Gathas consist of worship of *Ahura Mazda* ('Lord Wisdom') and an ethical dualism, Truth and Lie. It was a composition of earlier Indo-European beliefs.

Arianism was a Christian heresy founded by Arius in 4th century. Teaching of the founder was that god is unbegotten and without beginning. According to Arianism The Son was not generated from the divine substance of the Father but created like all other creatures as per father's will. Hence the relationship of the Son to his Father is adoptive. Thus it denies full divinity of Jesus Christ.

Gnosticism is an esoteric religious movement, which presented a major challenge to orthodox Christianity, flourished during 2nd and 3rd centuries AD. The word Gnosticism is derived from the Greek term *Gnosis* (revealed knowledge). It says that seeds of the Divine Being fell down from the transcendent realm into this physical world and are under bondage in human bodies. The spiritual sparks or seeds can return to the transcendent realm by attaining wisdom (*Sophia*).

Mithraism was a chief opponent to Christianity and became one of the major religions of Roman Empire. Mithra is the ancient Persian God of light and wisdom as described in the Zoroastrian writing, Avesta and later Mithra became the god of the Sun. It was similar to that of Christianity in baptism, use of holy water, its ideals of humility and brotherly love, the adoption of December 25, as Mithra's birth day, last judgement and resurrection. It differs from Christianity in the exclusion of women from ceremonies.

Mayas is thought that came in pre-Columbian civilization, centred about the worship of a large number of nature gods. A god of rain called *Chac* was particularly important. The supreme deities were *Kukulcan*, a creator of god closely related to the *Toltec* and *Aztec* and the sky god, *Itzamma*. Complete trust in the god's control of certain units of time and of all peoples' activities during those periods, were their significant peculiarity. It flourished in between 300 BC and 900 AD.

Zuni Indian is a North American Indian tribe constituting a distinct language family, of the south west cultured area. They live in a pueblo Indian reservation near North Mexico. In appearance, culture and social organisation they closely resemble other town-dwelling Indians. Zuni are industrious and are noted for their weaving, basketry and pottery making as well as their turquoise jewellery. They have strong attachment to ancient religious rituals, which are tied closely to the changing seasons and include special devotion to the rain. Advent of Christian mission in 1629 made serious threat to them.

Manichaeism is An ancient religion named after its founder, the Persian sage Mani (219-76?) which presented a major challenge to Christianity. Mani was born in an aristocratic Persian family in south Babylonia. His father brought him up in an austere Baptist sect. Between the age of 12 and 24 he experienced vision in which an angel designated him the prophet of a new and ultimate revelation. On his first missionary journey, Mani reached in India, where he was influenced by Buddhism. Manichaeism fought against Zoroastrianism.

Orphism was a classical religion in the 6th BC, mystic cult of ancient Greece believed to have been drawn from the writings of the legendary poets and musician, Orpheus. It was based on the myth of the god, Dionysus. According to Orphism, people should endeavour to rid themselves of the evil element in their nature and should seek to protect the Dionysiac or divine nature of their being, by following the Orphic rites. Through several lives, people have to prepare for their afterlife. People, who followed holiness, would be released from all evils and reunited with holiness for ever; and who lived in evil, would be punished.

Julia Memorial School began to teach lessons based on stories of the famous writers in order to reveal the follies of religious beliefs without following radical virtues of real life, as the old maxim, "Spirituality is the panacea for worries, only if it stipulates Dharma or equality and justice."

****

Chapter 16

Created by Imagination

"Listen…, now I shall read the thirtieth episode of the spectacular story written in *Eternal tranquility.* This section deals with the second guilt of mankind done on the planet, K'iche…," the master addressed the students with this introduction and started to read:

"Now it's four o'clock. Still the seminar is going on. It will not end before midnight, I think…," one man slowly came outside of the hall and said.

"Yea, it is a serious matter to decide. It will take time…" –audience waved head and supported.

All of them are in pleasant mood since today is the third golden jubilee of their arrival in this planet. Here the second generation has attained youth hood. Now Junior K'iche is representing his family name.

During this period one golden jubilee should have passed after the celebration of one millennium on the Earth.

On this occasion they are thinking about an everlasting monument to be erected for memory of their ancestors. That is why the seminar is going on after the stipulated time.

"Finally, it is decided to make a statue of God in one big sapphire…," one man informed the spectators about the decision taken in the seminar.

"Which God…?"

"God of all planets and stars…"

"Name of that God…?"

"K'ichen…"

"Form of K'ichen…?"

"bear a resemblance to man…"

"Why…?"

"Since man was created in its shape…"

"Who said this nonsense…?"

"It is the belief followed by mankind…"

"Is it true…?"

Their debate continued for long time but everyone could understand everything except truth. Though discussion was about sculpture of God, it ended in division of supporters and objectors. The supporters categorized themselves as believers and called the opponents as dis-believers.

Within five hours a statue of one hundred and fifty feet height was made with latest technology! For it, one big rock of sapphire taken from the cliff of the K'ichen Peak was fully used. It was believed that the mist-covered summit was saving the inhabitants by arresting lightning. The statue was erected.

"Even if the god doesn't desire, this will stand here forever…," the main orator of the inauguration said solemnly, while devotees were gathering before the statue and praying to god. Suspicious didn't participate in the function. Instead, they organized a group to teach about their faith. They cursed and blamed the supporters for destroying of all social values and goodness of mankind, being followed unaffected in the planet.

When the ceremony was over, falling of rain-drops had already started more heavily than ever before. Populace passively saw the unexpected dropping of fibril-fixed grape-stems. Breeze transformed itself into the form of tempest. Like demons, dark clouds leaned down from sky towards land. Their houses were trembled with tremendous thunderbolts. Gradually an atrocious fear foiled their courage and compelled them to cry and run home for refuge.

Bursting out planks of their houses in the heavy rain dashed their dream-land's bonanza. They began to realise sob of sorrows, which they never heard from ancestors. Glares of lightning blinded their eyes and its beams glittered on the head of the statue of K'ichen.

The sculpture suddenly became flame of a fantastic fire-ball. After an hour it burned and burst into grime and specks. The dust drowned the stadium and surrounded ferns in futility as stained sterility of a desert. The particles, red due to burning, spread and filled the ground as if dried spots of bubbled blood!

The supporters of the statue were blamed for all disasters and isolated from all social activities. On the contrary the followers of K'ichen explained that the calamity was due to the fury of God, K'ichen against the unbelievers and hence made another big sculpture and erected in the yard of the meeting hall. Prayers of penance were started and pandemonium broke out simultaneously when the news was spread around.

Names of religions descended into the society and divided the populace into different classes and sects. They reviled each other and residences of opposite groups were banned in each locality. From selfishness, almost all seven deadly sins entered into their mind, sprouted, flourished and grew into unbreakable thorny bush. Unexpected small spike of altruism tried to come up, but simply scattered by those sharp spikes around.

According to the changes of their attitudes nature's attribute also transformed apparently since man began to use natural elements and articles for making baleful things. The moderate climate and seasons lost stagnancy and became unusual. Severe hot and cold seasons began to appear. Faultless fertility of soil turned up down. Ultimately all organisms became unable to absorb sunlight except plants. Hence food became unavoidable to them and it caused soil-filth. When the vegetable kingdom failed to feed animal kingdom, some species of animals including man became carnivorous. This ended in the total eradication of all natural rules and values.

"Alas! Man is walking before all immoralities as emblem of all evils…," When malfeasances became numerous and unaffordable in the society, artificial laws and code of punishments were came into force. Religious discriminations and rites inflamed all other public atrocities and animosities.

"Now our planet, K'iche is not parallel to the Earth but in zenith, in the case of human life-style…," seeing the places of earth on the screen of the satellite station, innocent people indicted.

"This planet has now become precarious and later it will perish as hell…," someone said prophetically.

Social security vanished and people lost faith in themselves. Their thoughts were entrapped by fear of self-protection. They ran for security measures in all respects. Wooden houses were demolished and concrete structures were replaced. Huge gates and locks emerged. Above all arms and ammunition were made for newly constituted armored forces. Competitive mind persuaded them to fight each other and in those unfair actions several souls lost relation with their bodies. Various troops conquered places and put up their realms. Thus people were divided forever and became permanent foes.

Behind all those evil developments, religious fertilizer and spray of water were the hidden and unidentifiable elements; because those elements were, as venom covered with honey.

Those conditions and polarizations were transferred from generation to generation sequentially. Four hundred and fifty years elapsed. Now it is the fourth generation going on here. During this period more than three thousand years have passed on the Earth. Recently it is noticed that here also total length of lineages is getting down considerably.

The people have already learned to adopt all social, political and religious transforms from anywhere except real wisdom and truth during these eras. Religious modifications such as Crosalvism, Berithism, Al-Taqwa etc., attracted them also very much. They could understand everything including all transformations of religions, gospels and teachings except what real god is. So they failed to follow the real goodness and forgot what their ancestors taught through their truthful life:

"If no goodness, no meaning in having wisdom; if no wisdom, no meaning as being man; if no man, no meaning in religion..."

In every sense, life became distressing. Scarcity of essential things due to slit between supply of artificial products and demand, discrimination of social status, threatening diseases and such other numerous factors made their life so sophisticated and vexatious. The present situation can be read fully if we see the K'iche's family. Now the family has around two thousand members scattered into different places with different family names. K'iche –V is aged and lying in his death-bed. One of his sons died due to epidemic. Another son is suffering from an unidentified disease with symptoms similar to mental aberration. Died last year, was his second wife. One niece is a handicapped lady. It is a pitiful story:

In childhood, when she was visiting a zoo, tried to give some edible fruit to one bear, locked in a cage because she had studied that all animals are tamed as pets. Unfortunately it masticated her arm also!

In the case of another niece, life is very hard. According to her words, 'compassionate people are contributing money for her livelihood every day.' Others say it as begging. One nephew is running a small bookshop in which most of the items are about sexual affairs, commonly called as yellow books except some copies of the holy Bible, some periodicals and newspapers. Just as on Earth, now here also news papers and periodicals have special pages for advertisements, thanks giving to different saints, matrimonies, obituaries etc.

A teashop in a city is being run by another nephew, which s famous for dishes with wild animals' flesh and blood. When such flesh becomes deficient he will mix meat of goats and cows secretly. Since he is aware of sins, he goes and participates in all Sunday-mass in the nearby church with his specially designed holy Bible with leather cover, bearing all hardships of journey, occur especially on holidays in the city. Yesterday happened one of such grievance to him while returning from the church:

The incident occurred around 12.30 p.m. He and his wife were assaulted by the staff on duty at the toll-gate. When he hesitated to pay the levy, a scuffle ensued and a few youths armed with iron bars and wooden sticks roughed up the couple and caused extensive damage to his vehicle. He said that the toll-gate building was a heaven for anti-social elements, thriving on the sale of narcotics.

One of his grandsons is a pastor, who is more concerned about food rather than prayers and hence usually gets special meals from houses of devotees. Now he is sitting in front of a dining table in one follower's house asking about soup:

"And what's that…? Mutton soup by any chance…?"

"You're in for a special treat…," grinning Mrs. Lee ghoulishly stirring at the steaming vat with a glinting ladle.

"It's not just soup, but heart and liver too, flavoured with cardamom, pepper and ginger mix…," Mr. Lee explains.

"You don't mind ginger mix, do you…?" Mrs. Lee concerns about until the pastor shakes his head. The meal is going on…!

Another grandson is living in the famous historic ruins of the capital of an eastern region. The breathtaking beauty of the abandoned capital continues to charm visitors as an extraordinary and amazing creation of the Empire. So he is working as travel guide there, carefully showing magnificent landscapes adorned with clay and stone architecture, spotlessly green vegetations and towering mountain ranges to adventure lovers and romantic couples who are coming as tourists.

Thus all places in this planet now not only more or less resemble with those of Earth in life-style of human beings but become difficult to dwell due to various unidentified contagious diseases, adversity of atmosphere, diversion of land into barren deserts, deterioration of underground water level, ruin of flora and fauna, wrath of hot sunrays etc.

During the last decade several prayer halls and schools have closed for ever due to lack of members. Birth rate is declining and death rate is increasing in geometric progression.

"If this stage continues, we all will be annihilated shortly. No need of these records if remedial measures fail…," keeper of the birth and death records said.

"Portents of the total doom are appearing in the forms of pandemic and piercing heat…," some put hands on head with frustration.

"Real ill-omen is religious clashes. It swallowed more than fifty percentage of the population…," some others pointed against communal riots getting fired from one place to another rapidly.

"In the past, this planet, Venus was paradise. Into this Promised Land, man came with an assurance that no one would play against the natural law.

But what did he do? Even though all majesties were bequeathed to him, he brought up his selfishness and all other drastic evils as if emphasising the maxim, 'Leech will not lie on bed.' Now he is harvesting all of his misdeeds sown earlier by him...," someone cursed himself as being a human.

****

Chapter 17

Sacred Conflict

It is impossible to describe how much, death of Mary has shocked the entire village and Poorvapunya in specific. People are going with bowed head. Always her tomb is being covered with wreaths and flowers put by villagers. Pavement to the churchyard is filled with the weeping visitors who are waiting for their turn to dedicate red circlets as their hearts of love......!

Dropping tears of the people tells how she was loved by the parish. Mills and other working places are opened very late every day. Children are seen very lazy and sad. Folks are reluctant even to smile due to their grief. Her mother is lying paralysed on bed. Poorvapunya became regular visitor to Mary's residence to put flowers before Mary's portrait.

"Mind is always in the yard of quailing memories and man is always of mind......," Poorvapunya purported passively.

"As water ceases fire, grief won't but kindle......," persons' contemptuous talks flooded in the society.

"This event will tragically trigger off communal combat. It may end as last war grabbing last man's life on earth....."

"As fire in the Hell, sacred conflict is the permanent flame on our planet now......"

"Sacred conflict...?"

"Yea..., religious clash must be ridiculed with words worse than this......."

Days and nights went by; but the village remained restless and rampaged. Everyone's exhaling included infringe of unforeseen antagonistic animosity. In churches lanterns were not put out in the night, while minds of priests were burning throughout.

"Volcano, even if smokeless is an appalling one......," Pastor suggested.

"This is shame to Crosalvism..." someone murmured.

"We should retaliate very strongly against Al-Taqwiites........," revengefully one replied and entered in the yard.

"Our village should remain as a place respecting all pluralism and should keep peace and harmony...," One old man's voice drowned among the supporting applause to the Pastor.

A young chap crushed his teeth and roared:

"We must send those kidnappers to the Hell at the earliest...," anger surged up on his face.

"We should remain as a distinguished community, linguistically and culturally varied. We won't allow other religions to pour water into milk. If they do so, we have to separate it in the name of Jesus.........," priest's sermon followed.

Looking at the portrait of Mary, Poorvapunya kept silence for a while and returned to portico, filled with sorrowful memories.

"Contradict to the adage – time will efface all sadness – it would be an ever-flaming furnace in reminiscence..............," she whispered to herself.

As if it was heard, Michael told her:

"You are right, but grief will not draw the cart of life......"

"Can miserable memory be set aside.......?"

"No..., Poorva. But have to put it on one side....," Michael's philosophical concepts continued during the chit-chat, although she was not much interested.

She was dressed in white robe looking like a swan of seemliness.

Like seeing a lily on hand side, Michael stood to the magical mitigation of zest, when magnificent mind's attention beveled on the jigging jasmine in the garth.

Minds of them flew together towards the new horizon of unimaginative future. But all seemed to be real to them as if dripping the signet of his love on her lips.

By bearing new flowers, the lawn of love grew between Michael and Poorvapunya day by day. Despite meeting regularly, time seemed to be objecting even to inch before both of them. In a darkest night in the following winter when the entire village was asleep, Poorvapunya decided to elope with Michael.

The frightened village, due to the loss of Mary, before recovery from that misery, fainted gasping when heard the news of their fleeing.

As in a granny's tale, waiting for these dear one the hamlet's eyes became pale and old quite earlier than usual. Symptoms of Senescence began to see in every action! However when each outsider comes, it looked with deep-fallen sick eyes through grey hairs falling to the old cramped forehead and enquired about her lost daughters in frantic way.

That time, in one corner of another region, songs of proselytizing were rising. Poorvapunya was not the first or last person who got baptised there in the new church situated in that small town of Christian dominion known as *'the Cross Belt'*

While returning from the church, though she was holding a rosary which was gifted by clergyman, her face seemed to be unsatisfied and agonised about the conversion procedures followed in the church which were fully absurd and abuse according to her thought and belief.

Several sermons and seminars went by in the church while Poorvapunya was also one of the audiences.

Always she was seen indifferent with a facial expression, while participating, that 'these are only sacrifices for her sacred love.'

While weeks and months were thus going by, that year's anniversary came.

Decorated yard of the church and roadside with coloured paper- cuttings and palm-leaves excited people's mind of festivity. Everywhere Christian devotees lighted candles in front of houses and shops adorned with pictures of Jesus Christ and other saints.

Flag is hoisted to mark the beginning of anniversary of the church. Devotees are gathering in the procession of Holy statuette.

In large numbers people are marching from church to the main cross road and returning after making constabulation to the chapel, adorned with cupolas. Children are looking at decorated portal amazingly and walk for special holy mass in the late evening. Peoples seemed to be in a rush to see wonderful fireworks after the mass. This year the fireworks will be on competition basis so that everyone knows that it will be a greatest one.

Following an announcement, put out lights from all parts of the ground. While arising exclamation among the mob, various teams waiting for their chance with packed materials entered in the play ground.

"Will it happen this year also..........," someone pointed to the cupola, damaged in the fireworks last year.

"Don't say so; fireworks are not only in churches............"

"But what is its necessity? Dangerous activities are to be avoided by wise animals. Otherwise it would be the furthermost sin..........," ratiocination among the aged.

"If God's will is that, fire accidents will happen though there are no fireworks........," one of them argued by pointing his finger towards the sky.

"You are an old man with twisted thinking.........," another person laughed at him.

"You are about to step into sepulcher; But denying golden rules of the Church............"

By putting an end to their debate, crackers' continuous sound echoed in the air loudly.

Miniature rockets soared up into the sky and bloomed, spreading colourful sparkles in the air. Holly cross on the dome in the top of the church was shining in blue light of fulminating big crackers like star-pendants in hands of Archangels.

"How wonderful; look at that white light..., mummy...........!" children embraced mothers, seeing the sparkling iron ores of white lights whirling with humming sound.

Withering white rays, crackers blasted with huge sound. One of the splashed squibs fell among the crowd and exploded. Scampered mob's scared cry heard as another explosion! Here and there girls and kids were trampled down by escapers. Chain of bangs ended in couple of minutes. Shattered bodies were seen in the bloodshed ground under dark smoke of gun-powder. Hundreds were hospitalised. Portal of the church looked like an entrance of a consistent grave yard.

At last the atmosphere of gratitude paved way to gravity of grief.........!

Next morning-sun, rose behind the dark clouds seemed to be looking miserable over the village. Most of the houses were deserted because majority of the inhabitants were weeping in hospitals.

A heated dispute on the tragedy was followed. Assembled devotees in the church-yard, divided in to two sects. Opponents took an oath, not to allow crackers in future celebrations. Some argued that without programme like fireworks how can attract people to church-festivities.

"When number of festivals increases, number of followers increases...," another man commended.

"That is true; not only churches but also other religions are attracting people by these types of techniques just like torch towards bees at night ...," some nodded head.

"Are you traitors of church to say like that? Inner meaning of your saying is very awful. Do you think that church is leading people to ruin like bees...?"

"Why not...? You know how Agnes became nun...," he replied as an introduction of a long story of Agnes and tightened his turban on head as if getting ready to tell.

"This is not a tragedy but a curse on fake-believers among us. How many of us are regularly coming for Sunday masses...? Only few with will..."

Shall we take an oath that all of us compulsorily attend Sunday masses today onwards…? In the name of Jesus we will spread the message of Holy Spirit to each and every house in this village. In the name of His sacrifice, we will spread His blessings to all cities and counties…," all clapped hands loudly.

While saying 'Halleluiah', suddenly a Holy Cross fell down among them from top of the cupola as remain of the blast of eve.

They looked at the sky with amazement and said:

"Oh! What is happening…? What is the meaning of this broken cross…? God is giving us the duty to build a new cross-top…?"

The devotees admired God's grace and interpreted the accident as the most marvelous and greatest miracle that happened during the century! Aunt Sally and others talked to everyone about it all the way and so they could reach home only after sunset! But Aunt Sally is not finished her job. Aunty sat in a chair. It crashed.

****

Chapter 18

Aunt Sally's Snobbery

Michael's auntie named Sally is familiar to everyone in the place and the people used to call her *Aunt Sally* Not only name but also character reveals that she represents an average human being except in her superhuman height and size. Her behaviour like cupidity, pomposity, selfishness, envy, hubris, languor, stinginess, indignation, avarice etc. emphasises her human nature.

If anyone analyses a day of Aunt Sally, he will get full image and surely admit truth of the above view. For instance, she is old but treats herself only as middle aged, though puts small specs always to correct her defective eyesight, such as to identify spoon and fork separately without touching. Truly the glass increases some gloss to her face rather than hiding paled hollow-eyes. If anyone asks about spectacles, she would say with a half-smile:

"I am from the Midlands and was a middle school teacher till last year. Specs were a must to make pupils to obey with sharp looks and now it is to protect eyes from tropical dust..."

Any body puts a doubt about her retirement saying, "till last year...,?" suddenly she will say simply as if, likes to forget age, by looking at your eyes:

"Not last year, but a few years back..."

At this stage, it is better not to ask more questions; otherwise you won't get good answers from her. This doesn't mean that she is very cruel. But Aunt Sally believes that she holds an absolute authority over everyone as an Aunt since all call her Aunt Sally. Her words will always have such an implication.

Suppose she is getting up in the morning. Though she wakes up late with hesitation to wake, she will scold all others if they are one minute late. If it is Sunday, after daily routine, she will get ready by wearing most special and delicate dress to go to church, with great effort and will stand before the mirror several times in different poses with a sheer analytical skill.

When enters into street, she will look at other women devotees with envy and grudge if they are better dressed than her. She will tell others:

"See, followers of Jesus must be moderate as me. Look at that lady; she is dressed very vulgarly and stupidly. Doesn't she know that she is coming to church for prayer…!"

If anyone supports her she will be more satisfied to criticise further and it will lead even to blaming and scolding against their haughtiness by hiding her desire to have such a dress in mind. At the same time she will find some time to praise herself and to seek faults of others such as late-coming to church, slow walking, fast walking etc. she will say pointing at latecomers:

"Look at them; they are too late. If they are lazy in prayers, what would be in their daily life…? But see, I got up early in the morning even though it was so gloomy with cloudy atmosphere…"

One may think that Aunt Sally is more much interested to hear rumours about other's depravity and to explain weakness of her neighbours than attending Sunday-mass. Especially her super investigative power in finding demerits of others is admirable. If gets a chance to calumniate about neighbours, she will make it worst, vibrating and extraordinary than legends with her own imaginary additional contributions!

Suspicion is said to be her innate nature because each and every look has a mix with distrust. Hence her gazes would always be more piercing. But somehow she manages to look mildly at opposite sex and talk intimately with them, since she holds an unknown attraction in mind, which is considered by her as an allowance given by God only to her. Thus Aunt Sally is intolerant against all looks and gossips between other men and women. If anything comes to her attention like that, she will blast against it with a contemptuous look. She is very keen to catch such sights; almost all cases will come across her eyes. Sometimes Poorvapunya has also undergone such critical situations.

One Sunday, Poorvapunya was sitting right to Aunt Sally in the church near the Altar. During the prayer, Aunt Sally saw that one man, sitting in the opposite side, was looking curiously! She exposed her face slightly from edge of the shawl, which was covered on head and sat erect. But she noticed that the man was looking at Poorvapunya, since she was a newcomer after conversion, she waited for Poorvapunya's glance at him. When failed, she nudged and turned her attention towards the man. When poorvapunya looked at the man, who was smiling at her, Aunt Sally angrily advised Poorvapunya:

"Don't look at….; it's a bad habit…"

"I am not looking, but what can we do against others' looking at us…," Poorvapunya said in a low voice.

"You must sit calm and cover your body and face carefully with shawl...; understand...?"

Everyone knows that Aunt Sally is more cautious even about a silly thing if it is related with her wealth. The proverb, *Aunt Sally's cart*, means 'dead-weight and discounted fare' is popular among cart-men in the town. Because, if she hires a cart to go to town, will always forget to give fare after getting down from the cart. When asks for money, she will bargain until cart-man surrenders fully and returns silently with what, she gives.

No one says that she is a miser. She will eat several times a day and concerned only about times of others, coming to dining-room, reminding them the importance of diet. She will talk lavishly about extravagance, but curtails herself from spending at the time of purchase only, stating the quality of simplicity. As far as possible she will not stretch hands for others' benefits unless and otherwise she expects some higher return, but willing to seek help from others.

Slackness is her companion in doing things. She will get all things done by others if possible. In the case of works, she will always act as Aunt to give directions promptly and to scold if others even against silly mistakes.

Apart from seven deadly sins, she has other modern sins also like other fellow creatures. When she does a wrong thing, it will not be a grave one, but if others do, it will have height up to sky. She is alert to hide all of her evils and to discover the faults of others. Her particular skill, to leap into others' matters and quarrels, is clearly proved, in order to make them worse as much as she could. Her detractors' opinion is that she is quarrelsome and witty as if the literary meaning of the word 'sally' is making true in her case. The town has witnessed to her humours many times.

One day when she was returning from town, she entered in the cart while the cart-man was trying to tie the horse before the cart. Her weight in the cart's back, suddenly pushed up its front. The cart-man was hanging on the top! By seeing him she said bending her eye-brows:

"Come down man; this is only a cart, not a boat with driver's seat on the top..."

Another time, Aunt Sally was sitting in the front row of a sport competition ground, near to the starting point. Contestants were standing ready to run, behind their starting lines. Then Aunt Sally laughed with a shrill voice and within a while, sound of the signal was also heard to start. A man standing there with a signal-organ wondered that the runners were still standing unmoved! Then only he could understand that the shrill voice of Aunt Sally had made the runners deaf for a while!

Aunt Sally also, like all others, is interested to see sports and games except the game named '*Aunt Sally*', in which balls or sticks are thrown at a wooden dummy. According to her outlook, it is not at all a game but unlawful affronting seniors. Anywhere she goes to see sports; she will try to get one of the free tickets which are very special, to be issued to invited guests only.

On one occasion, she was standing in front of the ticket-counter of a boxing club. As usual she asked for a guest-ticket:

"Please give me a free guest-ticket…"

"Madam…, you want *Aunt Sally ticket*'…?" the man who was sitting behind the desk, pulled out his head over the glass shade and asked.

"Yea…, but how could you recognize me…?" she wondered.

"We all have heard that a lady has been coming for a free guest-ticket to see every sports and games in this town. So we call such tickets '*Aunt Sally tickets*'…"

She entered in the hall and seated in front line near the boxing ring. The boxers entered the ring and started fight. After some rounds, while the audience was enjoying the fight, one was about to knock down the other, Aunt Sally sprang up whirling fists in the air with a roar. All of a sudden, the winner-boxer also fell down! Even after the Referee completed a count of ten seconds, the winner was lying and looking fearfully at Aunt Sally as if afraid to stand up!

Like other common people, Aunt Sally has also personal grievances such as derelictions, derailments, dismays, disobediences, denials, dislikes and dark spots in life due to ordinary behaviour. There are so many instances for her general manner.

First of her usual nature is to start dealings with others by a quarrel. Suppose, somebody calls her for dinner, she will say:

"If others hear your invitation, they may think that I am a hungry beggar to accept such dinners. I don't need but accept your request only considering your good mind…"

When enters in a shop, she will take even the least wanted things and put them in disorder. Sometimes she will come out without any purchase, with a smile after making all nuisances to the shop-keepers.

She will object everything at first, without considering goodness or badness or others' interests. There is a rumour about failure of her married life, which stresses this point.

When her husband returned home one evening with some dresses for her, she threw away saying that the materials were not at all suitable for her. In another occasion, when she was invited for an outing, she said that she had already gone for day-trip in the afternoon.

Critics say that it is the great fortune of Michael that, Aunt Sally is coming to his house once in an year from London and not definite to stay here permanently. They also say secretly that Michael is her illegitimate son, who was brought up in an orphanage, only to hide her motherhood.

If anyone asks questions with evil intentions, she will reply:

"Who is an angel in this world? Everyone has human nature. I am not different from our society but only one among them. So I also have defects..."

Looking at her critical face in mirror, she may even dare to say:

"Really, Aunt Sally is a symbol of humankind..."

*****

Chapter 19

In the Dale of Sin

Mind of the village-dwellers were fenced with dark iron bars of animosity due to fanatic violence. Utter imprecations and scandalous tales spread like a jungle-fire. Seeds of revenge were sown by communal activists in the fertile hearts of illiterates. They looked at each other with fainted and dull face as an expression of contempt. Tranquility was overridden by chaotic betrayals and misdeeds in all corners of the village. Thirst of revenge grew like a monster in the minds of people and began to scrunch their wisdom and will. Wherever they met, turned eyes to footsteps only to avoid looking at each other.

Economic classifications and discriminations became manure to culprits as well as downtrodden to turn against the Riches, which suddenly crossed hands with anarchism. Money became the profound moderator of all justice and injustice.

All beautiful meadows and grounds gave way to markets, toddy shops, dance clubs, cupolas and religious centres, where all immoral activities got recognition and reputation. But no single library or an educational institution opened eye any where!

Selfishness and animosity filled in looks, voice and action altogether. Lost faith and belief among people irrespective of creed or class. Lost neighbourhood nature and true friendships.

Theft, bribe, superstitions, atrocities, racial discriminations, and religious festivals only to promote rites, along with religious clashes introduced vicious circles of public tribulations.

New forms of social evils also sprang up as new strong species of animals evolves, according to theoretical conclusions.

One day, astonishing news spread in the speed of wind all over the village: "In the night a wizard appeared in the town….!"

People wondered and looked at each other. They competed to make various fabulous stories about witches and wizards. Some told that wizards are souls coming from Hell. Some others explained that man who dies abnormally becomes wizard. Another fable was that wizards would be super-magicians like Warlocks and Charmers. Someone argued that Witches can create wizards...!! Many fables became popular within a couple of days.

Several people saw the wizard at night at several places at the same time. Some tried to shoot it. But at the time of shooting, the wizard would become a sphere of fire and disappear. Sometimes he will give sweets to hunters or frighten them from behind. Thus many hunters got fever due to fear and went to sick-bed.

According to the increase of fear among the people, vexation of the wizard became harder and harder. Above all, dacoity, house-trespass, and all other crimes began everywhere in the name of wizard by other criminals. Thus full anarchy became the social order. The real wizard, a Research-student of National Defense Academy in *Royal Empire*, at last surrendered with all of his equipments such as Fire-coat, Bullet-proof cuirass, Head-light, whistle, Helium air-jacket, Spring-boots, night-vision equipment, mask, gloves, Hat and so on, agitated in mind about the misuse of wizard's name by criminals.

He wrote in his surrender letter:

"Running from the reality is not cowardice but cowardice is running from reality. The highest man-made lie is prayer to escape from sins. Baseless belief is more dangerous than a double edged sword. The key of religion is not discovery of truth; but disability to discover. Rule with fear is worse than bondage. All these words are revealed from my experience as a wizard ..."

As the maxim, 'thrift of the poor is in coffer of the Rich'; accumulated all wealth in a few hands by illegal means. The gulf between the poor and the rich became widened making impossible to reduce it ever.

Behind the big bolted golden doors, creatures of immoralities got down from human-devils and number of such stories about the tears fell down on the cheeks of the village, *Gape Dome* were innumerable like Sony's tale:

After a small daydream during drowse in the afternoon she woke up as symbol of the vale of wealth. Rays of light were creeping with languor through narrow chinks of closed windows as if reluctant to see the sins of wealth. Pallor of deeply clotted yesterday's sins was not yet perished from lustrous eyes. Victimised frustration arouse out of social evils poured on was still spoil her pleasure. Her glimpse turned to door-glass gratuitously.

Beatings of heart became not so regular. In front of the mirror she stood tired, looking at her reflection.

"What does the world think about me? May be like a sparrow sitting in leafage of prosperity. What is reality? The little sparrow is shivering in the wind of evils expecting footsteps of death...! Anywhere she goes, all tribulations follows. Everywhere I can see welcomes hands having false affection with hiding brutality. All gazes are filled with ...," continued her solicitude.

Mirror reflected her body, shaped with time-created youthfulness, increasing eager and excitement! Anxiety flashed, and its reflection seen in the dark-blue beautiful eyes.

Slightly bent long neck seemed to be emblem of road of sins when she locked the hook of necklace.

She murmured as if self pacification:

"No good stories will come from the Rich, since the Riches have no good stories..."

Brightened eyes looked like sliding fishes looking for novel sweet things! In every slide there was an unknown force and attraction. Larger bent eye brows were shaking slightly with a welcome command to unseen arrows of love. Spout cheeks seemed to expect stamps of emotions. Reddish lips sparkled with mysterious smiles in the form of imposing love. Hair clubs falling down through shoulders seemed to be half-curtains all of her new blooming youth with hollow darkness. Attention slowly and slowly went towards her flowering youth.

"Curtains are not covering anything but uncover the curiosity to reveals. What makes a sin? How can it be conquered...?" she thought.

She stood as the sign of sins realizing that the curtain of wealth is veiling sins. She recollected the truth, 'sins are the sons of richness flourished with selfishness and superstitions. The false notion of human society which decided Galileo to stone to death is in the expectation of future preys'.

"Nowadays religions have become the root cause of sins...!" she thought about the recent story heard about the rash religious clash:

The St. Broth's day massacre, as it came to be known, destroyed an entire generation of Church-Group and their new leadership. The ruler, Mark was an exile in St. Broth Island. At that time it was the beginning of decline of the Church of the Reformed-Group.

After the massacre the island was really an island of broth in literary meaning due to the decaying countless dead bodies.

In spite of the wars, the enthusiastic growth in the religion had been seen over the following months.

The experience radicalized many of the survivors. They were reluctant to have a profound trust in the king, and unwilling to disarm. This feeling was high upsurge in the political rhetoric of the resistance.

There was high causality on both sides. Before long, the royal coffers began to suffer deficiency of funds and all the blockade and fight were stopped., Later the isle began to get ready for the ballot vote due to the pressure of neighbour islands. The treaty was disadvantageous to the Reformed-Group and left them certain to break it when they were strong enough.

Mean while Mark was collecting troops, money and support from other Kings, who were ruling their regions with strong hands in the North. Although they were Church-Groups, the Provinces were heavily Reformed-Group regions. When the anti-royalist fraction also began to play, the strength of war reunited with other small religious confrontations.

Day by day the numbers of corpses were increasing in the name of religions and finally the conflicts ended in total annihilation of Church-Groups there.

"By means of assassinations and accidents human flesh becomes cheapest. It is the human-meat-market only yet to come...," passengers mocked at the brutal killings.

"Why is the religion a factor in war when all the other species have little time for violence and yearn for peace. War-field can be created artificially; but a land of peace can't...," she thought.

Resonance of preach after the special prayer in Ramadan, began to rise from the nearby mosque:

٢:٥٥٢ اللهُ لا إِلـهَ إلاَّ هُوَ الْحَيُّ الْقَيُّومُ لاَ تَأْخُذُهُ سِنَةٌ وَلاَ نَوْمٌ لَهُ مَا فِي السَّمَاوَاتِ وَمَا فِي الأَرْضِ مَن ذَا الَّذِي يَشْفَعُ عِنْدَهُ إلاَّ بِإِذْنِهِ يَعْلَمُ مَا بَيْنَ أَيْدِيهِمْ وَمَا خَلْفَهُمْ وَلاَ يُحِيطُونَ بِشَيْءٍ مِّنْ عِلْمِهِ إلاَّ بِمَا شَاء وَسِعَ كُرْسِيُّهُ السَّمَاوَاتِ وَالأَرْضَ وَلاَ يَؤُودُهُ حِفْظُهُمَا وَهُوَ الْعَلِيُّ الْعَظِيمُ

(2:255 Allah! There is no God save Him, the Alive, the Eternal. Neither slumber nor sleep overtaketh Him. Unto Him belongeth whatsoever is in the heavens and whatsoever is in the earth. Who is he that intercedeth with Him save by His leave? He knoweth that which is in front of them and that which is behind them, while they encompass nothing of His knowledge save what He will. His throne includeth the heavens and the earth, and He is never weary of preserving them. He is the Sublime, the Tremendous)[iv]

"Allah is great. There is no God other than Allah...," she tried to recollect the meaning of that summons, told by Aisha, the only person somehow escaped from the suburban village, fifty Miles away from *Gape Dome*, after the Militants' mass attack.

"Then why do they show nervousness towards other groups of their religion, if there is only one God…?" but when she asked this question, Aisha had no answer but shivered in the horrible memory of the past.

Aisha could not complete the story as she fainted with fear while describing the brutal killings, of which she was an eye-witness:

"The intra-religious wars as well as intra-religious are often seen among Arabs over religion. But the same story repeated in our village. It was related with a rite followed by one Islamic group in the next village. They tried to put it in our place also but failed. Then their militants entered with arms…!

During the early hours of a Holiday morning a troop of militants came to Mooza's door; they killed the guard, then opened the door and rushed into the house. Mooza was dragged from his bed, stabbed and thrown out through window to the footpath. News and rumours spread wide and fast, and suddenly triggered a rampage between the Militants and the general population, believing themselves to be fully supported by the religious Heads. The neighbourhood militants played a very significant role in the slaughter. The killing went on for five days. During the period, the militants killed all the people and looted the entire village. After that massive attack, numerous tales of same tempest of atrocities were began to be heard from other suburbs…"

Within two weeks the tempest entered in *Gape Dome* and flew furiously than ever before. The first looting and intra-religious killing more among the Muslim groups occurred in the Grocery shop of Abdullah Hajji, in *Shoe Town* and was spreading quickly to each nook and corner: Like a bandit gang, the mob looted everything. They picked whatever they wanted and burned what they didn't.

Some pulled out wood piled shutter of the Grocery shop. By the time someone intruded in the shop by drilling the roof. Another took tea bags and cartons full of perfumes, jumped through the broken window and ran away.

"I enjoy harming others…," by pulling a loaf of bread in to mouth another man said.

"The advantage of looting by mob is that if we get punishment, it will be lightened…," one evil said loudly.

"But where your sin can be blotted off…?" Abdullah Hajji asked and cursed.

"Before hunger where is the place for sins…?"

"This hunger is the consequence of your *Taqwiite-group's* sins…," Hajji's elder son pointed towards the sky.

Before completing his words one person of the other gang cut off his arm with a long sword.

Pawn shop was next, much promising target for them. By pushing the guard sharply on the ground, robbers entered the shop. They pulled down the wall and like greedy wolfs, grabbed gold and silver jewelleries. Promissory notes, Agreement papers, Bills and Cheques were defaced and thrown to air. Tried to open iron cash-box but failed and angrily threw it away. Suddenly in thought of taking key, one of the looters kicked the shop guard. He became unconscious. Locker couldn't be opened since it was in guttered stage and key was unfit to it.

By the time the guard slowly opened his eyes and stared around. He identified one among them, a friend's son of the pawn shop owner!

"Hey, you too bastard…? How devilish you to do this …?" he roared with tantrum.

Darkening dusk was not a hindrance for their pillaging but seemed to be blessing as they couldn't be identified in the darkness.

In another corner, a sharp knife pierced into flush of a shop-keeper and blood splashed to nostrils with sour smell. He crept on the floor and pathetically begged for water. No one came forward to hear him.

While running in the darkness, those sons of Sins saw two sparkling eyes! One of the thieves came across a high tangle-mannered street beggar as he was the eye witness for their looting.

"You stab that silly man and come on or else we will be in trap…," other thieves screamed and ran away.

"Punishment for killing one person or a racial massacre will be the same…," with an ardour the beggar looked at the thief who was putting his dagger on him.

He slowly raised his slender arms and murmured:

"Butchery is a stain to humanity and it won't give happiness to our world for ever. If a wrong doer has to bear the pain of his deeds, he won't do wrongs…"

"With scanty meal in stomach and trifle bowl in hands, who are you to teach us…? Money only will give us happiness…," the young crook uttered.

The tramp looked at him with fervent eyes and said:

"You or your fanaticism will fetch nothing. You are all pledging pleasure and wandering for happiness under the roof of religious absurdities…"

Next moment his wrinkled body remained over white stones, like a glowing red feather in the darkness!!

Next morning, quad of the grocery shop-owner's house filled with a gathering, praising all the goodness of Abdullah Hajji:

"Hajji who was running the shop in nearby street died in previous night by the shock of plunder in his shop. He was a moralist to our community and deserves respect from all walks in this village. How high minded he was…?!"

People purposefully tried to forget about the adulterated food he had been selling in his shop.

All arrangements were made for the cremation as per Islamic laws without a single merge. Everyone's actions and facial expressions of his Islamic group were disclosing their firm determination.

Some selected men from the gathering washed his body with soap, by. After *ghusul*, Mullah came and wrapped cotton cloth over the dead body and was placed in the coffin and arranged *sandhog* (carriage of coffin) for taking to nearby mosque.

The procession started with holy hymns. All the way the *dhikar*, 'Laa Elahi Illalah', was dissolving in atmosphere as if all sins of the dead man were being absolved. When they reached in the mosque, face of the dead man placed towards West and devotees went for ablution. Imam and others stood behind. Their hands were raised to ears and they gently murmured: 'Allahu Akbar…' Then their right hands were placed above left hand just below navel and continued hymns.

After the prayer, the corps was taken to cemetery, where the new pit was awaiting for. Body was slowly lowered into the pit, which was prepared for the dead man as the last offering from his fellow-creatures. Thus the last moments of the cremation was sanctified by the hymns:

'Bismi-l-lahe wa be-l-lahe-wa'ala millati
Rasuli-l-lahe-sall-l-lahu'alayhi wa sallam'

Hymns echoed and re-echoed from the minaret. From a long distance it could be listened as if the Earth was recalling one more person into its heart.

****

Chapter 20

A Memo to a Forlorn Creature

As usual, Poorvapunya entered into her hobby. It was nothing but writing letter to a lonely dolphin, which was her beloved comrade while she was in the beach-aquarium.

She wrote in a grey-coloured paper with her old fountain-pen:

"I remember the day, on which I reached there with my mother, though it was about twenty years back, when I was about three and a half years old. It was really a fine morning with clear blue sky and cool zephyr, blowing slowly from the sea. But I didn't feel it so until one of the aquarium-keepers gave me sweet bread to eat, since I was hungry that much, after a full night journey. Moreover, that was the first day on which I got enough food to fill my stomach, after last three hundred and sixty-five days! Hence appeared, a small smile of joy on my lips and gleams in eye-corners at that time, even though that day was the anniversary of the first misfortune that befell me, like a landslide, which dragged away whole things on its way – my father's death.

Really it was a new world for me, that aquarium and its surroundings! All labourers and aquarium-keepers became familiar to my little heart within seconds with their affectionate looks.

Then I began to dawdle along that dreamy and sandy pace filled with aquariums, attractive plants and flowers, like a butterfly to which a small garden is an endless Eden.

Several new guests were coming and going in the form of aquatic plants and beautiful small fishes, brought from fishermen and sold for small aquariums.

When looking at them through glass-wall, I could see the unveiling true love and fear in their eyes, while gliding inside the water-tank. I thought deeply several times, why those poor creatures were kept in little tanks, curtailing their freedom, growth and natural life. When I heard one man's saying, "it is interesting to see...," I asked him:

"As you see these fishes as interesting articles only, it is the mentality, most cruel and selfish, that a man can..."

After some days another indigent mother came there with her child, as helpless as my mother. That was a dolphin, having a length of about three meters, belongs to Delphinidae family, with its calf. It was an attraction for the visitors and hence the mother-dolphin acted several shows per day for the aquarium-master's benefit.

I counted numerous similarities than dissimilarities between the little dolphin and me! That small dolphin was not he but she! Learned from the fishermen that her father had died earlier! She also came there with her mother! It was the famine that brought her to that bondage called aquarium! Her mother had to work for the aquarium-master's to earn their daily food! She was seen mostly very close to her mother as if a tail stuck to it!

All these resemblances made me befriended with that little one without delay.   Then I noticed the most wonderful resemblance between us that she was feeding on her mother's breast-milk!

Inchoate inquisitiveness about that little comrade immersed all other thoughts of my mind and directed me to the books on oceanography kept by the aquarium-keepers. Descriptions in the books were spectacular and splendid:

Dolphins eat one-third of their weight, in a day. Their diet consists mainly of fish and squid. They breathe through a blowhole at the top of the head, like whales. They are superbly streamlined and can sustain thirty-five kilometers per hour! They are able to dive to depths of more than one thousand feet! They are found in the shallow seas of the continental shelves and move around in groups called schools or pods. They are considered the most intelligent animals and have been used to rescue trapped divers.

Oh! My friend, little dolphin, you might not have known all these. You may be in grief of losing your mother. I remember that the misfortune happened in a cold morning. One stout man with sharp and crooked eyes came and bought your mother for another aquarium!

I realized that you were crying bitterly at that time as I heard your unusual constant clicking sounds. I thought that each of the drops in the tank was your tear! I tried to console myself with the maxim that 'everything will be effaced by time and hence your sorrow will also be mended gradually'. But you might have rewritten that saying as, 'time can erase everything except mournful memory of extreme adversities from life'.

There are oceans naturally made by god for thy living, but man is spoiling everything, he sees. Thus decreased fishes and squids in the area where you were living. Your mother was seeking food elsewhere, when she was caught by the fishermen along with you. First day you were too restless about the smallness of the aquarium when compared to sea. You might have forgotten all those stories. But your miraculous saving of your friend from drowning is unforgettable for me because that friend was I.

Now also my body is shivering while remembering those moments. I was not aware of the slippery steps of your tank, which was as big as a sea when compared to my tiny body and mind. I tried to stretch my hands against a beautiful reed-top. I don't remember what happened then. When I opened mouth for cry, water gushed into my throat! I was sinking in that deep water tank! I felt that the Lord of death was swallowing me into his large gullet filled with oily water! When I struggled for breath darkness filled my eyes! But all of a sudden I felt that I was floating on the surface of water! I realized that I was sitting on something like a soft and polished stone! Recognized immediately that stone as head of the little dolphin, my friend!

Later, I have heard several surprising stories about your ancestors, who had saved many of our sailors from drowning in oceans. Now regret to say that such spanking events may not be heard in future since your species at sea are at the brink of extinction. What threatens their existence today is marine pollution, depletion in their prey and hunting. Often they get entangled in fishing nets, once again pushing them to the brink.

You may console me saying that we all have to depart one day or other forever. But these are all the results of destructive actions of my race, by which so many other kinds of animals are struggling for survival due to global warming.

Mankind will also be annihilated from the earth due to global warming. Reason will not exist after the consequence.

The short-wave of solar radiation, absorbed by the earth's surface is reemitted at infrared wavelengths and is absorbed by carbon dioxide, methane, nitrous oxide, halocarbons and ozone in the atmosphere and then reemitted back towards the earth. This greenhouse effect (term for the atmosphere' role in helps to warm the earth's surface) is being disordered as the amount of carbon dioxide in the atmosphere has been increasing by average 0.4% a year because of the use of coal, oil, gas etc. and the burning of tropical forests. As a result, worldwide rise in temperature will occur by over six per cent by the end of the century. This will change climates of this planet totally and will lead to increase sea-level by minimum one ft., causing damages to natural vegetation. Even an increase of four per cent will cause devastating shortages of food and water and annihilate numerous species from the earth! But no pain arises in heart of man against these dangers, happen to other animals because he blindly teaches himself that 'all other organisms are created for man by his god'!

Discarding the life and existence of other organisms, tall smokestacks of industries, power stations and motor vehicles boost pollutants, such as sulphur dioxide and nitrous oxide, higher into the atmosphere instead of removing them. These chemicals react with sunlight, moisture and oxidants to produce sulphuric and nitric acids and come to earth as rain, called as Acid rain. It ruins vegetation directly.

Use of the industrial chemicals such as chlorofluorocarbons damages the ozone layer and it leads to exposure of life on earth to excessive ultraviolet radiation which can reduce immunity and affect the growth of oceanic phytoplankton. Other grave environmental problems such as radiation due to explosion of nuclear weapons, radioactive wastes from nuclear power plants, encroachment on wild lands etc., are also creations of successors of Homo sapiens. Their predecessors have made their own canon in the name of their own God, which treat world and its nature as their own wealth. That canon was the first sin made by man out of his selfishness, and its consequences have been carrying him to all sorrows thenceforth throughout generations. But with egocentric mind, manmade geo-customs to place him as supreme and put those laws as human-rites. Later generations converted those rites into their culture, which produced various faiths and beliefs.

I am writing all these with bowed head due to shame over those man-made macabre credos, the biggest blunder that happened in the world. Because, even after scientifically proved that mankind is one species gradually developed from other species, modern man also keeps the baseless imaginary fable about the direct creation of Adam (first man) with dust from the soil by god, in the secret corner of his mind!!

Since everyone can't be deceived forever, one day people will recognise the falsehood and foolishness of those fables, canons and beliefs and will rectify mistakes.

You know, at the time of departure from there, I was sad not about the destiny, which darted arrow of separation between us but about the above said stupidity of mankind, when the other aquarium-keepers said, "no need of grief in parting from a dolphin; it is only a fish, not a human."

The destiny, which separated us, was not a silly thing as we thought. When we were leaving, all of us believed that the partial paralysis affected my mother's left hand and leg, will be cured shortly and then we can return to the place of aquarium.

Alas! Till now it is not cured, but haven't lost our hope; as for human beings, optimism leads and persuades them to continue their life.

I like to lend that hopefulness to you also. If such a wish comes true, you will be returned to the ocean from where they caught you and mankind will apologise for their selfish deeds, went on by generations for eons, which caused damages to other species on earth. Then human race will not be antagonist to other organisms; instead, become saviour and conservationist of natural environment.

Thus, if wisdom of man paves way to world-equality, the earth will be the real heaven. Then sorrows of humans and other animals will cease and true happiness will come. That would be the actual salvation to man; for which the only thing he has to surrender are selfishness and imprudent faiths.

Dear friend, we shall have to wait for that day in which such enlightenment comes to mankind...."

****

Chapter 21

Tragedy Blooms

Nice and sleazy rays of the dawn looked at the beveling grass unconcerned but again and again.

Dews are dropping from the leaves slowly as the remains of last night's misty cold. Frail fragrance of flowers is flowing in fickle breeze. Butterflies are flying hither and thither with morning mirth. Some of them are swinging on the top of pendulating palm-leaf-stratums with half waving plumes......!

Faces of labiate-flowers are twinkling while leaning their head towards the gentle wind......!

"Like several, one more morning has come only to fade away as past........," the indifferent faces of pedestrians seemed to have been saying.

"Alas! This day is dissimilar to others...," smiled smashing flames from distant building-tops, drowning in fire.

Spread the violence and religious clashes like open fire in the oil field. From the volcano of it all types of smokes of evils sprang up, covered and darkened the society. Neither, within a while its response came from nook and corner of the village. People had to see secret séance and cartels in places considered being holy prayer halls crated down in the fire in nights. Small thatched and grass covered huts burned and fell down more quickly than big houses and castles. That was the only difference.

Seeing the maladroit religious-malady of mankind, the next day-break dawns:

As the balance of turmoil last night, near the old well, the small house of Angel also catches fire.

Pieces of burning hay-clusters begin to fall down on her cradle while Small child, Angelina called by her pet-name, Angel is sleeping in inside the house.

No one can be seen there except a pet dog, Mickey chained in front! It is barking as if calling her mother and father, who might have gone for work outside.

She is asleep inside the turtle without knowing the battle of fanatically mad mob outside and the house burning down in spreading fire!

If she knows…?

How can she escape as she is only a small child of ten months?

Oh! Her cradle is broken in the fire! It is falling down on the floor!

Ha! The beloved dog is crying and in one leap, breaks its chain and runs towards her!

To rescue her, Mickey is hopping towards the well dragging the cradle!! Really it was a very small pond which is changed like a little well by that poor family.

Into the mud Mickey pulls the cradle to and fro! It is trying to put out the fire on the cradle! By sharp teeth, it is pulling the burned cradle-cloth out of Angel. Her body is dirty with muddy.

With natural love, her Mickey is tonguing out the mud from her body.

Mickey is now groaning to wake her up and waiting for her awakening unaware that she has already wake up in the world of peace, remaining realities and questions towards the futility of religious clashes:

'The ugliest nature of mankind is being expressed through religious deports.'

"Can a religion create mankind? Can it be sustained without human society? If not so, it is the king of all evils created by man on earth; isn't it? Thought of justice or Dharma is the part of wisdom or the human thinking power. As mankind uses wisdom or thinking power, has to rely and follow the way of justice or Dharma. The cardinal concept or central theme of all religion is the way of dharma to be followed by mankind. In case any injustice happens in the name of a religion, that religion itself becomes symbol of *Adharma* or injustice. Thus justice is the obligation of human life. Denial of justice or dharma is the denial of wisdom; denial of wisdom is the denial of human life; denial of human life is the denial of religion. In other words, denial of dharma is denial of religion.

Dharma is not inactiveness, but selfless action.

Man who acts against dharma automatically expels himself from religion, since all religions fundamentally direct man towards dharma. Any injustice by a man, who has thinking power, cannot be cured by confession or by any means. Moreover if confession does not resist the man from doing guilt further, it would not be a confession at all…"

"Greatest tragedy is to worship God while swallowing in all sins...," one man assessed.

Since the religious thoughts had conquered almost all brains of the place, only a few were in a humanitarian way to look at and understand the Absolute's illusionary world. They said:

"Look at a dense forest; land allures with profound and endless elegance.............!

Gurgling streams meandering through rock-straits and falling from high cliffs like flow of eternity from the heaven, gliding fishes against the falling masts from trees, calm natural pools filled with faultless water where sprouting lotus are smiling towards the rising sun, perfumed sandal wood's spreading glory, pasturing frolic deer, covey of birds and butterflies imbibing the nectar, majestically moving elephants, burrowing rabbit, chattering squirrels while climbing, chirming cuckoos on climber-huts......;even in a small pond variety of creatures are living amicably.

All are living in concord making their dwelling place as paramount paradise in its best. Here equanimity and enormous tranquillity goes hand in hand without withering others' will and pleasure.........!

But in this big world only for mankind, life is a struggle! Man as an intruder destroys the entire piece of mind in their blessed sovereign empire. They are gifted with equal privilege, but man is counting their life with canon of cruelty. He felt good to kill animals but they feel grief in being killed. Man has set his attitude to annihilate them from earth. But what they may think on mankind? They also have a right, not alike but more, to live on this earth as they are the creators of cardinal living conditions on this planet. But that right has no value even as of a sword in the hands of human being. When we pouch animals to attain our material success, they helplessly defend but finally surrender to death........."

The villagers, who heard about the pitiful death of the little child, Angelina, gathered in the street. They took one oath:

"We are all human beings, no need of discriminations, hostility, and prejudice. Church or Temple or Mosque, they are all equal. The true love and affection as well as sacrificial or helpful nature are enough. We are all happy...," smile entered on mouth of the people, thinking that, is this true theme of Islam, Christianity, Hinduism, and all other religions.

"Realising truth is equal to realising God...," they embraced each other with overwhelming joy

Rising up, the sun in the East, as if to witness their good and remarkable promise.

"Beginning of mankind is not from religion. Sustenance is not through any religion or creed. It will survive even if there is no religion. So religion is not a necessity. Nothing is in this world as of religions. If say, idols or churches or mosques, they are all made up of earthly things by artistically skilled men. Nothing is to discriminate man from man. Beliefs and ideas may be different and are put forward by intellectuals only to direct society to goodness. Really what the geniuses had done was to show and criticise the evils prevailed in the society in which they lived. Those criticisms were not meant for inter-clashes or supremacy over other religions or beliefs. Religions have no right to over-power each other as man has wisdom to take his own ideas. These beliefs or ideas will not give betterment to society if life of each exempts good way and values.

The biggest truth is before us. Our life is not to play with religious futilities and to fight each other. Look at animal kingdom. Even though they have no wisdom, there are so many species living in harmony than human beings.

All religious books, sayings or gospels approve the truth that in the beginning of mankind there was no religion. If it was a necessity, God should have bequeathed it to the first man. Regarding the origin of mankind, it is proved that modern man is the successor of primitive man who had no refined wisdom...," they solemnly declared.

"See our village. It is the queen of hamlets in the world..."

"Which were the first and eventual waves of religious tide in the village...?" they tried to recollect the culmination of ugly past days created by futile religious clashes.

"The first was reconstruction of a ruined temple. Its story is very puzzling...," one man pointed towards the hill and continued, "look at that high hill, the northern border of this village. It has rooted a deep cultural identity to this village. Behind this greenery covered hill, recalcitrant but a relishing river, the sole witness of all changes, is lined as a lace.

When the 'K'iche day' comes, the entire valley blanketed in unusual way! The K'iche Flower, blooms only once in twelve K'iche-years. The K'iche plants are seen in this hill-cliff only..."

On that day, banquet of flowers will be seen everywhere at the mist-capped aperture of hill cliff...! Other jungle-plants will also be covered with coloured leaves and flowers almost all over the place.

Dancing musk-deer, languorous butterflies and the natural tranquility of wildlife, attract people in large extent not only of this village but of distant places.

Thus splendour and spectacular beauty of this valley beckon on this day to the entire villagers to her cradle of enchanting beauty blessed by K'iche.

Usually some youngsters used to gather on the flat rock there. In a cold winter, after gushing of heavy torrential rain, along the hillside water-falls created several white veins to cliffs and glory to valley, painted in lush green.

Next day when they stepped on the rock, they saw an astonishing thing that happened there. Some parts of an old ruined temple were clearly seen near a small lake surrounded by thousands of K'iche flowers enhancing the beauty of the ruined temple!

In a gentle breeze bunch of flowers and aroma spread in the air. Valley looked like flower plane.

"This time, the exotic K'iche plants bloomed quite earlier...!" They wondered.

"Oh! Its fragrance is so powerful it makes me faint...," one of them waved hands.

"I may become romantic...," another man thought.

"I will inhale the entire fragrance to my nostril...," one began to inhale loudly.

"Heavy rain has created sprout of these rare flowers in the valley. Sale of these flowers will fill our stomach..."

"No my friends; it is the blessing of Flora*, Goddess of flowers to us. We ought to reconstruct this temple...," those who gathered there, expressed different opinions and thoughts.

Religious passions in hearts divided their friendship. Strong walls of selfishness and estrangement sprang up in their mind.

Few Saindhavas gathered under a huge banyan tree in the evening. Decision came out to renovate the temple in large scale by collecting money as charity and donations.

Coins flew to their treasury from all parts and even from people living in utter poverty.

In a new moon night four villagers trekked to the hill top with an old temple worshipper to do initial poojas (adoration) and other offerings as marks to start renovation.

"No one knows about this, I think...," the worshipper revealed his observation.

"Yea, so we are doing these poojas here now...," one of them said in low voice and looked around in the torch-light as if confirming his opinion.

In the dim light they saw two persons running away into darkness. Few carved stones were seen in packed state about six hundred feet away in the dim light!

Next day, there was heavy tension mounting up to evacuate seven Muslim families by Taqwiite leaders, at that place. Then only it was clear that a new mosque will be constructed there, in the way to this temple-hill.

All Muslim families were evacuated and their slums were destroyed. Scholars of Al-Taqwa asked them to vacate, to avoid criticism from the Islam community, as they all like to have a mosque there.

Their house-holds were forcefully dumped into bullock carts along with children and olds.

From next day they had to stay in the courtyard of a nearby mosque as refugees; assured rehabilitation in another place.

They had lost all expectations when two weeks passed without adequate food and care. Thus, no place to go, no rehabilitation, no food, they were thrown to street. No compensation and no fair deal were happened because their religious leaders believed that vacation was an obligation and sacred deed of Muslims as in the Jihad (sacred war). To them construction of mosque near one temple is one of the important actions in Jihad.

They had to sit on roadside without any help. In the unexpected heavy down pour one old man among hopeless, died of cold while sitting on the pavement.

Men came from mosque with bier to take the corpse. But the refugees objected in a very strong way.

"We are all Muslims; we must obey Allah. Corpse must be buried according to our religious custom...," Taqwiite leaders appealed.

"Is the Islamic custom related only with burial of a man who has lost everything for his religion...?" harsh words were thrown over the refugees.

"We lost everything. Where is our house...? Our cattle...? Our very means of life...?" their astringent cry resounded in the entire valley.

When their strike became hard, Taqwiite leaders declared them as outcastes from the religion.

At last, as the climax of their protest, the dead body of the old man was cremated with oil and fire-wood by an only Jain family in that village.

"Come to our Temple...It is blessed with the universal love. All will be safe there...," while bringing the refugees to their temple, one said.

"What changes have come to you when Taqwiite leaders declared you as outcastes? We saw nothing else. Religion without humanity is cracking madness. If so, all shrines can be termed as simple dark mud-moulds..." another man commended.

There were many smiling faces to receive the newcomers. Children were bathed and put on new cloths. Age old persons were brought to beds for rest.

Ladies were consoled. Youths were asked to take division of lands for house construction. More over all words of Jains were involved basic human-love.

No one asked the newcomers to convert to Jainism. On the other hand they were eager to know about Islam so as to analyse how far a religion can go into blindness of belief and cruelty like Al-Taqwa.

"Al-Taqwa is the religious transformation of conflict, not of concordance..."

"Now conflict is the concord of religion as cactus's touch-wound..."

"When religious conflicts become causes of corpses, it will only be a catalyst for decay of humanity..."

"If anyone has to die for a religion, that religion is the sole incarnation of slaying..."

"Uncompassionate religions have no cession over man in the name of canons..."

Their conference deliberated dictates of Qur'an, various religions and their origins.

"For social administration, instead of reformation, religions were used in the name of God in all periods. That was the fundamental mistake done by various religious head quarters. They forgot the natural truth related with life of organisms such as the tortoise immediately after birth on river bank goes to river not because of the knowledge imparted to it but as per the inborn sense..."

The deep thoughts of Vardhamana Mahaveer (founder of Jainism) were disclosed before the guests and refugees as new feast of knowledge:

"Even though Mahaveer was born in 599 B.C as a prince in Bihar. At the age of 30, he left his family and royal household, gave up his worldly possessions, including clothing and become a monk.

He spent the next twelve years in deep silence and meditation to conquer his desires and feelings. He went without food for long periods. He carefully avoided harming or annoying other living beings including animals, birds and plants.

His ways of meditation, days of austerities, and mode of behaviour furnish a beautiful example for monks and nuns in religious life. His spiritual pursuit lasted for twelve years.

At the end he realized perfect perception, knowledge, power and bliss. This realization is known as keval-jnana.

He spent the next thirty years travelling on barefooted in and around for preaching people the eternal truth he realized. He attracted people from all walks of life, rich and poor, kings and commoners, men and women, princes and priests, touchable and untouchables.

The ultimate objective of his teaching is how one can attain the total freedom from the cycle of birth, life, pain, misery and death and achieve the permanent blissful state of one's self. This is also known as liberation, nirvana, absolute freedom or Moksha.

He explained that from eternity, every living being (soul) is in bondage of karmic atoms, which are accumulated by its own good or bad deeds. Under the influence of karma, the soul is habituated to seek pleasure in materialistic belongs and possessions; which are the deep rooted causes of self cantered violent thoughts, deeds, anger, hatred, greed and such other vices. These result in accumulating more karma.

He preached that right faith (samyak darshana), right knowledge (samyak Jnana) and the right conduct (samyak charitra) together will help to attain the liberation of one's self.

He organized his followers into a fourfold order namely monk (sadhu) nun (sadhvi) layman (shravak) and lay woman (shravika) and later they are all known as Jains.

A living body is not merely an integration of limbs and flesh but it is the abode of the soul which potentially has perfect perception (Anand-darshana) perfect knowledge (Anand-jnana) perfect power (Anand-virya) and perfect bliss (Anand-sukha).

Mahavir was quite successful in eradicating from human intellect the conception of God as creator, protector and destroyer. He also denounced the worship of gods and goddesses as means of salvation. He taught the idea of supremacy of human life and stressed the importance of the positive attitude of life.

Jainism existed before Mahavir and his teachings were based on those of his predecessors. Thus unlike Buddha, Mahavir was more of a reformer and propagator of an existing religious order than the founder of a new faith.

Lord Mahavir's idol is escorted by the symbol of a Lion..."

The Muslim audience, while hearing the eloquent speech about Jainism, began to think about different religious beliefs. They understood the folly of quarrel in the name of faith and sheer insistence of religious customs. All existing wrongs are to be changed in order to pave way to goodness and true worship, which are not harmful to other species on earth.

"Man's ability is to do wrongs by knowing wrongs...," one of them suggested.

"Man who makes hell on the Earth has no right to say about heaven...," they told themselves as if realized the truth that, killing of animals are not justifiable in the name of god. Follow Dharma is the cardinal duty of an individual. Social equality is the mark of a good civilization. True prayer must be a stimulant for man to refrain from agitating others but to consider helpfulness as one's duty. See all religions as true and equal instead of blind beliefs.

They murmured:

"Religious faith without humanity and harmony is imprudent…," a beam of brotherhood glimpsed in eyes of the refugees. They felt freedom from all bondages of religions.

"The ultimate freedom is inborn…," one man remarked with delight.

"That freedom can be attained only if we study about other religions to have realistic view that there is no meaning in religious beliefs and devotion if it does not accepts the natural equality of all living beings.

"Prayer for goodness becomes good only when the goodness is in actions…," another man revealed his vision.

"Just as men kill animals there are no man-killers since it is clear that men will act as man-killers themselves…," one of the refugees showed irritation against religious hostility and clashes.

"When Mohammad Nabi told his disciples that not to make their stomach a graveyard of animals, he was mistaken because he believed that his advice will be followed by them…," One refugee expresses amusement.

Al others joined in the sense of humour.

****

Chapter 22

The Vortex of Exhoration

Gentle breeze was blowing steadily from the expansive lagoon in the receding dusk; white shadows of free-wheeling egrets scatter on the water surface, frilled by the twilight. Nearby the majestic river, *Sarasa* was flowing swiftly with gurgling sound, graciously making wavelets and bubbles by bumping brightly on brinks of rocks. Murmuring of tender leaves in zephyr seemed to be their greetings to the coming night.

While returning from the market, Poorvapunya remembered the poem and plunged into the thought:

> 'Heaven is the Earth; ye Men,
> Unless of Absolute's splendid
> Realm and real values often
> Just undermine as your greed.'

Once it was a gracious vegetable market known as *Mango Market* and now as *Butcher market*. In those days of serenity and innocence, passersby could have been seen in the early morning gathering there with baskets and bags filled with colourful fruits and fresh vegetables.

Various stalls of the market were much highlighted with banana, beans, marrows, root-vegetables and tomatoes but now blood-oozing flesh pieces of buffalos, goats and cows are hanging in front of butchers, blood stained knives held in whose hands are piercing into dying poor animals' throat! Head of dead cows with bulging eyes are adorning their shops as if looking at the new culture of mankind, folded in foolish religious rites to hide unforgivable cruelty.

She turned her squint to the front street, from those shops fearing that she will cry otherwise. Alas! The sight which greeted her in the front street was heartbreaking one. Alice's husband was bringing their old cow towards a butcher shop! When saw Poorvapunya, he pretended to be a stranger, but the cow lowed loudly since she was too familiar, as if animals can't forget neighbours, like human beings.

"There was no other way to give Easter egg to my children tomorrow..." – he told Poorvapunya with shivering voice looking at her fiery eyes in order to hide his deceit and humbuggery towards that poor innocent animal. The cow was seemed to be frightened but followed its owner, as having some belief of safety in him!

"Man's wickedness is unpredictable even to his fellows, then how can about other naïve animals...?" – Poorvapunya said to herself as if bowing head before the cow with shame since she is also one of that crooked species.

For a moment she looked at the cow. Tears were drifting from its frightened eyes just as depicting its life in a nutshell. Suddenly, flashed a memory into Poorvapunya's disappointed mind about the past days of Molly, the milk-maid and of her cows in the hamlet, *Kalpam*.

Fates of Molly's cows were also like this. This old cow was a small calf leaping in the yard of Alice along with her children imparting them happiness and with the consideration as one of them. Later it became a foster-mother to all and began to give them milk and brought up Alice's children along with its own calf impartially but with more affection till become old. Alas! Now it is being lead to butcher to become foodstuff for them!

Poorvapunya recollected the song written in **Eternal Tranquillity** about human's cruelty and hypocrisy:

> 'Turned to this world, a little babe, I;
> As the weakest creature here of all
> Oh! With human grottiest form, lay by
> Folding half within a shabby shawl.
>
> Calf and a cat and a cock-chick born
> At that time as my friends, all beauteous
> And very healthier to stand and own
> Better play of their living, courteous.
>
> All of them came to my quilt and vast
> Pitiful look cast ov'r my frail state
> But poured sterling love on me with fast
> Selfless service, all for my own sake.

Grown up by Nature's grace and help
They! To act as per attribute's will;
Cock daily crowed to waken me up,
Cow fed me every day with sweet milk.

Kitty played along with me all days
Mighty as to jump over my head
Straight away came, in chilly night's haze
With a majestic look, to my bed.

Yearned to become as them auspicious,
Alas! As chick no gold plumes and wings
Sprouted; or not my face came precious
As the cat; so wailed I, like bell rings!

Merciful Lord, to melt my grief, pent,
Poured on me wisdom for worthiest life;
One by one winters and summers went;
Matured my mettle and Bone then, safe!

Wore a Suit, wild-dress of mankind soon;
For a fun threw the cat into riv'r,
Cut old cow's throat for meat as a loon,
Ignored! She was my foster-mom ere.

Telling my guiltiness, cursed me, God;
Fell into worldly hard sorrows thence.
Called me the Lord then; calmly I bowed
Realizing my sins and cons'quences

'Take my life and save from this vortex
Of all exhortations made by Men...,'
Implored so humbly! Oh! Shook vertex
Of my chill hands and ended move-yen!

She couldn't face the distressing cow and turned eyes towards the end of
the road to conceal her tears. In a mechanical mood she walked with quick
steps as if longing for escape from this world of injustice.

Since it was Sabbath day, Jews were returning from the synagogue after prayers. She noticed a Jew coming towards a nearby house after attending the prayer. He kissed the wooden cascade, which was mounted on the right side of the main entrance of his residence, by putting hands on it and to lips.

She thought:

"It is *Mitzvoth*, the inscription written on skin of cow, put inside the cascade. In this age of paper, why can't it be written on paper? If they think about durability or attraction, even sheets of metals could have been used. If sanctity is the matter, part of an animal's body should not be taken in any case especially while man eats flesh of such animals. When compare skin of cows or goats with that of man, skins of those animals have sanctity, durability and attraction, but in that condition, man has no right to use and to award divinity to these superior elements than that of him as he claims that he is the supreme in all kinds…" whether god likes it? Then how can be said that these animals are created by God? God is happy in this slaughter? Oh! God!! What is this?….?

When she was crossing the street, Marcus came that way. She quickly tried to move back as if frightened. Knowing that, Marcus made way for her and told her:

"Don't be afraid, you go…; I become mad only against the follies of religious customs, which are the social evils and mislead mankind towards the darkness of damnation…," pointing to a nearby Mosque he continued, "hear the teachings resonating from that mosque. They advise that if any hindrance occurs to anyone to do *Hajj*, it is compulsory to sacrifice an animal and until the sacrifice reaches the destination, should not remove his hairs. If he becomes ill or has any disturbance on head, he can remove hairs, but if so, to compensate penance, charity or oblation is enough. If takes rest after *Umbra* to *Hajj*, he must immolate an animal, he could get, for penitence.(Page 50:196)…"

She also heard the announcement from the Mosque.

"How can a man get merit by oblation of animals…? Instead immolations would be pure sins…" –face of a poor sacrificial cow sprang to her mind and understood that Marcus was saying the truth about such foolish human teachings. She remembered an odd story of immolation which prevailed as a customary practice among Saindhavas:

****

Chapter 23

An Illusive Symbol

Reiterations of incantations seemed to be continuously resonating chants rising in the air, over the river, *Sarasa* and making its surface wavy! Wrinkly wavelets were turning into golden by mingling with narrow rays of the morning sun and mysteriously disappearing in that magic spell! A mythical story came to Poorvapunya's mind.

The river, Sarasa is believed to have been flown from an invisible location of The Mountain! The legend is known to every villagers of **Gape Dome.** The mount was a living being once! He was in solitude for several eras. The God of mounts, when pleased with his service, made a River-girl by a magic wand and gave him. He brought up her in his cavern. In a hot season, while he was outside, the pretty River-girl went out of the cave and ran to the valley seeing the panorama. When he returned, searched for his beloved daughter and failed to find her. In that severe grief broke down his heart, body became brown by clotted blood, and soon he died. Seeing her father's tragic death, tears dried up lasted in her eyes! That time onwards, in summer, the mount will turn into brown and eyes of the river will dry up due to deep sorrow!! People believed that the God of mounts could be pleased with special *Yagam (offering ghee, grain etc.to sacred fire)* on the river-bank during the summer. Always a cow with one horn would be selected as the sacrificial animal!

On the river bank, they had been completing all arrangements for the immolation and were under complacence believing that all prosperities will come to their land anon after the sacrifice.

Flames of sacrificial fire (*Yagagni*) were glowing more and more. Within a *Nazhika* (24 minutes) the sacrifice, a cow, which was tied to a pole near the *Yagasala* (a place for conducting yaga for sacrifice) would be put into the fire as alive!

163

Agnihotri (person who conducts immolation) was pouring ghee again and again very speedily into the fire! Suddenly an old man appeared and asked:

"I am a Brahmin *Bhikshu (wandering saint)*; today this is the fifth place I visit for alms. From all other places I got nothing. Kindly give me something, charity…"

"This is a Yagasala; you can see that there is nothing to eat here…," the helpers of *Agnihotri (one who is doing fire rituals)* told him waving hands.

"In the case of a beggar, there is no difference between a house, a street or a *Yagasala* to get alms. Above all, according to custom, as you all Brahmins know, a *Bhikshu* is restricted to go to five places only in a day and even if he gets nothing, he is prohibited to go to sixth place on the same day. So be compassionate towards this poor…," the beggar stretched his arms.

The helpers and Agnihotri felt that they were in a dilemma. They began to sweat thinking about the curse of the Brahmin if they couldn't give him something.

Looking at their perspiring body and at the pot filled with ghee near the fire, the beggar said calmly:

"If you don't mind, please give that ghee…"

"What? That is for *Homam* (to pour into fire); you can ask for any thing except that…," they requested humbly.

"If so, give me that cow …," the mendicant looked at the cow, which was lowing innocently.

"It is *Yajna Mrugam* (symbolic sacrificial animal), to be sacrificed. It can't be given to anybody…"

"Sacrifice that animal means you are offering it to Agni. *Havis (offering ghee to fire)* is the offering to *Devas* (god & goddesses). According to belief, a hungry man approaching for food is to be considered as Deva. Hence no unfairness in giving the cow to me…," the beggar argued politely.

They suspected him as a Jonah and decided to drive him out of that place by ridiculing him. They said:

"You are asking for the cow. Really, *Atma* (immortal body) of that animal is called 'cow'. So you may take the Atma of the cow…"

The beggar went out.

Suddenly the cow fell down and died!

The Agnihotri and his helpers were surprised. The helpers ran to the beggar and begged for his mercy and apologised for their teasing:

"Pardon us for our unwitting mistakes. Please be kind enough to save the Yajna Mrugam and allow us to complete the Yagam (immolation)…"

Then the old man came back to the Yagasala and asked them: "What is meant by Yagam and Yajna Mrugam...?"

"We are only following the custom. From ancient period, the custom of immolation is being followed by people of different religions. Several such instances can be observed in the history of mankind. In Vedas, Bible, Qur'an etc. there are many stories about it. We are not aware of the exact meaning. Kindly tell us..."

"According to polytheistic belief, man is offering his valuables to his deity, which represents the giver of all his prosperities. In the case of monotheism, such offerings are supposed to be as per the request of God. But both of these beliefs are wrong and stupid because the God or the deity, according to their belief, is supreme owner and giver of all glories; since offerings from man, as man is also one of its creations, are not needed. If the offerings are for man's satisfaction, such argument is utterly absurd as oblation, offering, homage, ritual slaughter, immolation or lustration means killing of an animal whatsoever called.

In many ancient religions, immolation played a central role, such as ancient Greeks, who sacrificed animals like goats, horse, cattle and sheep! Before the Spanish conquest, the Aztecs offered human sacrifices to the Sun God, consuming average twenty thousand lives a year! During the Vedic period, Hindu priests offered animals, plants and humans in sacrifice. Human sacrifice was in practice in ancient China. But Buddhism didn't practiced sacrifice. In Judaism, sacrifice was essential and established for expiation of sins and thanksgiving. Isaac's story in the Bible tells that God asked Abraham to sacrifice his beloved son, Isaac to test his faith. When God was convinced the perfect obedience of Abraham, God accepted a ram as sacrifice instead of Isaac.

Veneration of fire is the most renowned earliest forms of religious worship as the material manifestation of fire spirit. Every mythology narrates how fire was brought to mankind. Semitic peoples propitiated their Fire-God, Moloch by immolating their first born children! Among the early Indo-European people, Fire-worship was the central part in the religious rites. Likewise, 'Id al-Adha' is a major Islamic festival, usually marked by the sacrifice of a sheep, coming seventy days after Ramadan.

Thus all kinds of sacrifices, whether putting an animal into a sacrificial fire or cutting of throat on a sacrificial altar, are mere killings and not different from other types of slaying such as strangling, stabbing, poisoning etc...," the old man explained.

"As you said, if Yagam is wrong what would be the right way to pay homage to our Deities...?" they asked with regretful voice.

"Since Deities and other forms of idols as well as God, described by various religions are only personifications of different concepts and beliefs, no relevancy and space for such questions about sacrifice…," the mendicant pointed towards the dead cow.

"If so,   reparation of sins…?" they stood as puzzle-headed.

"The term, Sin denotes an action if the doer knows that it is harmful to others. Elaborately speaking, sins include all actions of which consequences are affecting adversely on any other organism directly or indirectly, if done consciously about such consequences. As human being is able to think about the significances, results and effects of his acts, he is liable for all of his actions and all consequences are to be borne by him and his successors. So sins can be compensated only through rectifications, remedial measures and keeping goodness in future. Sins can't be cured by other sins such as immolations or by prayers…," the old man smiled.

"Then what do you say about God and religions…?" next question arose from them.

"God is neither a creator nor a creation. It is the inert and eternal basic energy which includes the whole macrocosm, which involves one physical world or transformation of positive energy, another part of negative energy waves and basic energy part. Hence all organisms are transformations of positive energy, every species have equal significance though some may possess much sophistication. That basic energy is indifferent to all.

Man realised various aspects of his actions or *Karmas (action)* and their results as well as many terrifying natural powers and his uncontrollability over them such as wind, rain, waves of sea etc. That wisdom made him obedient to Nature and thus he changed his way of life suitable to a social life. That way of life gradually transformed into a civilization named Sanadhana Dharma. Afterwards, tale-based customs were introduced to induce people to follow Dharma. Those tales as well as dependability of life on fire, air, water etc., made man fearful and he began to cry for help from these different natural phenomena. It paved way for various thoughts and thus later he made several concepts regarding natural powers, imaginary forms and gave names for them as God for his benefit and selfish actions. Fearing that he will be punished for his wrong-doings, he set customs, rites and prayers. Discarding the reality, for his benefit and for escape from sins he confirmed his beliefs. To make others believe and compel them to follow customs, taught about unreal resurrection, afterlife, heaven, hell etc.

Faiths, which tell about afterlife, are utter foolishness, since there is no such life. But all consequences of actions are to be suffered by the doer and his successors. So they must be careful to follow goodness or *Dharma (right way of living)* in doing actions or Karma

"A true religion must be the product of scientifically proved culture based on virtues, equally beneficial to all living beings in mundane life...," he continued by looking at their curious eyes.

"We are in chaos! How can we believe your words...?" they interrupted and gazed at him suspiciously.

"Come and see...," he led them towards the fire. He put his hands over flame and took burning embers slowly with both hands!

He ordered them to put their fingers over the flame as he did. All of them pulled back their hands with a cry of pain. He asked:

"If small burns on your finger give you this much pain, then can you ascertain the horrible pain of that animal while burning to death...?"

He walked towards the body of the cow and suddenly vanished as if mystically dissolving into it. While the Agnihotri and his helpers were standing astonished, the cow stood up alive and the Yagasala caught fire!

****

Chapter 24

Cribe of Nameless

Summer flowers bloomed again and again. Quill of seasons brushed bilateral tints on life, which is penned in the case of cosmic time-circle. Poorvapunya realised paling colour from her cheeks and cheer from eyes.

Dark shadows of sorrowfulness began to make her days gloomy.

"Squabble will be prospered without any stimulants……," Poorvapunya remembered the adage.

The degree of difference and quantity of conflict grew very widely day by day between Poorvapunya and Michael. It seemed both of them were competing in babbling and blustering.

Initially, problems were not much significant. Most of the disputes were settled before going to bed. But their difference in faiths and status increased with the arrival of their first child.

Discordance between them became an obstinate obstacle to infant's baptism.

That day Poorvapunya was very angry. Sometimes she grumbled like a parakeet in a cage. She was sitting in a dark room as completely isolated from outer world.

"Instead of baptising my kid and turning me to your fake religion you must convert to *Hinduism*……," she raised voice.

"Your *Hinduism* …! Never heard in the history as it happens……," Michael laughed.

"Not heard…? It's lie. Blaming others is nothing but self-deception. It is one of the main defects of a selfish mind…"

"Now I am saying about religious history…"

"Let the history be changed by you in this way….," Poorvapunya suggested.

"Hah...; Poorvapunya..., in the case of followers of the majestic path of church, children should follow their religion. In our case, first baby must follow the religion of his father and other things can be decided when second child comes......," he tactfully replied.

"You can follow *Crosalvism*; no hindrance. But where is the permission for me to enter in your temple? This reveals the highness of Christianity ....." Michael waved his fingers as sign of victory.

"First, you think about Humanism. At the time of birth everyone is Hindu, as there are no formalities to become a Hindu. Man-made rules and regulations will not be absolute as man himself is incomplete......," Poorvapunya tattled.

She closed her eyes and chanted

मनुर्भव, जनया दैव्यं जनम्

-Rigveda 10.53.6

(First you became a good human being then only to divine being),,,,,,

"If I had married any one from *Abrahamic cult,* it would have been better for me. At least could have flown together.........," Michael shouted.

"Then why didn't you do that...?" she questioned.

"You, rat...; don't think that I had fallen in the spell of your beauty. Your question hides such a hint. Really I had been carrying out our agenda successfully. Now I don't care what would happen to you......"

"What agenda...?" she surprised.

"You fool...; Agenda of conversion. We are doing these things to carry out this holy agenda......," Michael's face gleamed with an arcane arrogance.

"You nasty betrayer...; I feel this world as stinging due to these kinds of devilish actions of brutal person like you......," she continued, "Life and love can't be shut in the dark room of Religions. Marriage is not an alliance with reticent religious or communal platoons. If you were married to a lady from *Reformed-group*, could you have compatibility with her class?"

"That is only inter-church alliance. You don't teach about our *Crosalvism* or Christianity...," Michael's voice hardened.

Baby's long cry for breast-milk or time of lunch or call of neighbours didn't interfere in their disputation. Both of them were not willing to put down the mace. Most of their sayings were answers without questions.

"First of all you need to believe in real human life rather than fighting for dirty religions. Because of you I repudiated my mother, my friends, my village, my job, my Brahmin-cult and everything.....," she plainted.

"You, cretin..., stop your screaming...," He roared like a frantic foe.

"You are an oaf. Who said that Jesus is the founder of Christianity? Before Christ, there were so many religions like that. It is really a baby of parent religion, *Judaism...*," she jested.

"Your Hinduism...? What a hell it is. Out of those innumerable gods, who is real and who is unreal? Have you thought about that bosh before...? Michael challenged her.

"Gods like Krishna or Ram are really personifications of attributes or Dharma. Siva*, Vishnu* and Brahma* are epitomizing the eternal Cosmos' compendium and stages...," Poorvapunya tried to teach the truth, though she knew that it is like trying to train a puppet.

"If so why we see hands and legs like us in their pictures...," Michael tried to stir the matter more.

"Pictures are manmade. Moreover in pictures, various virtual concepts are depicted in forms most familiar to man...," reflected insight in her words. Once again she closed her eyes more deeply and chanted more silently

औम् न तस्य प्रतिमा अस्ति
यस्य नाम महध्यशा

-Yajurveda 32.3

(There is no statue required for God as God has no shape)

"Don't go to cave. Give correct answer. Otherwise surrender...," he waved head.

"I am not a fish to swallow your gaff. But you are an idiot to walk before the dog. Your Jesus had legs and hands. Really he was not God's son but a good Christian opposed social evils and folly canons of churches. That is why he was crucified..."

"What you said, bastard? Who are you to question our church...?" Michael stood up. his teeth grained, fist crushed, slap flashed.

Even after Poorvapunya felt unconscious and her cheeks were swelled by his hard slaps, he was still afflicting her. As a rutting elephant, he trampled vessels and households. His gale of anger continued until the peeling of pillars of their comfortable life-domicile.

At last she realised that living there was impossible due to the nutty nature of Michael and decided to return home. She got down from the doorstep with a broken-heart.

In melancholy mood Poorvapunya walked with tired steps through the street. There was no one to recognize her. She told herself:

"In the middle of this mob I am alone. Perhaps all these people are creeping to the unknown future carrying own burdens of life, like me. All faces are gloomy and darkened! Past bitter story of betrayals and infidelities might have been turned their faces as mementos. No flower can stand without withering in hot sunrays. Then what about our world, standing over the flame of religious immoralities...?"

She asked looking at the sun going to set:

"Oh! Sun god, are you also moving towards the west to return home like me? You will come tomorrow. But I have nowhere to go...; if everywhere there is fire then where a poor creature can go...?"

While walking into the narrow muddy road in deep darkness with a small bundle on hand and holding her tired sleeping kid on hip, the road seemed to be closed before her. As dawdle, but with caution her forlorn journey continued considering not to harm her son's safe sleep.

"My meek child, what harm have you done to this world to get this much sorrowful life...?" dripped tear-drops from her eyes.

Lassitude provoked her mind. Memories spooled back. It seemed bellowing in ears, the echoing footfalls of eons.

"To mankind even a single day is equal to an epoch...," the maxim intervened along with memory of Mother, childhood, friends, school, village........! The chain of recollection elongated endlessly as unending pathway that takes nook and corner of her village. But it was hurdled when monsoon-clouds entered in the sky of reminiscence:

In the gush of monsoon, small slushy water passages are being created and meandering streams' overflow are making them straight. Snow-white waterfalls from mount tops created by the new rain, appeared to be celestial life-porridge pouring from heaven through hill-tops. Greenery and paddy fields are drooping gently in the lullaby of winds coming from dales bearing fragrance of newly bloomed flowers of *Parijatham (heavenly flower)* lushing on long foothills.

Pasturing cows on distant hill seemed to be small differently coloured stones moving among bushes and grass lands. The coruscating virtuousness reflecting nearby meadows on the smooth faces of dews are depicting the whole hamlet's miraculous vein.

Gradually, small flame of imagination began to glow like burning hay-stack. Memories turned up down. Found attribute's attractive seemliness as ineffable:

It is not rhythmically flapping wings of stark-flocks, slowly flowing and disappearing among the flakes, but is the waving hands of earthly born little angels, going to sleep in the sky-crib! Bats flying,,, around banana groves are not seeking nectar inside the sheaths but singing songs by seeing newly blossomed bunches. Bees are not crooning around floated ponds with new-fangled reddish lilies and lotuses, but are telling heavenly tales in melodious voice. The farmers striding wooden tread mills, are not watering paddy fields but filling exuberance to their future Spence. Parrots are not chirping but greeting all other creatures with sense of equality.

Chill of the midnight-breeze called her back to reality.

'Clink-clink......clink-clink........clink-clink........'

In the tranquility of darkness, jingling sound of bullock carts, moving array towards the town to reach before aurora, seemed to be booming, in her ears. Aloof, slightly flickering lights a, ppeared to be the glimpses of faint flamed lanterns hanging below carts,' axis. Slowly, cry of crickets began to hear "Oh! At last reaching my hamlet......," she stopped for a while with surprise as if a horse is bridled.

Though tired of long walk through out night, an unknown novel vim conquered her. As if greeting her to native town, the morning star smiled at her from behind the eastern mount. Poorvapunya deeply breathed deeply like a deer which had escaped from the den of wolf; but her motherly mind woke up. She sighed by patting on the head of her sleeping son, drooped down to shoulder as half dried strip of a jasmine stem.

While entering the gateway of main the street an ominous, scene welcomes her. Because never has seen that lane in such a hampered state. She looks sharply into the bleary slim bluish light of early morning.

She realises that something is blocking her legs from moving forward! Scattered body of a middle aged woman is lying half nakedly on asphalt-cask! Her lips are cut off. Blood is still gushing from shredded wounds and spreading around through tattered attire, as if the last remains after a rude attack of wolfs in the darkness!

By seeing the horrible sight she shivered in panic, clung kid to breast and ran frantically and frightened. Streets were deserted. Shattered stones and sticks were lying as aftermath of pelt and conflagration. Somewhere still big red flames and fume-coils were rising from burning shops and hutments. Posters, harbouring prejudice of own community, on electric posts and walls were the main newcomers along the street as festoons, welcoming all disasters.

She stood wheezing near the outer wall of the temple and looked everywhere as if, she saw it for the first time. Her body was painfully trembling with fear. Anxious glance flew to the meadows like midge towards sweets.

Scrolling over several odd scenes at last her eyes fell on a house entirely ruined and almost ground to fall down, which was a citadel of dreams where she had knitted an imaginary future.

Slacked thatches and termites-eaten reapers are lying here and there in the portal, filled with grass and gushing mud. Big black millipedes are creeping on pillars, covered by darkish mosses. Half-drowned roof, in the spoilage of huge attacking wear and tear, seem to be an antic old fainted big ant-hill...!

With an anxiously beating heart, Poorvapunya called her mother but it emerged as a half-cry:

"Ma....Ma....., where are you, Ma....; I have come.....Ma...."

She was panting with to see her mother.

Groaning words hurdled in her throat and hushed. However, as a lush waterfall from mount, shriek flew out.

But her lamentations were returned unanswered.

She cried bitterly.

Strange faces appeared over nearby fences. Peeps through half-closed windows were followed.

Two women furtively looked at and came out by stooping down from one of the nearby huts.

They enquired:

"Bint, who are you? Why are you crying...? This tot...?"

Hearing her questions about her house and mother, they narrated all past events.

She was shocked to know that her mother had passed away two years back. In the very first night, she was eloped; mother became paralysed and was in death bed unto last breath. In her case, the adage was true, 'no need to regret on death but to rejoice on relief from regrets.'

The story filled deep darkness in her eyes.

Somehow she managed to sit in the ramshackle veranda. It was changed in colour with moldiness. Small evergreen plants, growing through slits of broken stones of the little porch, bowed head as if looking at her with an unknown compassion.

Hours rolled by...

She was crying like a small kid even after the veil of nature was covered everywhere during its course, since couldn't convince the reality to herself.

Poorvapunya trudged in the vague way, towards the banyan tree in front of the temple. She reeled from side to side as if her mind frazzled with frantic thoughts.

She sat beneath the Banyan tree for listening to her mother's call. she could not believe mother's demise!

Her mind realized that an enraged orphanage is approaching with opened gigantic mouth to swallow.

She looked at favorite baby, sleeping in her lap. Suddenly, her motherly affection raised its hood.

Patting and embracing kid, she murmured:

"Nay, my child…; I don't allow you to be an orphan. You must grow…, grow bigger than anyone in this world. Thus you have to put out my orphanage by bringing back all lost springs including ……"

"Yea, your Papa will also have to see you as a grown up youth. But…..," her thought stopped in a hurdle of doubt:

"How can he recognize you…? Oh, it doesn't matter…you will be looked alike him. Moreover who can't have identified one's own son…?" she tried to console herself. "When see you, he will come back as a good man with refined mind. As old maxim, it is true that son is an angel who saves parents from Hades…"

Poorvapunya began to rock her child by holding in fore-arms. Like all mothers, she also crooned a lullaby in a low melodious voice forgetting all sorrows and surroundings when the child clung to her arms and started to weep as if his sleep was hampered:

> 'Isn't the lamp of Queen of night?
> Or the little lamb of it?
> Isn't the Lord of lotus flower?
> Or there loaded nectar, fair?
>
> Isn't the Godly jewel-bit?
> Or the divine glory of it?
> Isn't treasure of fondness-sea?
> Or its gift, Theo granted me?
> …………………………..
> …………………………..
> Oh! My infant, sole gold of life
> You are all in all to me…'

Days are coming and going for your growth. All these plants and flies are for your benefit. World is the play yard for you. As the days rolls by you will be a boy, able to walk and run. Then,

> 'Nightingale's call will wake you up;
> Beams of dawn will be first sight; soon.
> Granny will be at step, for help;
> Naughty pal-chats make you play-loon.'

Like all mothers on earth, I will also be in the heaven of happiness by seeing your countless comedies of childhood:

> 'Run with others, as rabbit jump;
> Fun with muddy soil on thumb;
> And it's fall on forehead-top
> As odd sandal wood paste drop.
>
> Turns to my knees when belly burns;
> Horns your mouth for breast-milk; Moon's
> Beams of love will then fill my bones –
> Son's naughty eyes are Ma's joy-boons.'

Lull made the little child sleepy. Her song was lush with imagination. Fatigue of long journey put her eyes half shut and ears deaf. The banyan tree appeared to be refuge for her by branches spread thickly. Cluster of dry leaves, fallen below, made a quilt. Tiny leaves waved fan. She leaned on an aerial root. In the lap of world she was appeared to be an infant drowsing slowly...

Echoing hollers thrashed in her ears as thunderbolts ample enough not only to wake her up but also to frighten as a rat before a cat.

She listened. Sound of rattles seemed to be coming nearer and nearer.

"They dug out our temple, stole our girls and converted them to satanic cult to disgrace us publicly....," bawling became more clear.

She could see flambeau coming closer.

A gang of persons with sticks, swords and plastic cannas came that way. All looked like armed men from an Armada.

Abruptly hostile mob rushed towards her from other side.

"Whose chick is this...?" one of the gang chuckled.

"Couldn't you see the delicious hen…? Now you can see how she will be pinched in my hands…," one man looked at her with an evil smile and his fingers touched on her right cheek and passed through neck and below.

One of them leaned forward and forcefully took her kid. He projected his mouth and jaw like an animal.

"Please give my kid…" she begged before him.

Colour of his eyes looked like sun in the dusk. He roared and poured kerosene over the child and asked another man to set fire on it. Darkness entered into her eyes. Cry was crushed in her throat. She felt, full black everywhere, losing hope to live and all wishes are going to be burned to charcoal.

Suddenly, the first gang bounced upon and gruff fight began. Several heads were cut away within seconds. Bloodstained knifes struck and pitched on bodies again and again.

During the clash among them, somehow Poorvapunya took her child and escaped. She ran as fast as she could but some extremists followed her. She ran towards their opposite hillside through grass covered slop. When they reached near, her leg struck against a stone. She fell down and rolled into the steep cliff. Though she had held her son with both hands, the child slipped away while rolling.

"Alas! That sweet fruit has damaged. Now she would have become the cluster of some broken bones…," one of the terrorists expressed his frustration.

They returned with luscious lips like wolfs which lost prey after a long chasing.

"Whomsoever, killing is easier than protecting. Killing is much easier than keeping …," one of them said thoughtfully.

At that time another group marched towards them in dramatic garb and easily overpowered the first gang. Dead bodies of their group were taken away by the military uniformed persons saying Arabic slogans loudly, "Allah…. Allah…."

"Take the bodies into our Bungalow of mystery without delay…," the senior person ordered to his assistants when heard bawling from other sets.

Everywhere innocent panic-stricken people were running helplessly discarding whether it is day or night. Tragic events other than religious killings became not at all impressive. Religious leaders tried maximum to squeeze the situation and turn it in favourable to their community.

Jubilant marches of communal fractions were colliding in cross-roads. People began to keep knifes for self protection. Fleeting gangs for aggression seemed to be symbols of communal strength. Frightened villagers moved apart.

Few decided to evolve a solution for the culminating clashes. But no one was gallant to bridle the horse of violence.

Bloodstained yards of Churches, Mosques, temples and other religious places were filled with crows and vultures. Rising-sounds in the morning became vociferation of crows. In isolated corners foxes also dared to stretch leg.

Narrative consequences began to be visible, like group cremations discarding religious ceremonies; burial of several dead bodies in one pit, new temporary hospitals, tents and so on. Common markets were divided for each class.

"If anyone comes to another market, runs by opposite class, he will be cut into pieces…," even small children repeated the sentence to by heart.

Some Taqwiite groups arranged refuges. In those camps also they were cautious to execute their religious customs strictly. Widows and deserted infants were rehabilitated at bamboo paneled centres. Most of them were with broken bones, swollen out from wrinkled skin. Frequently the leaders came to analyse situations and to recruit youngsters who are willing to become martyrs for their religion.

Since the leaders were not concerned about others, refugees' voracious stomachs couldn't ever fill with the stingy food served to them. Severe distress and shrunken stomachs became a terrible sight but always those camps were silent because everyone was aware of the punishment for making noise – piercing hot apex of sword into eyes.

Day by day scenes changed according to the spreading of clashes such as, in one place hunger-deaths, in another place looting and setting fire and in some places warfare training. In one street, one group was threatening women of the opposite race to walk nakedly into the road, while huts of the other groups were burning down on road side. Nowhere could see food materials and wells containing good drinking water. No medical shops with ample stock. No silage for cows to eat. Everything was polluted and destroyed.

Viewing the rapid changes coming to the culture of the hamlet, main chit-chat of the common folk was about future ethnicity and exaggerated predictions:

"Now human doesn't eat human-flesh. It is a state of civilization. If deficiency occurs to other edibles, this civilization may also change because existence of cultures has no infallible stability"

"In a nutshell, at present the persons who die, is a lucky man since he can escape from this *Gape Dome* village, the real Hell…," by seeing poisoned well, one man said.

"This will happen to whole world soon. This small village is only a symbol of total ruin…," another man observed.

In the weekend, new symptoms of another tragedy were visible. As a bad omen, morning-sun rose in the cloudy sky and its pale rays hesitated to come down.

Untidy atmosphere unleashed epidemics. The diseases entered as ally in all places in a frolic style and marched to slums and streets.

People were compelled to receive these new visitors by denouncing their own fate.

Uproar of the epidemics disturbed the rich and the poor equally. Remaining peace also turned up down. Each disease began to take lives as its own share in each minute with search for enumeration of victims.

****

Chapter 25

Doorway of an Untaint

When Poorvapunya opened her eyes, real wolfs were sitting around her. She looked at them with a groan of pain because of the injured and bruised body, still shivering with fear of terrorists.

"Yea, eat me dear animals while alive; I don't care. It is better than being killed by those brutes in nasty way ...," she murmured in a half-conscious stage.

The small rays of the noon-sun, creeping through dense leafed thick tall trees of that jungle, had begun to dry blood on wounds of her body.

With a deep moan she returned to consciousness.

"Where are you...?" Her arms were groping for her child.

With all strength, she got up and looked around. All that time the wolfs were sitting around and looking at her! She watched them carefully.

"No, these animals are not sitting around their prey. They came here not snuffing the smell of blood drops! May be calmly watching their new guest! Real natural love is emitting from eyes of these animals...," feeling a security she looked!

Her eyes turned into darkness of the dense forest. Her wavering legs moved fast.

"My child..., where are you...?"

Her faltering echoed and re-echoed as if the woods have undertaken her misery. She could have realized the truth that 'nature is the Neptune of the ocean of absolute love', when those wolfs followed her as pet dogs.

Her wandering continued. She couldn't find her way. No way among shrubs and highly crossed thorny bushes. Cicadas' shrill sound entered in ears as fearsome noise.

179

Above all, even Midday was quite equal to night since the thick woods obstructed sunlight. Even then she continued to walk seeking her son hither and thither until she fell down and became unconscious.

A twig fell from a tall branch as a symbol of the dried scion of human virtue; trembled down in the tempest of taboo of Tantrum-era.

She regained consciousness when large group of wild fowls flapped near and fell on her, fighting each other with beaks and talons, making clutter as the usual evening wild scene.

Caressing of gentle dusk-breeze daubed dampness on her face.

Seeing a quaint face before, she puzzled and woke up!

An odd face gleaming in ecstasy of wisdom! Indescribable benevolence flowing from his eyes is deeply permeable into the heart. Eyeshot, perforating into fraternity of all minds seems to be sign of sanctity as well as safety. His forehead daubed with sandal paste, shining like alabaster from heaven, depict the divinity of denunciation. Neck is decorated with decorous *Rudraksha**. Tufted hairs reveal the radical mystery of hermitage.

As a chant of humanity she heard: "Do you know, what brought you here...?"

Even though his voice felt as an oracle, she looked at him with reverential fear.

"Nay...! Where am I? Oh! Bhagwan, where is my kid...?" She cried like a child.

"Caught hold of by those devilish......."

She collapsed down like a lark which had lost its limb and memory slipped in to darkness.

Rhythmic ritual incantations woke her nerves again. That time she had been received by the sacred door of the Ashram and brought to the Ayurvedic treatment centre of the hermitage to medicate her wounds, by disciples as directed by the Sage.

"This is the beginning of my life in a new world...," she murmured while past days' memory flew into the baffled darkness of thought, like chattering bats in a cave.

Reminiscences of childhood glittered more as it consists many memorable golden moments of the school-days.

Other disciples greeted her and began to hear her stories interestingly to pacify her. She continued:

"On the first day, when I entered in to portal of the Lower-primary school, holding hands of my mother, crying little crows, sitting on the big tamarind standing high in the courtyard, were the interesting thing than the people gathered there because I also made a cry to go home. Children with different coloured dress, sitting in array seemed to be pieces of rainbow clubbed together.

In the floor a girl with a big rosary on neck was sitting near to me. Her name was Mary. She became one of my best school mates. You can't hear her story without tears..."

While Poorvapunya was narrating with quaver about the pitiful death of Mary, other disciples could not control their tears. Not only noteworthy flourished with matters but also hopeless dreams were included in her narrations.

Her story filled with immaculate words was penetrating all hearts like the fragrance of mint chilled with cold dews.

"My life thus faded away like nugatory dreams of a mad man...," she had been sobbing like a small kid who had not seen the cellars of life even while others were telling fables filled with billows of dolour, in order to pacify her by opening the sanctum of life-woe.

Even while hearing their words, she was reviving memories of home-days, which were flowing to mind:

"From the yard, I plucked leaves of black sweet basil and tucked into my luxuriantly curled dark hair. When saffron rays of setting sun hit on my nose studs, its rays flashed to luscious lips. As a cuckoo skipping on cornfield-ridge, I headed towards a small shrine in the farther end of the paddy field.

After the downy rain, drops of water were trickling down from grass-leaves and branches of trees in the twilight. I walked through slush, green dyke and swampy soil. I splashed water with mud-covered feet. Drops steeped up in the air like golden granules and fell down to wet soil.

I viewed that the usual evening sceneries of the village was unchanged that day also:

In the natural square pond near the temple, frolicking kids are smearing oil on their body gently and diving into muddy water. A naughty boy is jumping over a calf and slipping down into cow-dung and hear bowling sound in full magnitude. Tired poor plough-bulls are not yet allowed to stop pulling shares in ploughing paddy fields. Storks are following in the mentality of boss, chattering to them. A plough-man fully covered with mud, is angling with a hooked earthworm. As solitary drummer, a wood packer is hollowing a palm trunk.

I reached a small shrine made in thick stone under a huge banyan tree. Idol was embellished with garland of white basil and deep red flowers. Wick was burning in a lamp nearby. I burned camphor and prayed for a while in ardent and immerse devotion. I bowed and the priest touched on my crown of head and blessed.

When the Sun disappeared from the horizon, darkness painted on ground. I returned from the temple yard and walked quickly to my house.

When I reached home, mother was preparing pith of plantain as a curry to gruel.

"Poorva, today I am on fasting. So have your supper earlier….," heard mother's low voice.

"Ma…, today is not Monday. Then why are you ….?" I was anxious.

"Don't you know, on all full moon nights I observe fasting…?"

"Ma…, but in almost all nights you are not taking food…" I argued.

"Who knows fasting is a way to hide poverty in a divine way…" I heard mother's murmuring in pensiveness while going to a reed-mat to sleep.

'Who has created poverty? God…? No, if it was God, there should not have poverty to good people. Then by whom…? People are making their own…? No one will select it for himself. If so, the riche people are making poverty by holding wealth of others…,' thinking about the substratum of poverty, with contempt towards Riches, I went to sleep.

That time also, in the zenith of deep blue sky-avenue, the full moon was effusing effulgence while passing, like Queen of night…," Poorvapunya stopped her narration for a while.

Remembering the stories, she had read earlier, she continued:

"If the tale of **Eternal tranquillity** comes true, it would be a tragic end of mankind on our earth also just as it happened in the story of planet K'iche! Now human society is going that way of ruination by all means… where human beings go, there tragedy comes…"

****

Chapter 26

Re-visit with Repentant

Orbit of the K'iche planet is changed to a nearest circle of the God of Light. All places have destroyed in the continuous high tremors of the planet except one suburb of the capital city. High temperature of the atmosphere became uncontrollable even with the help of air conditioning mechanisms even inside official buildings and houses. Finally the remaining few inhabitants of the suburb decided to return to Earth on next Christmas day.

For the mission Mr. K'iche-VI was selected as Shuttle Commander and Mrs. K'iche as Pilot along with another crew, since they were the trained astronauts of the control station.

As the day for returning came nearer and nearer, sadness of people came at the brink of cry due to nostalgia.

"Today is Christmas Eve. But the planet is seems to be quiescent because no human being is here to celebrate Xmas tomorrow except us…," Mrs. K'iche, who has been suffering from paralysis since last Monday, couldn't complete the sentence due to desperation.

Mr. K'iche-VI and his wife escaped from the previous day's explosion of the Thermal Power Station situated near the satellite station followed by strong quakes.

Their narrow escape was a surprise:

His wife requested him to catch some frogs from the field for their special dish. She said:

"It's not very well known but, in fact, frog-meat is the most delicious of all…"

While he was searching for frogs in the muddy field, his pet dog, Samson caught a small rabbit by its own effort and came back. That time he heard the bang. He fell down in the vibrating shock. Somehow he got up and ran towards his home with the bag containing rabbit and frogs.

Back-door of the kitchen of his house was seen open among the totally broken down building.

Threw away the bag and he entered into the room, calling wife with a large cry:

"Dalia….dear Dalia…….."

She was groaning and trying to get up from the floor but couldn't. He carried her outside. She was injured not seriously but both of them cried loudly for help.

Alas! Nobody was there to hear their wails.

He wandered everywhere to see whether anyone had survived. At last he recognised the truth that he and his wife alone are the living human beings on the planet. This new suburb of the capital city with a small population was remaining after all calamities but totally ruined in the previous days explosion. All inhabitants are buried alive under the constructions fell down to the ground as mounts of dust.

"What shall we do then…," Mr. K'iche covered face with both hands and wept deeply.

"Today, weather is unaffordable. Heat is as high as to inflame even soil. Changes in the magnetic field of our planet and increase in the energy output of the God of light made this land barren, lifeless and unlivable for all organisms! Then how can we live…?" Mrs. K'iche evaluated the situation and took the compact edition of the Bible from her pocket.

"We are alone. Where can we go…?" Mr. K'iche turned his face.

"That is what I am also thinking. Can we return…?"

"To where…?"

"To Earth…"

Earth? I am sure, the situation may be most horrible there.

"Is it possible for us to take such a bitter decision…?"

"Anyway we have to judge…," she insisted while reading the Bible.

"Power of judgement is not with us. Dear Dalia, if we choose to vacate, it is just as that vacation of Adam and Eve from Aden. Main difference is that they were compelled to vacate as a result of their own sin but we are for our ancestors'. They hadn't Bible on hands but we have at the time of vacation…"

"Instead, they had promise of salvation and an end to their woes at a later date. Now the Bible saved me from death. Thus it will help us …"

"But how...? In this blast all other remains of the station were also destroyed except the space shuttle. There is no message sending mechanism; so that no contact with the Earth...," Mr. K'iche explained the difficulty.

"If the Shuttle is working properly no need of another control station as it is fully automatic. Shall we try...?"

"Yea, if stay here we will die soon. So let us have a challenge to escape...," Mr. K'iche shared with her braveness.

They entered the shuttle and examined whole equipments and parts carefully thr, oughout the night. In the morning when they were about to get down, heard the alarm from the shuttle for journey!

"It is Samson doing the mischief...," Mrs. K'iche pointed at their pet dog, which was biting on the starting button playfully.

"Then we, have to arrange all the other things for journey...," Mr. K'iche showed uneasiness.

"Everything is ready since the journey was planned earlier. But God has sent his chariot for others before this..." she murmured with regret.

When they entered the shuttle, their eyes were filled with tears of indescribable so, rrows. While putting seat belt, the poor dog peeped into the helmet-glass, above the belt, wonderfully. Thus they started journey with bowed head in complete silence except the sound of booster rockets.

During the, journey, machines had taken full control over them since they had to obey all orders of the shuttle's automatic control systems. They seemed to be the parts of those machines; that much both of their faces were swollen over and above the normal puffiness during space-journey, due to melancholy mood.

For a while their imagination reached to the scene of reception by earth-dwellers when lands on earth-station:

"About fifteen centurion years have passed on the earth after the beginning to do, micile on K'iche planet. Now it may be only a part of their immemorial history. How can they believe that we are also human beings...?" Mrs. K'iche looked at herself with anxiety.

"But we had consultation with them until last one thousand five hundred years according to their arithmetic calculations...," Mr. K'iche reckoned the period from which the break of contact between Earth and the K'iche planet due to the absorption of all types of waves and light signals by an unknown object in the space.

"Anyway o, ur landing will be a surprise to them...," Mrs. K'iche waved head.

"Though we enter unexpectedly, I think, their radars will detect our shuttle, at least when we cross the margin of biosphere of the Earth...," Mr. K'iche explained.

"If they know about our unsuccessful end of domicile on the planet K'iche, I think they will blame bitterly and curse us by putting hands on head. That much our ancestors have ruined all our heavenly life...," intense grief reflected on face of Mrs. K'iche.

"Don't think so dear; it will only be a joke for them since they have already made their own earth a nasty hell than any other place in this physical world., Instead of blaming, they will shake hand for our victory...," Mr. K'iche laughed.

"What victory? Don't say such cruel jokes..."

While landing on the Earth, on a floodlit runway in the early evening darkness, Mrs. K'iche felt the pull of gravity unaffordable due to her paralysis. She held Mr. K'iche's hands tightly and looked at him nicely as a the mark of farewell. Slowly her holding hands became loose. At last when she was brought outside of the spaceship, she was dead.

Weeping uncontrollably as a child, Mr. K'iche followed the stretcher in which h, er corpse was lying, while the pet dog was growling unusually.,

"This is not only a tragic return from the golden land of glories but also a regretful go back to the glob of man's useless wisdom...," Mr. K'iche lamented in half-conscious stage.

"For further proceedings needs some money...," Attendant stretched his left hand for bribe while pulling the stretcher.

"Money...? What money...?" Mr. K'iche looked at him angrily.

"Sorry sir, you may not have money with you; but any other valuables...," Attendant reduced his voice.

"You take everything, left with me by God; take my life also if you can...," Mr. K'iche tried to control his wavering legs to walk towards the entrance.

When crossing the gate, he stopped for a while and turned back as if waiting for his wife to come. Then his hollow mind directed him to follow his dog, which was crossing the road against road-signal.

"Are you following that dog...?" the traffic guard asked loudly.

"Yea, that's my pet, Samson..."

"But do you know whom that dog is following...?"

"It is following its own will..."

"If so its will is death..."

"Why..."

"Because it is crossing the road without knowing the signal; it will be knocked down by vehicle coming from other side…," the guard roared.

"If it's the will of God…"

Mr. K'iche also crossed the road, looking on the route-map, while the guard was looking furiously.

At last his travel ended at *Tin-Metro,* the old city, in the *Land of Mesoamerica.*

He stopped before a very old museum. Once it was the college of astronautics which was fully owned by *'K'ichemoor'* family.

He was stopped at the gate by some security personnel:

"Where are you going with this dog without permission…?"

"I think this is a public place…"

"It's true as you think; that is why dog is not permitted…"

"Why…?"

"Have to keep safety and silence here…"

"Look; it is keeping quiet…"

"So, be more careful; on the other hand, barking dog will not bite…"

"See, I have put its mouth-cap…"

"In your place, is mouth-cap enough to get permission for a dog to enter into a museum…?"

"There were no such rules, but here mouth-cap is necessary to all; I think…"

"You are coming from…?"

"From *K'ichemoor* family…"

"Sir, as you are from *K'ichemoor* family, it is the latest astonishing news that the family is not totally eradicated in the inundation that happened five centuries ago as i read in a book once…" one of the security personnels laughed loudly and danced like child with joy.

"Then, can I go inside…?"

"Welcome to the oldest museum in this continent…"

He could identify the large colour portrait of the founder of that college of astronautics, hanging on the wall. It was of Mr. K'iche.J.Santler. From there he got information about address, location and land-mark of the *K'ichemoor* family.

It was in the evening, he reached the village, which was twenty kilometers from *Tin-Metro.* As per the graph, got from the museum, he came to the turning point of the cross road towards west coast.

"Sir, if you know about *K'ichemoor,* please tell me where it is…?" he asked a man on the road.

"Yes I know; it was nearby in the Eastern coast. But now it's in the sea…"

"In the sea…?"

"Yea, in the Atlantic sea! It's a long story…"

"You mean…?"

"One thousand and five hundred years ago coastal area about half of the village was swallowed by the sea in the flood, which is considered to be the second after Noahic flood…"

"Oh! My God…"

"See; that church is made for memory of the inhabitants, who died in that calamity…" the man pointed towards a church near the beach.

K'iche entered the church and enquired after introducing himself and about his past history:

"Now My wife expired. Where have to bury her body…?"

"Though you belong to K'ichemoor family, now they have no membership in our, diocese or family-grave in this churchyard. Once they had, but after the flood no one was here to give subscription to the church. Hence their family-grave was auctioned for higher bid…"

"What can I do then…?"

"You can get membership after baptism as per canon…"

"Baptism again…? If the canon insists I can; but my wife…?"

"If she was not dead…"

"But she is dead…I say, she died as a Christian…," K'iche intervened with anger. "Then no way according to our canons…"

"No way because your cannons killed the true Christian and the Christianity…," he turned back and slowly walked towards the beech, which was gleaming in the golden twilight.

He continued walking over the wet sand and sounds of waves were becoming higher and higher. As on the K'iche planet it seemed to be melodious and glorious to his ears. While looking at the horizon abstractedly, he saw his wife calling by gestures into the faint-light…!!

While others were eagerly hearing the tale, bell rang with long sounds as if imitating the night-owl's hooting from distant wilderness.

"Next time I shall tell the remaining part of the story…," Poorvapunya turned around and thought.

*****

Chapter 27

The Final Interment

The chilling mist of the December morning had not yet vanished. Sexton of the church was going to ring church-bell since another man also died in the village.

"This is the fifth bell today; then how many before dusk...?" he asked himself with astonishment.

Sexton put left hand in his pocket and tried to reckon the coins. Usually he was very much pleasant to do the job because of the thought about the count of silver coins, which would fetch out of each funeral.

Unfortunately, Money got were much less than the normal rate including the fourth rich man's case that day, in last four burials, but somehow managed to collect more, only due to the increase in the number of interments.

He thought about the fourth man whose burial was done just half an hour before. That old man's death would have happened before several months. In fact, everyone in the village was expecting that death, true to say, wished severely. Moreover, he had received last sacraments several times. People used to say by seeing that old man's struggling:

"How long a person can be in the death bed and this is of course more than enough..."

The old rich man, the only money lender of the village, was a much impressive person both inside and outside his community. Vicars and crosses bowed before his money. Almost half of the dusty sand and moor land in the village were captured by him and his influence extended even to the altarpiece.

Lamentation was much noisy and loud enough to reach even outside the village. All the villagers flew to his house as if a flood-gate was opened. Face of the people paled, feeling that their golden time will suddenly fall in a nightmare after the death of that rich man.

According to custom, some persons gathered and took his corpse for last bathing and dressing. They washed the body and wiped with a cotton cloth, which was dipped in spirit. Body was laid on a decorated wooden coat and a golden cross, brought from nearby church, was kept in between his crossed fingers, covered by embroidered socks. A bystander opened pages of the Bible. *Sankeerthanam (chanting lines)* began to resound everywhere. The Bishop and Vicar rushed to the place in a cab. A deep silence suddenly covered over the mass. Then funeral prayers started and were seconded by those who gathered there.

"Our church is deeply distressed in this death and praying for his soul's eternal peace…," the Bishop reminded in his short preaches.

"In the case of diseases, garrison of palace is not a hindrance to enter…," Vicar added as revelation, "in moments of joy and agony we must stand united and spread the message of Jesus Christ to each and every village…"

The choir group loudly sang songs and its echoes reflected in the air as if grief of the soul.

Funeral procession started and all slowly moved to the churchyard. Due to heavy rain in the previous night, portal of the church was covered with mud.

Some of the devotees pointed out:

"Rain will come after the death of good persons as a symbol of the World's grief…!"

After final prayer, closed lid of the coffin and was taken to his family's necropolis, which was exceptionally built very near to the right side of the portal.

Handful of soil was put on the coffin by the Vicar as if repaying debt of the entire land, which was donated by him to the Church.

Even after entering the church-yard, the sexton had not finished his thought about the rich man, since he was so much fond of richness. With much distress, pulled out his hands from pocket after reckoning several times, the coins gained on that day, his eyes were eagerly searching for another call for funeral ceremony.

"Fortunately, next one is coming…," seeing a small crowd, he told himself with delight.

A group of people came holding a hearse on their shoulder to the burial ground outside the fence of church's approved interment-land. All of them seemed to be in a hurry.

No procession….!

No mourning….!!

No religious rites….!!!

While the sexton was looking with astonishment, one of them said in a silly manner:

"No time to stop. We have to come here for another burial within half an hour. Only half an hour past now, another funeral was done here…"

"Then what about our rites and customs…?" sexton asked with anger and curiosity; "How soul of the dead will go to heaven if you do this uncustomary things…?"

"Are you not living in this place; don't you see the dying people by the epidemic? After costly treatments, how these poor people can bear other burial charges also…," the crowd ridiculed Sexton.

"You, unbelievers have no entrance to our church or heaven. Otherwise, somehow collect and give money to church and get a place in the approved ground for the dead man's burial…," he examined carefully the small gate and lock of the church-fence, to confirm whether shut and locked correctly.

That time another small crowd was coming with a corpse to the place outside.

"This cadaver is of a poor sexton of another church. He was admitted in the hospital yesterday but died today morning. All of his family members died earlier. So none is to bear expenses, but you can arrange for the funeral inside the fence as he was a sexton …," one man coming towards the fence, said.

At first the sexton was shocked, but thinking about the money to be spared from his pocket, he abstained from offering customary burial and said in a low voice:

"Please go to the church where he was sexton; that is the only way to get approbation…"

"How is it possible…? It is far away from here. Dead body of a man, who died of epidemic can't be kept for long time. Moreover he belongs to the same group of church…," they argued in the tone of begging.

"No contention; go there; no other way…," sexton waved his hands and went away.

On the way the sexton noticed the crowd, around a hearse in the yard of nearby Mosque, with envy because of the thought about money that would have been earned if it was a Christian funeral.

"Whose body is that…?" he enquired though there was no curiosity to know.

One man came near the steps and told him the real story:

"The rich man in unconscious stage was admitted in the temporary hospital yesterday evening by some unfamiliar youths. They returned soon, after entrusting a big gold coin box with the doctor, saying that they have to bring another man. Immediately after their departure the man died. Then the doctor certified that it is a Muslim and informed us to bring the body for burial. But now the *Imam* and others are seeking whether the dead body is of a Muslim or not..."

"Why a Muslim's body can't be identified...?" sexton pointed his finger with a puzzling look.

"The cicatrice of *Niscar* (prayer) on his forehead is not clear because skin is totally burned and darkened due to the application of medicines. The only evidence is circumcision. But some other religions also follow that custom..."

When the deep aroma of costly and rare balm pasted on the dead body, entered into his nose, sexton thought whether there is any provision to proselytise a dead body.

"What are you thinking about...," observing the long silence of sexton, the other man asked.

"Nothing else...; if compare with the event happened last week in *Shoe Town*, this is not at all serious. That was an unbelievable occurrence...," sexton patted his throat to enter into the story.

"A dead body was handed over to the relatives from the private hospital, where there are special arrangements for keeping bodies in freezers. It was of a Brahmin youth who died one week before. The body was keeping in an air-tight coffin, in the mortuary till the arrival of relatives from a distant place. Nowadays that hospital is not taking much care about the preservation of bodies of the poor, since they are getting many bodies from rich people to keep. More over people are taking back bodies before contracted dates, giving full payment for the whole period, as dead bodies of persons who died of epidemic must be buried as early as possible.

When the body was taken back, it was in half decayed state. Special order was given by the Superintendent of the hospital that the air-tight black polythene bag should not be opened, in order to protect epidemic from spreading. Somehow all the Hindu customary rites were followed and the body was cremated. In the presence of relatives, the body burned down to ashes along with fire-woods. While the relatives were wiping tears and returning with grief, a messenger ran towards them and handed over one letter from the hospital. In the letter it was written:

'Please return the body as it is not of your relative. It is of a Muslim youth. The misplacement happened because two bodies were kept inside one box in order to save space and to carry out more orders considering this special situation. Your relative's body had already been destroyed after three days by our mortuary-keeper as usual practice. Unfortunately he forgot to fill the polythene bag with separated organs and wastes from the operation theatre. Sorry for the inconveniences caused to you. With regards.............'

Sexton walked quickly through a short-cut to reach home thinking that next call might have come for funeral.

On the way he saw another sight. There, a house was burning, but none of the watching crowd was trying to put out fire! Sexton wondered and opened mouth to cry for help. When the sound blocked in throat, his eyes filled with darkness. One old man came near and pacified:

"You might not have heard. Here one death happened one hour before by the new type of epidemic, which is the most powerful ever had seen. The specialty of this disease is that if anyone touches or see the body, the disease will be transmitted to him immediately! So there was no other way except to set fire the house along with the dead body in it.

"Then how did you know that he is dead without seeing...?" sexton's curiosity increased.

"No need of seeing. Doctor had said that everyone will die within an hour after the appearance of symptoms...," the old man waved his head as if he was an assistant of the doctor.

Before completion of the story by the old man, sexton had started walking with anger against all Christians who were avoiding customary burial rites.

On the other side of the road, Marcus was walking towards another place, where people were dying due to spreading epidemics. Sexton didn't look at him straight, though recognised.

Marcus saw a strange sight:

People are clambering across a small wooden bridge to force their way into a mass funeral! Volunteers, wearing towel across nose and mouth as temporary face masks against the stench of rotting flesh, are lowering cheap wooden coffins into shallow graves quickly!

"Oh my God, this is the coffin of a baby...!" one of the mourners wipes tears and cries loudly while grave-diggers lowering one small coffin into a pit. Someone showers Rose-petals on the coffin.

In the meantime a stranger, seemed to be a Taqwiite priest, comes and reads out verses from his religious book! When Marcus reached near, he said:

"That's the least we can do for Al-Taqwiites if any among these people..." Marcus smiled.

After looking sharply at the beard of Marcus, as if suspect him a Taqwiite, the priest put his bag containing his religious book, in Marcus's hand and said pointing towards another distant grave:

"Please keep this for a while; I shall pray for and come back soon..."

Marcus noticed, in another corner a man was lighting lamps near the graves as per Saindhava rites. He slowly moved towards that man. On the way he got some ritual books of other classes from another place. He reached near the lamp and suddenly burned the books along with dried leaves, lying on the ground! Seeing that, the man, who was lighting lamps, ran towards him and tried to put out the fire. In his attempt, his ritual book fell down and caught fire!

Marcus laughed and said loudly:

"These are more dangerous than epidemic-viruses, which are the causes of all ruins in this world. Let them be damned in their graves calmly..."

The Taqwiite priest roared against Marcus and ran back towards him. The other man asked furiously:

"Who told you to give your bag to this mad man...?"

Looking at laughing Marcus, walking slowly out of the grave yard, the priest murmured:

"Oh! He is a mad man; I didn't know at all..."

Number of epidemics increased day by day. Deadly diseases entered each nook and corner of the village. Schools and public inns became temporary hospitals. Religious headquarters and prayer-halls were seemed to be altered as religious sanatoriums for upper classes.

"High walls of castles are not hindrances for disease and death to enter...," poor people reminded upper class against their unwillingness to help in such a critical stage.

"Every day the Sun is setting after seeing numerous settings of human beings in this village nowadays...," people lamented.

"As if, a flower smiles today, tomorrow falls, a man sees today tomorrow dies...!" reflected sadness in the words of the masses.

Lamentations of the populace rose from different parts began to echo as the loud cry of the hamlet!

Death dared at everyone and became the common portent. Life of the village was stagnated totally since no house was free from disease.

"Passing of dead bodies and hearses are not a special scene now. If we see the bustle in front of coffin-shops, we may think that people would have recognized the usefulness of coffins. Shop owners reduced length and width of coffins as far as possible but increased the size of letters showing religious names on coffin-covers...!" Marcus observed with contempt.

Though there were no such coffins for Hindus, smokes from burning pyres continued to rise from the south corners of their houses. The most pathetic situation was that there was no one in some houses to do post death rites as those were the last ones in the houses. In some places people took outsiders as successors on contract, like rented vehicles.

Perhaps, this may be the reason of new boards in some places saying that, 'Rental heirs available here'.

Without tears one can't see the pitiful conditions of some other slums and the poorest inhabited places:

There mass funerals and dumping of bodies in big pits are frozen sights in every turning of the roads! Hindus, Christians and Muslims are lying altogether with persons of other sects without any untouchability, discrimination and hostility! All are receiving simple and same burial, free from all religious rites! There only atmosphere is calm because the poorest innocent people may not have time to think about religious customs and vanity apart from appetite and famine, which are common to them all.

Mighty poverty and attack of epidemics would have turned others more human and culture of unity or due to neglect from all hard core religious thoughts; these people are showing common sense to accept others. Here these people have no holyday's celebrations, controversial to upper classes, which make even deaths as auspicious occasions for entertainment and pomposity, irrespective of religious classifications.

Anyway, their unity seems to be a good sign emphasising the maxim, "A single spark is enough to fire the whole stack..."

Within a week the thunderbolt of pandemics reduced population as well as religious discriminations and clashes considerably.

"One natural contagious disease will easily gobble all artificial religious diseases, fundamentalism and fanaticism, like an elephant eats grass-buds. Oh! Here number of elephants is more than grass-buds...!" Marcus laughed and cried simultaneously with delight and sorrow.

Diseases were recognised as common enemies of the village. Before these common foes, communal classes and religious segments were compelled to cooperate. The unity and harmony started in this remote place but before long found same sort of ray-bits in other places also.

People themselves made willing not to close their ears before the words of peace and equality because they feared that total annihilation will occur shortly if these miseries are cankering villagers with the most fatal weapon.

"Who will disarm this enemy...? "No one knows...," people asked and answered themselves with astonishment and agony.

"Diseases become social calamity when they are not objected by men unanimously...," Marcus roared loudly.

From the countless tragedies the villagers realised the truth that, only by the incarnation of humanity can put an end to this disaster.

"We recognized the danger of religious conflicts at last. Alas! By that time we have lost our neighbours, relatives, parents, brothers, sisters, children and even ourselves...," persons lamented.

"Ourselves...?"

"Yea, we became deaf and blind by the potation of folly religious hymns..."

"When we get this remarkable human life for salvation, it is necessary to live in harmony and love. If something hinders, even though they are religions, then must be resisted and thrown out from the society since they are the real enemies of mankind. Without harmony and love, nothing will give salvation. If we, human beings, are not able to show kindness towards our race on this earth, how can we believe that we are able to rescue others into heaven, if there is such a one...?" one said as if golden clarity came to his thoughts.

"Spiritual ignorance leading to religious beliefs is the greatest misery to mankind..." another man applauded.

The innocent public woke up from communal giddiness and slumber, and decided to enshrine love and fondness in their heart. They collected scattered grains of natural love and sowed in the land of social conscience, ploughed by hostility. Esoteric humanity sprouted and began to grow to a divine lush green plant of civilization. They observed:

"Any organism without real knowledge can be termed as cloddish ninny, even though it may be a man..."

****

Chapter 28

Indefinite Passing Way

After Poorvapunya had left the house, it seemed to be an isolated inn to Michael. Indefinite

"How can I escape from this cursed earthen range...," looking at the house, Michael put his hand on the head with anger.

He became a stranger to that house later because of his late arrival and absence. Gradually, doors and windows were seen closed always. Alcohol was so close to him always. In highly intoxicated stage he forgot the way to his house.

At last Michael returned to *Royal empire*. There was no one to receive him since he was then a man with bare hands. He sought for a chance of some pennies at least for livelihood, but he was driven out from everywhere.

One day, before midnight when he was sitting under a street light, fainted with hunger, a Christmas carol troop came that way. He looked curiously at the coloured glossy dress of the mob, remembering his childhood days. Suddenly, he dived back into the darkness.

The procession was lead by clergies. Devotees were following them singing carols all the way according to the tune of drums:

"Jingle bell jingle bell jingle all the way..."

The group of drummers were walking rhythmically behind them. Pipers moved after them making carols through their pipes melodiously:

"Oh, little town of Bethlehem...

...."[55]

Light of the lamps hanging from Christmas-trees increased the glitter of the procession. Michael silently followed them.

---

[55] A famous Christmas carol

A huge gathering was formed in and around the church and in its portal. Surroundings of the church filled with pomp and gaiety. The church-bell rang for the holy mass. The entire Street plunged into festive mood.

"After midnight mass there would be delicious feast in houses everywhere...," Michael thought.

Suddenly, his eye-brows rose in delight. He stealthily entered the clergy's bungalow through an open window and looked around. A furnace was still flaming as if lending a dim light to the room instead of the dead lamp hanging on the wall! The sight awaited there for him, really shocked him and stopped his breath for a while!!

Loafs of bread, fried turkey, roasted potatoes and backed brown cakes were making a parade on the dining table. Every thing was arranged properly. He justified:

"This is the true spirit of celebrating Christmas and the way we do have in this Royal empire..."

Michael came out with a long eructation from there just before the completion of the midnight mass. There after he tried several tricks to fetch his daily food. Even then he didn't stop enquiry for a job and money but all efforts were unsuccessful. During the wandering, his face was darkened and grotty by midday sunlight. His criminal look and theft-experience put him in the gang of notorious smugglers who were traitors also. Gradually he became a full time worker among them. When he was enquired about future consequences, he said:

"Darkness is insignificant before a blind man..."

On one occasion, he was at the brink of death! He was carrying the smuggled gold from the boat to a destination on the shore as planned earlier, in the night. While swimming with the bag, he noticed one torch pointing towards him! At once he realised the danger and dived down after connecting the floating pipe with nose. Immediately one speed-boat passed over his head!

Then he felt difficulty to breathe! He realised that the pipe was cut by the blade of the boat! Since the boat was patrolling there it was not possible for him to come out of the water surface. He saw death face to face but dived as fast as he could. When he reached the shore, he saw the patrolling party, trying hard to detach the pipe from the boat-engine.

Illegal arrival of cash drowned him in extravagancies and immoral life. He did numerous crimes, small and big. He was put to jail and underwent severe punishments. Illness and diseases grabbed his body as well as mind. Later Michael was exiled from his country to a distant island named *'Solity Isle'*, for sedition and all his property was confiscated by the Government. In the strange new place he became the most unwanted element to the society and hence was expelled from everywhere he went, even from the group of beggars. He had to sleep with empty stomach on footpaths. His awkward figure became the usual scene on the street-culvert.

After a few years, somehow he managed to escape to Poorvapunya's village. While walking towards the village-town, he wrote in his small diary, the story of his miraculous escape from *Solity Isle*:

"When I was exiled to that island, I thought it would be better than solitary confinement. The soldiers threw me to a deck on the port in midnight. As I was half-starved and fully tired, slept there; it is better to say, lay unconscious. When I opened eyes, I saw people going with angle-hooks and fishes, caught in the early morning. I smiled at them with expectation. In reply all of them spited on my face with contempt. I could see their criminal mind and nature and understood that most of them were exiles.

After some time, one man asked me to carry one fish box to a small tent nearby, seemed to be a fish market. I followed him with the box on my head. Several time I got headache and was about to fall down. When reached the market, he put three coins in my hand and pointed to a corner place where a man was sitting behind a big tin-plate, filled with boiled fish and wheat.

Thus, I became a porter there. The word, starvation faded away from my belly. I was the box-carrier to a man who came there every day. Came to know that he was a laundry-man, who became too familiar. One day he invited me to his laundry to work there, offering food and shelter. Shelter was a small earthen mount adjacent to an ash-filled oven behind the laundry. Laundry appeared as old as that island It was only an enclosure of some ant-eaten and lose broken wood-planks, fully covered by dust and fumes. It was very difficult to identify the laundry during night especially in cloudy day because of its faded dark colour. There was roof only in rainy season, with a temporarily fastened old cloth-pieces tied together.

But that hideous pace, like a gloomy dark cloud, was keeping inside a new light to my life. One day that lightning flashed: I saw a Ship-cleaner's pair of dress among the clothes taken for washing. The cleaner's identity card was in the pocket. I noticed that the photo was identical to that of mine. With deeply beating heart I opened mouth with wonder when read about the identification mark, written on it:,

'One black mole on left cheek.'

As an unbeliever, I groped several times on my left cheek. My eye-lids closed half with an idea.

While walking in the evening towards the ship, anchored in the port, only prayer in my mind was not to come across the actual cleaner there. The captain smiled at me and waved hands when entered. One crew shook hands and asked me to go upstairs. Most of the people inside it were walking in an intoxicated stage. Some of them were even struggling to keep clothing on their body. There were numerous places to hide my body. So that I tried many places. That cumbersome job took that night from me and hence when I stepped down to another port in the next day before dawn, my eyes were pale due to sleeplessness.

In the dim light, people gave me way with respect along the road looking on my cleaner's coat. Though I was proud of wearing that coat for a while; soon recognised the danger in it. Suddenly I disappeared behind a building under construction, pulled off that coat and threw away. The cold wind of another world had begun to cool my body that time. That was the beginning of tide of changes to me, which were really wanted by my will.

Everyone knows that law will not leave me free if they catch me from any country. But to recognize Mr. Michael is not easy but impossible now, since the past life have changed me that much. The change occurred to me is not only to body but also to mind. I will not have answer if you call me Michael because I have changed my name to most deserved meaningful word, *Manual*. As the literary meaning of the word 'manual', my life shows how to operate the machine of life. You may argue that change of my name is unlawful and non-religious. Then, I have one question to ask; 'what makes all other names lawful and religious if one doesn't accept as his own…?'

It is not easy to describe all the changes that occurred to me but shall say some of them. I was fatty and wheat complexioned. Now I am a man of living skeleton covered by black-wood coloured skin. My face was round and flushing like rose apple. Now it is long, rough and shapeless like a yam grown between two thick stones. As very thin roots, few hairs are on the top here and there and beard only for name sake. Holes of my very old rag type cloth are filled with dust.

In the case of my mind, it is totally changed or reborn. Now it holds the naked facts of human life and bears natural truth. For instance, now the 'Ten Commandments' in my mind are as follows:

1. Before you begin thought, beware of the matter to think.
2. Before you say something, say the benefit out of it.
3. Before you start anything, believe well about cause and consequence.
4. Before you stop a work, best to confirm its completion.

5. Before you eat, better to comprehend what it is of.
6. Before you take rest, must have worked till that time.
7. Before you laugh, keep ready to weep again and again.
8. Before you wish, belt the will with your own wisdom.
9. Before you fight, block the enmity of your own life.
10. Before you die, bequeath all of your victories to death.

Now I believe in the delicacy of life and realise the equality of all organisms..."

Michael carefully kept the diary in his pocket and said to himself:

"This is not only for your reference, dear Poorva...; but also for our son. I have to confess all my sins before him also..."

His mind turned towards the past memory and tried to recollect the shape of his son. Crying face of the small child reflected in memory.

While walking, he noticed the changes that took pace to the town and people.

Everywhere, he could see the horrible remains of a monstrous disaster, not yet completely vacated from the place.

"Really, the village is in a ruined state struggling to sustain the remaining small number of populace...," he observed.

Instead of old thatched houses, only ramshackle walls and broken floors could be seen.

As if the relics of past glory, some huge concrete buildings and structures were standing high   on roadside. Instead of beautiful shadow-trees, high fences with locked iron-gates were bulging into road on both sides. People were too much cautious about their safety.

"Can they protect them if they themselves revoke morality and justice...? Morality is the mother of social security...," he thought.

"It is not possible for me to recognize places. All faces are strange and no need to walk in disguise here...," Michael wondered.

The scene of more grown and spread branches of the banyan tree before the old temple put a pause before his walk. He sat on the marbled vestibule of a newly built tea-shop under the tree.

One day, he heard a fable about Poorvapunya among other gossips of the people, gathered there to take tea in the morning. He could hear about the hermitage and disciples. Curiosity made him mad but controlled and prevented himself from asking more questions.

While returning from there his mind was totally agitated. Face of Poorva and his son frequently flashed to memory.

He thought and tried to imagine the changes delineated by ages on her:

Face should have become slightly round due to lush cheeks. Otherwise it should have become pale because of monotonous. Eyes might not have undergone any changes. But eye-brows might have lost its curve; or else should have curved more due to long impatient waiting for her husband. Hairs and curls might have been turned half-white; or age would have bowed head before her unbeaten beauty. Otherwise it would have been preserved as a golden gift for her returning Hubby.

He looked at himself and felt ashamed of his ugly shape. He cursed himself for all wrongful deeds done in the past. At last he tried to believe that all sins will be pardoned by Poorva as she is the goddess of humanity.

In the evening he joined with a group of people going on that way. They were new migrants going to another distant village. It is like one settlement was being plucked from one place and planted in another place.

"This scene of transferring one village to another due to religious conflict is not the first or the last...," one man explained to Michael.

"We lost everything. They plundered even our earthen pots and ladles made up of coconut-shells. All of them will be dammed...," curses of women heard in loud voice.

"Who are those nasty elements than devils...?"

"Al-Taqwiites..., except whom...?" one grimaced with contempt.

"But you...?"

"We are 'Al-Juma' group', the original followers of *Muhammad Nabi* and *Qur'an*..."

"They are also arguing that..."

"But what is the evidence...?" anger in one old man's voice.

"I think you also have no evidence...," Michael expressed his doubt.

Hearing the words of Michael, the old man walked very quickly with a feeble look.

Michel viewed the long march of the people behind him in the circuitous way:

As if the chaotic human life, some of them were on foot, some on carts, in array with feelings and imagination about the new place; loaded horse-carts and bullock-carts; Camels and donkeys carrying bundles of households; slowly walking Olds with support of sticks, calmly following their pet animals like cats and dogs, some women carrying kids covered by coloured towels in arms, some holding hands of small children with one hand and holding bales on head with other, and youngsters leading sheep and cows as shepherds......! Flashes of sorrow and prospect in all faces simultaneously!!

But a veil of affliction seemed to be covered on those folks. It was clear from their faces paled with fatigue.

"Oh! Man-made burden of life is the biggest bale to mankind. Religions are competing to see its seeds in human society...," thoughts made in him irritation towards religions and abasement of being a man with religion.

Self annoyance while recollecting past futile deeds for his religion made him more and more weak and dragged to thoughts about abject death and last moments to come to such a person like him.

New small rills of muddy water on the side of road due to last nights heavy rain had not yet stopped flow, through which dry leaves were slowly floating. For a moment, his eyes concentrated on. He told to himself:

"Your aspects determines your place in the society"

Wavering legs seemed to be telling that he is a wizened leaf floating through the gully of generation. Tiredness grabbed all of his memories and hops. Footsteps on stepping stones became more and more weightless. Leaning on a climbing stem he looked at the passengers, surpassing him and disappearing away from sight. At last he became fainted and fell down.

Dews in cold midnight fell down on his chill body from tips of tree leaves as if the last tear-drops of Nature over a man's sorrowful life.

****

Chapter 29

God in deep silence

Poorva Punya was disturbed very much. Memories of violent street chased her and haunted her heart. She felt though her nostrils were still filled with the smell of burning flesh. She was dipped in the sea of deep sorrowfulness. Poorva Punya had lost her last hope to live.

She went inside the hermitage and sat for a while. Her mind was completely distressed. She came out with a determination.

Sitting under the huge banyan tree gave some relaxation to Poorva Punya. It was a clear farewell to one more dusk in that small hermitage.

She decided to take deep meditation.

Initially she stretched her body completely then kept her right leg over the left. Spine was erected. Hands rested on the lap with palms facing up ward and eyes were closed. The top of the index fingers were made gently to contact with the thumbs of both hands to make chin-mudra (the thumb and forefinger form a ring and the three remaining fingers are curled into the palms of the hands). As her body relaxed, she chanted Oomm. Ooommm. Oooommmmmmm....

She was made conscious of her surroundings. She had seen the shape of her body. Muscles of neck, shoulders and chest were relaxed. She felt as if she were alone on this earth and experienced as if she didn't have any muscles and organs inside. Her mind travelled around the place she sat and the room in which she was sitting. Around the ashram, her village and the land of Ganges, and across the continents. She took wings to fly like a bird. She was elevated to the sky high above moon...and above sun. Now felt feathery weight. She thought of the earth in which hundreds of thousands of creatures' lived and living.

She saw the sea of sorrows and the faces of hopelessness.. helplessness... worthlessness....

What are all of us doing? What for?

For the sake of living we all fight one other...kills for fame and name. for wealth and health. Things of cruelty years back and today have no difference and even in years to come.

What for? What is the benefit ? Who is winning after all? She laughed at it... she laughed to herself...laughed at everything. She felt ashamed of everything...

Like a prophecy, a spark of thought has came to her mind.

Her spiritual antenna worked!

When will this life on earth ends? Will what I read in *Eternal tranquility* ever come true?

Here in the land of Ganges people are fighting in the name of God and religion, forgetting the real apprehension such as famine and poverty. If it is so here it is so in whole world.

Future catastrophe appeared before her.!....??........!!!

The sun will spite more fire to the earth. Each day and each year Mother earth becomes hotter and hotter. Across the earth millions of people will be left with hunger if rain fails to come and seeds fail to germinate. Harvest will become a day dream in draught-stricken fields.

In the *dark Continent* people will flee from place to place in search of pure mighty water.. Failed rain will wipe out crops. Food will be miles away from reality to them. Malnourished children will collapse and die in the dusty deserts and rest there for ever like black rocks. Even in poverty people will fight in the name their ruthless religion in some places and for wealth in other places! What a shame. Refugees from war tone areas of west Asia and eastern Mediterranean will flee to Western Europe and North American continent. Whole world will be dotted with dirty and shabby tents. After rolling of years, refugees will form small groups and will fight one another and with host community. Even in their homeland people will became refugees. People who hail from rich places will come and offer food and clothes in the name of charity to countries that were looted by them once. Hunger and malnutrition are the worst enemies of our time. Two major religions on this earth will be in a big fight in the coming years. Now religion is synonymous to violent extremism. Brutality is spreading like a forest fire. On once side of the street ambulances rush to save the last flame of life and on the other side humans are be-headed to obey the 'will of God'. Real human beings are the most endangered species on earth

She thought. The world would be more peaceful if there were no religions at all. Now preachers now guiding believers on various methods to follow and adore God. How to believe in God. These preachers are really Intruders in our thoughts on God. A lion may sleep with a deer, but two religious thoughts will never move together. We need to have God only not religions. God does not judge us based on our religion but our action in life. We don't have any holy books at all. We do have personal experience with god. She thought..

The face of her mother came to her mind. On all Mondays her mother used to say 'Today I won't take food and I am on upavasa[56] But in future hundreds of thousands of innocent children might take upavasa in most of the days due to the lack of food if we would purposefully ignore them.

In the coming years economic gap between the West and East will be narrow but across the globe, there will be a huge difference between haves and have- nots. Major wealth of the world will be embraced by a few corporate only. Things might be deracinated in the near future. All resources on the earth may be used up. There may be extinction of species, due to destruction of eco system, drying up of. water resources Pollution in river. Interestingly people spending money to rejuvenate simultaneously clear felling trees in once side and re-planting in other side. What an irony. Irony irony everywhere!

Oh God! What a hell Mother Earth will become in the future!!

Depletion of forests commonly happening everywhere. Now desertification is starting in Amazon rain forests and it will go even to Siberia. After three decades world population will be 10 billion. Means 10 billion nostrils alone will pollute our atmosphere. Violence and immorality will increase all over. Even small girls will be rapped and killed. Water will be polluted. Birds and butterflies in huge numbers will die. If the hole in the arctic grow further and bigger, it means the Sun, the god of light may became a ghost of harmful radiation. Air pollution will hit life very heavily on the earth. The whole world goes polluted with dreadful gases and this earth becomes a gas chamber. Due to entropy both internal pressure and external pressure are increasing the entire soil is submersed with poisonous chemicals. Earth becomes an unfit place for cultivation. Catastrophe might come to marine life also. Creatures of blue sea disappear for ever due to over fishing.

Birds will no longer chirp you to wake up and butterflies will no longer make you happy with their multicolored wings.

We are moving to an era of darkness!

As I have seen many colourful butterflies around in my early years. But where have they gone? Nowadays there are very few butterflies with their beautiful wings. During my child hood, lots of birds were in my village kalppam. Birds once sang have now completely disappeared. I would awaken to the chirping of birds on the nearby trees. The carol of countless birds has

---

[56] https://en.wikipedia.org/wiki/Fasting_in_Jainism

stopped for? In spring, there were singings of cuckoos all around. But now it's very rare for our ears. Their silence is shocking.

Poorva Punya made a deep sigh!

They are too quite in the water frontage of Saras. Butterflies and birds might taken to the root of death. Mighty creatures can't tolerate pollution and heat waves. Some times they might escape to polar region. If polar region also becomes polluted where will they go? What will be life on this earth without birds and butterflies? my earth will be like hell. Pollution is stealing fragrance of flowers. in future no one can see kissing of butterflies on flowers?

. In the era of massive radiation, the situation of the butterflies became very deplorable. Will they are deprived of their beauty and shape due to radiation? In future butterflies will born without or with a small antenna then they can't feel presence of flowers and thereby pollination?

Even very small rise in temperature is un-bearable for very sensitive creature like butterflies. As such, butterflies will shelter in the polar region of the south or north but never to the East or West. How can they think of the East or the West where the worst human creatures are living. A world without butterflies! What beauty is left in this earth then? Butterflies vanish in vacuum!! But before disappearing into the blue sky, they give a signal- signal of imminent danger. 'Hey Human being your habitat is getting unbearably hotter. Shady trees and flowers having nectar are fast disappearing. Oh man, do something at least for your own sake'. But who is going to hear? In fact who has got time to? As pollution increases, the fragrance of flowers gradually fading. Flowers without aroma- then how can they attract butterflies?

Contamination affect birds also.

Poorva Punya took deep breath

Greedy humans are squeezing the last drop of blood from Mother Earth. The world is now a battle field between prey and predators. Excessive use of soil will end in a big tragedy, and it will be another terrible issue we are going to face in the coming years. If seeds are not germinated in the soil how can we quell our appetite? If overfishing destroys the entire marine wealth how non-vegetarians survive? Will they eat one other? Or they might eat gold and money? That is the only way left for them. Due to global warming the surface temperature of the earth increase day by day. Water level on the earth may rise to plunge islands like Mahal[57] Dvip, Nihon[58] or Moloka'i[59] for ever. If

---

[57] Imaginary name for Maldives

[58] Imaginary name for Japan

[59] Imaginary name for Hawaii

atmospheric temperature increases there will be no ice formation in the Arctic belt.

Ice in the mighty Himalaya will melt for ever then it will results to heavy floods in the whole land. The water tower of the Himalayas will collapse which means the entire the land of Ganges may be washed off. If the ice in the Arctic and Antarctic melts islands and low lands on earth may be submerged.

I think earth will be the most unfit place to live on if we continue to ill treat it.

Who is to be blamed for this? Who is responsible for famine?

God? Or Satan? Is mop it the work of devil alone? If not then whose? In the name of God satanic persons work through and try to destroy the tranquility on earth. But God is in deep silence watching everything.

"The soil is dying very fast. Chemical manures and insecticides are killing our soil. Due to climate change desertification faster than expected. How harshly we are destroying the natural habitat of birds and animals! Have we ever though how difficulty the birds undergo in making nests. How many days and nights do they spend to complete their domicile. but who has time to look into all these? Why should we worry over the sufferings of the silly birds? Corns is the staple food of birds. But grains are being sprayed with poisonous chemicals. What is the fate of the birds which feed on them! Either they die or escape to the un-known!

Who want a world without birds flying about in the sky and butterflies which can't imbibe nectar?

The sky in the Levant and eastern Mediterranean terrified with missiles and cartridges. In this land now creatures of birds and butterflies has completely vanished. Everywhere there fire machines are flying.

'Small children's in war tone area will put their hand-up even when seeing even camera. Moan of machines pervade all over. Let the progress of human race be marked by these and together we can wait death bell of human race!

'If we continually abuse earthly beings then we will be retaliated by nature very soon. Even in the coming years spring may come on earth but with a difference! Spring with no fragrance and so silent. Winter, Autumn and Summer will follow but will be deeply muted!!

'Man is polluting not only the soil but also the sea, which forms largest reservoir of food. The blue sea spreads all over the world. But cities big and small and millions of people dumps tones of waste in rivers and destine to sea. The sea may be called by different names but there is only one sea which engulfs all of our waste materials. Countries both in the East and West are competing to pollute the sea with plastic wastes, chemical wastes, nuclear wastes, oil leak from ships etc. All these take the lives of aquatic organisms. about half of the marine life has been expired in fourty years. Seventy five percent will be destroyed In coming twenty five years. Then?

When watching the spirit with which man is hunting the marine creatures, one might feel that they are solely for the use of men. Millions of fish are caught daily for men's greed. Due to large scale fishing and dumping of waste, the sea wealth is exhaust. What will man do once it is totally drained? The soil is already breathing its last. Somehow when seeds are not going to germinate in the future people will be left only to prey up one another!! we will become man eaters!! Modern cannibals!!But has man got time to think of this? How can, someone who can't find peace at his own house exerts for world peace?

Why should we yearn to live for one hundred years in this world. A world where family bonds are crumbling, where wives and husbands deceive each other, where even young children are not spared from brutal massacres, where pupils are shooting down in class -rooms, where teachers are burned alive before students, where mosques are bombed, where children's are hijacked to mass religious conversions or are used to quench sexual urge, where innocents hands are armed for attacks, where children are abducted and amputed by doctors for thrown them for begging.

What a world this is?

Rich people are lying on huge money mountain while millions of people are dying due to starvation and malnutrition. The crying of innocent children resounds everywhere. But nobody is listening. We continue praying to God to bring heaven on earth. On one side tons of food grains are being burnt for want of warehouses and on the other side millions of children are dying of starvation for want of just a square meal. What an irony! Once a photographer has been honored with a renowned award for flashing a dyeing girl due to starvation, awaiting an eagle for her flesh. But those award judging panels have failed to see a hidden eagle that is eager for recognition. People are really dying for awards and recognitions!!

We are claiming that medical science is advancing, but great catastrophes are awaiting us. Cancer, kidney failure and un-known diseases spreading across the world, and so called science is yet to find solutions. And when science finds the solutions then more and more un-known diseases come up.

We need to change our food habits. Even though we are herbivorous by birth we are living like animals. Carnivorous should eat meat since its physical structure is supporting it. But if we eat meat and its fat then our body balance will collapse. Our cholesterol level will increase. The heart will fail and stroke will hit brain.

Advocates of progress are turning our earth into a virtual hell. While satisfying their thirst for power and greed the rulers and the leaders of the world commit unlimited number of sins.

Why should one wish to live longer in this world which is literally a hell? It is said that the earth has life expectancy of further 3.5 million years! It may be true but who need it, if we can't live on this earth happily even for ten years? If we can't live peacefully then what is the claim of putting man on the moon or sending vehicle to Mars? We may find a planets which is bigger in size and equal to earth but never will there be exactly like our Mother Earth!

In the coming years, the entire world will be troubled by the forces of separatism, terrorism and religious fanaticism. Who will solution to these ? Who can give real answers to these?

God?

Why should God bother ? All the issues are created by man and not by the Divine Creator. Man is created all these problems. He created religion and it created most of the problems. The greed of man made this world a hell. Man has to minimize his greed to make all natural resources available to coming generation. Man has to free God from religion. He has to reject religion and accept God. God must be made free from the chains that religions have bound. Or together we can sing.

"Nearer my god to thee before dooms day"!![60]

Someone preaches that the Son of God has taken all sins of mankind. If the Son of God took all the sins at the time of the crucifixion then how and why is sin numbering again and again? Around the world why are people in unrest. The land of Ganges should push out religious from clashes and even whole world! Destruction of holy places has become a passion now days.

In Gandharadesham extreme radical fundamentals are eradicating one other. Semitic land is a burning pot for Muslims, Christians and Jews for more than two hundred years. And in plateau of desert Muslims are shedding blood among themselves.

In Mahavamsadesam The Hindus and Buddhist are in animosity and in land of *white elephant[61]* the turn is between Muslims and Buddhist.

The Land of freedom remains as sanctuary to accommodate all talented people to settle and grow. Bur for how long? Let us see how the Land of Letters and Sheer of Wisdom turns their ear to be political asylum in the years to

---

[60] https://en.wikipedia.org/wiki/Nearer,_My_God,_to_Thee
[61] Imaginary name for Thailand

come. The Land of Wine Yard was well known as the cultural capital of the world but the same land is now spirited with religion rather than spirit of wine.

It is a matter of intolerance. Intolerance breeds violence, rebellion, vandalizing and looting. Human beings are inviting hell to conquer Mother Earth. That is why cruel human-beings are turning this planet a most unfit place to live for themselves and their fellow beings.

Is religion is the only reason for fighting? Not always. People are even fighting for nothing? Why did Michael fight with me?

It was not the name of religion alone. Human intolerance will be a big problem in the coming years. Torturing other beings has become a matter even in the family life. What a married life it was. My married life was just like walking on the edge of a sword. Those two years were a life under Gillette.

Whether God wills to listen? Never! Never! Never!

Why should God answer our problems when most of the problems are only self made.

God is in deep silence seeing all cruelties with deep un-happiness inside. God only listen to the voice of the innocent as God is also innocent. The Innocent will never appeal before God to get anything for their own benefits as they are so innocent.

Divinity has to come from within the mind. Actually, God is within us. We should be as pure as an angel, Only then we can experience the presence of God. If we go for deep meditation and yoga we can make a relationship with God. God is not the doer of our happiness or sorrows. These are our state of mind and it is ever changing. We need to find God within us. God likes silence. Silence is the true language of God. The more we speak, then more God be disturbed and God will move away from us. But who will listen?

Thought came in the mind. Poorva Punya contemplated on **Eternal tranquillity.**

What have I read that has come true on the earth?. If what is depicted in the last chapter may happen?. Then what is the meaning of me to live on earth?

Oh! that is why Mr. K'iche flew to Venus?

Oh!! that may be the meaning of the inscription that Mr. K'iche one read. It once again came to her memory.

tzuhtzjo:m uy-u:xlaju:n pik
chan ajaw u:x uni:w
uhto:m il[?]
ye'ni/ye:n bolon yokte'
ta chak joyaj

She remembered her mother once told her that this is Kaliyuga, the last yuga where all evil things would happen on this earth.

The water in *Sarasa* was once so crystal clear but now it seems like flowing of dark oil. When the factory came to the village things have changed. In the future more and more factories may come to my home town. Then population will increase there by the pollution also My *Kalpam* was once a peaceful village. Even in deep poverty, dwellers lived very happily. No one harmed anyone and people used to help one anothers as much as they could.

She strongly believed that sometimes tragedy would happen in the near future as what was depicted in the ***Eternal tranquility*** and sometimes it would not. What ever is mentioned or not mentioned in any books, the end of life on this earth will of course come about very soon due to the acts of man... whether the end comes or not is not my worry I must leave this hell. It will be good for me. Anyway, to whom should I convey all these- it I talk about Mahapralaya[62] or if I mention about forth coming tragedies then who is going to believe me? Only Marry can but she is no more!

The face of Marry came to her. She smiled at her dear buddy.

She thought "Even though I am not Jesus or Buddha to make preaching and even though I am not a prophet to make my statement or to create a religion or to get followers".

My poor villagers are trying hard to earn their square meal each day and whether they live or die is not all their concern.

She knew that her thoughts were odd. Rarely odd. odd thoughts are always called as mad. If your thoughts are not like those of the majority of people, then people will think you are odd and finally mad. But in the lunatic asylum you will be get red-carpet welcome as all of them there are odd and mad. But all there have great concern for the earth and earthly beings. That is why they are mad!

'Maya's once predicted doomsday on 12th, December 2012. but it not happened. May be their calculations and assumptions are misinterpreted by scientists of today's or Maya's assumption may little bit out from reality. One more thing is that the modern calendar is quite un-known to the Mayas, but it doesn't mean that we have escaped from the catastrophe. If we continue ill treat mother Earth the way we are doing now, then surely dooms day will come very soon.

---

62 https://en.wikipedia.org/wiki/Pralaya

Do we have any solution? No?....
But yes!

Natural disasters can't be clogged, but manmade tragedies can be in our control. They can be minimized and their impact can be watered down. We can't change our solar system. We can't stop the earth's rotation or the twinkling of the stars, but we can do quit a lot of things to Mother Earth. Epidemics can be controlled. Spreading of unknown diseases can be guarded. Environmental pollution can be stopped. Global warming can be lessened. Desertification can be stopped. Over fishing and over hunting can be re-thought. Water can be keep clean. Merciful thought can be developed towards our fellow beings especially towards animals and birds. Only then will the birds and butterflies be back to our earth. Let animals and children might live happily on this earth. We need to go to the forest. See its wonder. How happily birds are flying there. As a divine being we must go and enjoy its tranquility. The forest will give fabulous energy to your inside. you just have to embrace a tree. Embrace trees as you can Apart from that look at the eyes of animals and birds. Let them feel that you are not their enemy. Let them feel your humanity. Let them enjoy beauty of innocent love. Start loving innocent creature around. Let them feel that you are here on earth to love all creatures. Then our earth will again turn into as paradise. There is no heaven above the earth. There is no hell below earth. Heaven is here and hell is here.

Her thought landed to the soil. She enjoyed great tranquility.

Poorva Punya was in a search of a solution to quell violence on earth. Suddenly a flash of thought came to her. 'If whole world follows Vedic culture, then it could be better to all living beings and non-living things. Let all other living beings consider human beings as their friends. We may consider all living beings as our companions. Let all living creatures remain friends for ever in this planet.

ओम इन्द्रं वर्धन्तो अप्तुरः
कृण्वन्तो विश्वमार्यम्
अपगनन्तो अराव्णः

Rigveda 9.63.5

(First we must purify ourselves and transform the divinity to all humans to make them divine beings...Turn all human beings as aryas/ noble.

The only way to get happiness is to avoid religion and accept God in one's heart. See and realize the presence of God within and around. Practice meditation and yoga as a way of life. Embod your body and mind to make the whole world as Vasudhaivakudumbakom[63].

She took a deep breath. A moon-lash flashed on her rosy lips.

---

[63] https://en.wikipedia.org/wiki/Vasudhaiva_Kutumbakam

Chapter 30

Eternal Tranquility

Daybreak With the horripulating songs of jungle in splendor, blue-cuckoos began to fly from mountain-tops to valley:

'Greeneries are seen thickened and thickened
Sinking in the emerald green
Congealed dews – fell on mountain's head
As deep thrill – are moping off clean
By Dawn, peeping from close behind
The stratum of mountains' scenes…!'

Blaze of lighted lamps began to spread from the cottages of the hermitage. Lamps of Soul-realization through Sanathana-Dharma, the Hermits, were coming out. Disciples have already started for their *Prabhatha-Vandhanam (morning adoration)* the usual prayer in the morning on river-banks.

Thus routine of the day has started.

Poorva Punya and other recluse began to adorn the main entrance of the Hermitage. All the women entered the yard by frisking steps appeared to be encouraging each other and enjoying their decoration work.

One of the loners decorating outside of the entrance quickly ran inside.

She said: "An anonymous person is lying there. Don't know alive or not…!"

"Let us look at him….," Poorvapunya and others walked towards the outside of the entrance.

On the grass-covered small ridge near the pavement, a man was lying. They walked near and observed closely.

While others were looking excitedly, Poorvapunya noticed the familiar black mole on his left cheek. Michael's face entered into her memory. She closed her eyes and stood still for a while. All past days passed through her mind within seconds.

The drop of tears could not be forbidden though she tried as much as possible.

At last controlling all sorrows, she murmured:

"Valuation of everything is based on relativity. Years ago, this man was so affectionate to me. But later, Michael became anonymous by his perversion to me. That is why according to God's will, he ought to have stopped his walk for ever before entering in this hermitage to see me, though he might have been refined at last…"

Then what can we do…?" others crossed fingers with anxiety.

"We must finish our decoration and go back. As usual, this man's funeral will be done by the concerned local authorities…," Poorvapunya reminded and turned to the doorway-decoration.

Like a hover in river, she was floating over past, confused in memories without any control throughout that day.

"When death reach nearer, past memories will flash in mind…!" she recollected mother's words with a shock.

"Oh! If end is coming, let it come. Though I didn't become a recluse but follows an ascetic life. So I am not afraid about my bereavement…," she told as if consolation, half to herself and half to other by standers.

Suddenly, one more ill omen thought came to her mind. that is about her grandfather's death, of which she happened to witness in childhood. She began to describe it without any request from others:

"Early morning, I had not been awakened. Mother ran to porch and cried loudly. I hadn't ever heard such a cry of mother and so woke up with wonder and ran to her side. When I reached near the old wooden coat of grandfather, in the corner of our very small vestibule, with small height, grandpa was shivering slightly and breathing deeply. I could not understand it was his last breath; but seeing others' cry I also cried bitterly. Exactly, I didn't know what happened then, but heard about it later while father narrated the event to mother. He said that while the people gathered from neighboring houses, I was standing almost clinging to mother and as far as covered by her cloth-fringe with fear. Most of the people who came there seemed to be addicted to false notions. One among the populace reminded seriously the superstitious belief that death in the morning is a bad omen because there will be another death in the house shortly.

Body was laid down on the floor. Somebody closed his eye-lids. Another man wrapped around apex and chin with a piece of cotton cloth. A coconut was cut into two pieces and filled ghee in one and lighted a wick in it on head-side. It flickered as if its flame was half cut with grief. Incense-sticks were burning. Read scriptures from *Ramayana*, the epic.

Later the body was bathed and dressed with white new cloths. Forehead was adorned with sandal paste. Body was placed over a big plantain leaf near the plaza. Then all people were allowed to give last respect to the departed soul.

Later, The corpse was taken to funeral pyre after completing obeisance and *Poojas (act of worship)*. After placing on pyre-wood, wood-pieces arranged fully. *Poojari* (a priest offering worship) chanted Hindu rites one by one. As the eldest son of the dead is authorised to do the last Karmas, my father went round the pyre three times, holding a hollowed crock full of water. On the completion of third round, the urn was thrown backward towards pyre. Then holding a small flambeau walked round three times and at last lighted on the leg side of the pyre. Thus fire received the mortal physical body.

While the material existence of grandpa was ending forever in the Last Home, its glittering flames were reflecting in tears falling from eyes of all the populace, who were weeping uncontrollably. Without ability to grasp the reason of their grief with my two year old brain, I was setting eyes on everybody sympathetically and anxiously...!" Poorvapunya's depiction ceased for a while.

Her worried mind put her in a dilemma of thoughts. She couldn't select which matter is to be recollected or which is not to be.

She felt that the day was longer than it could ever be.

Even after midnight she was not asleep but looking lazily through small bamboo grilled window to the clear blue sky, filled with shining stars. After some time, without her will a small slumber slightly closed her eyelids.

A lark was singing in the clean blue sky above her.

Owls hooted as if competition, from nearby tree-tops. Splendour of dreamful sleep departed her all of a sudden. She gazed at others. They were all sleeping.

Pournami (The full moon) with pale face had already entered in the western horizon. Falling meteors seemed to be the silver flowers drooping on earth tacitly from the sky's curly hair.

Cool breeze was wandering with sandal perfume, telling stories to plants and flower-petals. Leaves and grass-tops were shining like silver bits. She gazed at the distant big pool near the threshold of the hermitage. It was resplendent with bloomed lilies and blue lotus-buds. Fringes of the lake were decorated with luxuriant garden-plants. Calves were strangely peeping into the frontal.

"Dear my buddy, why are you all crying? Have never seen your eyes filled with tears! We were all living here in peace and festivity but now...? Oh you, my favoured ones; can't you stay without seeing me even in night...? Don't be afraid; even the Lord of death can't separate us. Otherwise, who will dare to divide the affection of attribute...?" she murmured.

It became an auspicious sight when a few leaves of *Parijatham* (as per belief Parijatha tree is a heavenly tree otherwise known as tree of sorrows) fell in the still water of lotus-lake. By its tender touch, water thrilled with sport and ratification. Lily-filaments shook and shrank while moonlight was making silver rings on small surges. The ripples on water seems like a silver blanket.

Ambience covered with mist, attained a heavenly divinity while an exotic song of a solitary skylark resounds in the air from far away according to the rhythmic twinkling of stars.

Poorvapunya realised the change of impulse in heart-beat as the sign of longing to see her mother. She beveled to and fro like a child to lay her head in lap of mother. She saw her mother, stretching both arms and gleams of affection flowing towards her like cool and tender lilywhite luster coming from the world of stars. Her breath became deep as if inhaling heavenly fragrance with delight. Her heart beat became uneven and lost its rhythm.

Did she hear mother's hail? Perhaps...

"Ma fooo...fuuu..., let me come with you... Thousands of Aeons may come and go but I won't depart you ever...," she murmured as if in dream and turned eyes towards the entrance as if searching for someone.

"Ye....ss eeeee.., all my relatives, don't rush; please move a little; my son is coming..." Let him also to come to this place of tranquillity...," she struggled to muster all strength.

Did she see her son? May be...

"My son, till this time, where were you hiding, after giving unbearable twinge to your mother...?" her whisper had enough sound to waken others.

It was a lonely journey to unknown!

But a journey for eternal tranquility!!

They saw chill body of Poorvapunya lying lifeless! An unfading smile was still remaining on her lips; and eyes were darting a susceptible squint towards the door as if looking for someone!

Moon buried deep in the blue clouds.

The next day, golden streaks of dawn veiled over the hamlet, at liberty with all religious thoughts...! The morning sun was rising in the eastern horizon to set west for those still living on earth to eradicate ignorance to, light up knowledge and proclaiming, the inception of a new immaculate Eon.

****

End Notes

[i] The Hebrew Bible
[ii] The Holy Qur'an
[iii] The Holy Qur'an
[iv] The Holy Qur'an